Praise for *Once*

A brand-new Regency romance from
beloved bestseller Jane Ashford

"A near-perfect example of everything that makes this genre an escapist joy to read: unsought love triumphs despite difficult circumstances, unpleasantness is resolved and mysteries cleared, and good people get the happy lives they deserve."

—*Publishers Weekly*

"A bit of gothic suspense, a double love story, and the right touches of humor and sensuality add up to this delightfully fast-paced read about second chances and love's redeeming power."

—*RT Book Reviews*, 4 Stars

"Well-rendered, relatable characters, superb writing, an excellent sense of time and place, and gentle wit make this a romance that shouldn't be missed... Ashford returns with a Regency winner that will please her longtime fans and garner new ones."

—*Library Journal*

"It's so nice to have one of the premier Regency writers return to the published world. Ms. Ashford has written a superbly crafted story with elements of political unrest, some gothic suspense, and an interesting romance."

—*Fresh Fiction*

"Jane Ashford's characters are true to their times, yet they radiate the freshness of today."

—*Historical Novel Review*

The Three Graces

JANE ASHFORD

sourcebooks
casablanca

Published by Sourcebooks Casablanca, an imprint of Sourcebooks, Inc.
P.O. Box 4410, Naperville, Illinois 60567-4410
(630) 961-3900
Fax: (630) 961-2168
www.sourcebooks.com

Originally published in 1982 by Signet, a division of The New American Library, Inc., New York.

Printed and bound in the United States of America
VP 10 9 8 7 6 5 4 3 2 1

Contents

Prologue

THE THREE MISSES HARTINGTON SAT BEFORE THE
schoolroom fire, sewing sheets. Though their
surroundings were decidedly shabby, the dull brown
carpet worn and the furniture discarded from more
elegant apartments and earlier times, they presented a
charming picture. Their close relationship was evident
in their appearance; all had hair of the shade commonly
called auburn, a deep russet red, and the pale clear
ivory skin that sometimes goes with such a color.
The eldest sister, who was but nineteen, had eyes of
celestial blue, while those of the two younger girls,
aged eighteen and seventeen, were dazzling green.
An observer would have been hard put to pick the
prettiest of them. All were slender, with neat ankles,
elegant wrists, and an air of unconscious distinction
that did much to outweigh their dowdy gowns and
unfashionable braids. He might perhaps venture that
Miss Hartington's nose was a trifle straighter than her
sisters' and her mouth a more perfect bow. But the
second girl's eyebrows formed a finer arch, and the
youngest one's expression held the greater promise of

liveliness. Altogether, there was little to choose among this delightful trio.

Silence had reigned for some time in the room as they plied their needles with varying degrees of diligence. Having lived together for all of their lives and served during that short period as each other's only companions and confidantes, they knew one another's moods too well to chatter. And nothing of note had occurred this day to cause discussion. Miss Hartington had had occasion to recall her youngest sister to her work once or twice, but otherwise the circle had been silent. The afternoon was passing; soon it would be teatime, and the girls would put up their sewing and join their aunt in the drawing room.

A sound at the door across the room attracted their attention. It was followed by the entrance of first a very large yellow tomcat, then a smaller gray tabby, and finally three kittens of varying hues, bounding forward awkwardly and falling over one another in their eagerness to keep up with their elders. Miss Hartington smiled. "Hannibal's family has found us already," she said, "I told you it would not be long."

The youngest girl wrinkled her nose. "I cannot understand his behavior in the least. They are not even his kittens."

Her middle sister smiled. "But he has adopted them, you see, so they are all the more precious to him."

"I don't see why you say that," sniffed the other. "Our aunt adopted us, but we are certainly not dear to her."

"Euphie!" Miss Hartington looked shocked. "Mind your tongue. How can you say such a thing?"

"Well, it is true. If she cared a button for us, she would let us go about more and visit and… and do all the things other young girls are allowed to do. Indeed, she would bring you out this season, Aggie, as she should have done last year."

"Hush," replied her sister repressively. "Aunt has done everything for us, and you must not speak so of her. If she had not given us a home when Father died, we should be in desperate straits, and you know it."

The youngest girl sighed, shaking her head. "Yes, I know it. Not but what Father showed a decided lack of sympathy, too. Only think of our ridiculous names. He can't have considered what it would be like to go through life being called Euphrosyne."

Miss Hartington frowned at her, but the third sister laughed. "It was not he, Euphie. It was our mother. Aunt Elvira has told me that she was inspired by a passage the vicar read aloud to her just before Aggie was born. From Homer. How did it go? Something about the three Graces." She concentrated a moment, then quoted in Greek, translating for the others: "Most beauteous goddesses and to mortals most kind."

Euphrosyne Hartington wrinkled her nose once more. "Well, I never knew her, since she died when I was born, but though I do not wish to be disrespectful, I think she showed a shocking lack of sensibility. It is very well for you two to tease me. Your names are not nearly so queer."

Her middle sister smiled again. "I suppose you would prefer Thalia? I must say it seems just as burdensome to me."

Miss Hartington rallied at this. "Well, neither of you

was persecuted by Johnny Dudley as I was. He could never pronounce 'Aglaia' properly, and he used to dance around me singing 'Uglea, Uglea,' until I thought I should scream. He thought it excessively witty."

"Johnny Dudley," echoed Thalia meditatively. "I have not thought of him in years. What became of him, I wonder?"

Aglaia shrugged. "I daresay he is still in Hampshire. We were both eight when Father died and we left the county."

Exasperated, Euphrosyne jumped up and faced her sisters. "How can you sit there calmly chattering about nothing?" she exclaimed. "What are we to do?"

Thalia only looked amused, but Miss Hartington said, "Do about what, Euphie? Please try to control yourself; you mustn't fly into a pelter every second minute, you know."

Euphrosyne put her hands on her hips. "Someone must," she retorted. "I am tired of hearing about propriety and what I must do and must not. Sitting meekly in our rooms sewing will do us no good at all. We must make a plan, Aggie. We must *do* something!"

Thalia smiled at her ironically. "What do you suggest?"

"Oh, if I only knew what to suggest," Euphie cried. "You are the scholar. Surely you can tell how we are to escape this dreadful situation."

Aglaia looked bewildered. "What situation? I declare, Euphie, you get no conduct as you grow older. What are you talking about?"

"Can you ask? We are trapped in this house. We never go out; we meet no young people, only Aunt's crusty old friends and the cats!" She directed a venomous look at Hannibal where he reclined luxuriously in the window seat. Ignoring her, he yawned hugely and began to lick one of the kittens. "What is to become of us? How are we ever to marry, for example?"

Thalia laughed. "Take care that Aunt Elvira does not hear you, Euphie. She would give you a thundering scold for presuming to think of marriage."

Euphrosyne whirled to face her. "Oh, sometimes I think I hate Aunt Elvira." This drew a shocked gasp from her eldest sister, and she hastened to add, "I do not, of course. She has been wonderfully kind to us. But I get so angry. She never cared to marry. I understand that. But she cannot expect that we will feel as she did at every point in life. It is selfish of her to keep us hemmed up here."

Thalia sputtered, "Never cared to marry? You are a master of understatement, Euphie."

But Miss Hartington looked disapproving. "You are exaggerating all out of reason. And you should not encourage her, Thalia. We often go out; we are certainly not prisoners in our aunt's house. And she does what she believes is best for us and gives us all we ask. Did she not engage special teachers for you, Euphie, when you wished to continue your music beyond what Miss Lewes could teach? And did she not allow Thalia to study Greek and Latin and anything else she wished, again with special, and very expensive, teachers? I think she has been a very generous guardian."

Euphrosyne pushed out a rebellious lip, but before she could speak again they were all frozen by a bloodcurdling shriek coming from the direction of the drawing room. Hannibal leaped up, his fur prickling, and spat. The shriek came again. Thalia stood, and Euphrosyne started toward the door. There was a patter of footsteps in the hall outside; then the door was thrown open by an hysterical maid. "Oh, miss, miss," she gasped, "it's your aunt!"

As one, the sisters hurried down the stairs to the drawing room. In the doorway they paused, for there was clearly something very wrong. They could see the top of their aunt's head, as usual, above her tall chair before the fireplace, but most unusually, they did not see any other creature.

"Where are the cats?" asked Euphie, voicing their puzzlement. They had never seen their aunt's drawing room without at least five, and more commonly ten or twelve, cats. And now there were none at all.

Aggie hurried around the chair, stopped, and put a hand to her mouth. At this moment, the maid caught up with them, and seeing Miss Hartington's expression, she screeched again. "That's just how I found her, miss, when I come in to ask about the tea. Gave me the nastiest turn of my life, it did. She's gone, ain't she?"

Aggie, rather pale, nodded. "I think she is. But you had best send for the doctor."

The maid ran from the room.

Aglaia's sisters had joined her by this time, and the three girls looked down wide-eyed at the spare figure in the armchair. It would have been hard to imagine a greater contrast. Elvira Hartington was, or had been, a harsh-featured woman, with deep lines beside her mouth and a hawk nose. In death, her face had not relaxed, but held its customary expression of doubting disapproval. Her hand was clutched to her chest, and her pale gray eyes stared sightlessly at her nieces.

Aggie shuddered and turned away. "Poor Aunt Elvira," she murmured.

Thalia took the old woman's wrist. "Cold," she said. "She is indeed dead, and has been for some time, I think."

Aggie shuddered again, but Euphie merely stared at the corpse curiously. "She does not look peaceful," said the youngest girl. "I thought dead people were supposed to be peaceful. Aunt looks just as she did before giving me a scold."

"Euphie, please!" said Miss Hartington.

The other looked abashed. "I didn't mean anything. I wonder what happened? She seemed fine this morning. Remember, she was going to write a letter to the *Times* about Wellington?"

"We are at least spared that," murmured Thalia.

"I don't know," replied Aggie. "She seems to have been taken suddenly. The doctor will tell us."

"Well, I am only sorry for St. Peter," added Euphie, looking sidelong at her middle sister. "She will probably tell him he is not at all what she expected and is used to."

Thalia choked back a laugh and turned away as the maid came hurrying back into the room. "Dr. Perkins will be here directly," she said. "Should I send for anyone else, Miss Hartington?" She spoke to Aggie with a new respect, as her new mistress.

Aggie put a hand to her forehead. "No, I don't

think quite yet... Oh, you might send word to Miss Hitchins. She will want to know immediately."

"Yes, miss." And the girl was gone again.

The next few hours passed in a kind of muddle. The realities of death soon depressed even Euphie's spirits, and by the time the doctor had come and gone and all the details were settled, the three sisters were weary and silent. They went up to bed much subdued, for all of them had been attached to their aunt, whatever they might sometimes say.

The next morning, two early visitors arrived almost together—Miss Hitchins and their aunt's solicitor. The former, a forbidding woman of fifty-odd, had been Elvira Hartington's closest friend for many years, ever since they had met at a meeting of the Feline Protectionist Society and discovered like feelings on this important subject. Miss Hitchins often gave her friend's nieces the impression that she disapproved of them, though she remained unfailingly polite, and they greeted her with some nervousness on this solemn occasion. She pressed each of their hands in turn. "So sudden," she murmured. "Poor dear Elvira. None can count himself secure in this world."

Miss Hitchins looked even more somber than usual this morning. She habitually wore black, but today, she had added a black bonnet and veil to her customary dark gown. Her gray hair was washed out by this attire, and her pale skin looked whiter than ever. All of the girls were relieved when the solicitor, Mr. Gaines, came in behind her.

But even the usually jovial Gaines seemed oppressed today. "Tch, tch," he said as he returned the sisters' greeting. "This is an uncomfortable situation. More than uncomfortable. Outrageous, I call it. But she never would listen."

Euphie exchanged a puzzled glance with Thalia.

"Each of us must face death," replied Miss Hitchins reprovingly. "And we must all endeavor to do so with Christian resignation, as I am certain Elvira did."

"Oh, death," said Mr. Gaines, dismissing the question with an impatient wave of his hand. "I daresay, I was speaking of the will, you know."

Miss Hitchins's eyes sharpened. "The will?"

The solicitor scanned four pairs of unblinking eyes. "None of you knows? No, of course you don't. She left that to me. Just like her, too. I've been urging her for years to change the blasted thing, and she always said she meant to. But she didn't. And so, here we are, aren't we? Outrageous."

"I don't understand, Mr. Gaines," said Aggie. "Is there some problem with my aunt's will?"

"There is, and there isn't. And I shan't say another word until the reading this afternoon. If you'll excuse me, I'll go to the library now. I want to go over Miss Hartington's papers as soon as may be."

"Of course. I'll…"

"That's all right. I know my way." Mr. Gaines started out of the drawing room, but in the doorway he paused. "You'll want to come for the reading, Miss Hitchins," he added gruffly. Then he was gone.

Miss Hitchins looked highly gratified.

"Whatever can be wrong with Mr. Gaines?" wondered Euphie. "He is not at all like himself. I have never seen him so abrupt."

Aggie shook her head. Thalia stared at the doorway where he had gone out, a worried frown on her face.

"Oh, I daresay he ate something that disagreed with him at breakfast," said Miss Hitchins brightly. "Men are sensitive to such things, I believe. Women are really much the stronger sex, in spite of what they say."

One of the cats, who had returned to the drawing room when their former mistress left it, stood up on the mantelshelf, stretched mightily, and leaped to the floor, evidently intending to go out. Miss Hitchins bent as it passed her and held out an eager hand. "Cato," she said, "there's a good puss. Come here, Cato."

The cat, a large gray, turned his head fractionally, eyed Miss Hitchins's fingers with a distinct lack of enthusiasm, and passed by and out the door. A black cat draped over the back of the sofa yawned.

Euphie made a slight choking sound, and Aggie said quickly, "Would you care for a cup of tea, Miss Hitchins?"

The older woman straightened and indicated that tea would be welcome. Euphie made a face at Thalia, who shook her head slightly, though she too smiled.

The following half hour was very uncomfortable, and the girls were painfully wondering if Miss Hitchins meant to stay to luncheon when she got up at last and took her leave. "I shall return in the afternoon," she told them, "as Mr. Gaines has asked me to. I shouldn't have dreamed of doing so otherwise, of course." She pressed each girl's hand once again. "If there is anything I can do, you need only call on me," she finished, and the maid showed her out.

"Whew!" said Euphie when she was gone. "I

thought she was settled for the day. What a dreary woman!" The girl fell back on the sofa dramatically.

"Euphie!" Miss Hartington glared at her.

"Well, it is the truth, and I do not see why I should not tell the truth, even if it is impolite."

Her sister opened her mouth to reply, then shut it again. The question seemed too large to grapple with at this moment.

"I wonder what is wrong with the will?" said Thalia, who had been sitting in a corner, very quiet, for some time.

"What do you mean?" asked her younger sister.

"There is something wrong with it. Mr. Gaines said as much. But what?"

"He said, 'There is, and there isn't,'" responded Aggie.

Thalia nodded. "Yes, but that means there is. Why bring it up otherwise? Oh, I wish he had told us. I shall worry about it all day."

"But what could be wrong?" Aggie frowned. "Our aunt was always very careful in business matters. I am sure all is in order."

"In order, yes. But for whom?" Thalia was also frowning.

"What do you mean?"

"Never mind, Aggie. Perhaps Mr. Gaines was right. We should wait until the will is read. Come, let us see if Cook has managed to make us lunch today, or if she still has the vapors." And with this, Thalia strode out of the room. Her sisters followed more slowly, looking concerned.

◦✦◦

The group that gathered in the library at two for the reading of the will was not a large one. Besides the three sisters and Mr. Gaines, there were only Miss Hitchins, Cook, and the two maidservants. No one counted the six cats; they were everywhere.

Mr. Gaines sat at the wide desk, spectacles on his nose and papers spread before him. He seemed to have some difficulty beginning. He cleared his throat twice, adjusted his neckcloth, shuffled the papers, and finally picked up a document and held it before him. His expression held both distaste and disapproval.

"I shall now read the last will and testament of Miss Elvira Hartington," he began. "This document was drafted by me some fifteen years ago and signed in my presence and those of reliable witnesses. I may say at the start that I believe it to be perfectly legal and binding." He cleared his throat again. "'I, Elvira Hartington, being of sound mind and body, do hereby…'"

He droned on through several paragraphs of legal introduction, and the three girls were just being lulled into a kind of drowsiness when he read, "'Therefore, having no direct dependents in need of my fortune, I hereby bequeath all money and property remaining after certain small bequests to a trust to be set up for the care and benefit of my beloved cats.'"

Mr. Gaines paused and cleared his throat once again. Everyone stared at him incredulously.

"She is leaving all her money to the cats?" blurted Euphie.

"I fear so, Miss Hartington." Mr. Gaines shook his head. "I told her time after time in the last ten years that she must change her will now that she had taken you into her home. She always agreed with me. I know she *meant* to change it. But, the fact is, she didn't."

Euphie stared at him, stricken. "Everything to the cats? Nothing to us?"

The solicitor grimaced. "You see, miss, you were babies when this will was written. And your father, the baron, Miss Hartington's brother, was quite well off. She couldn't know that he would die without providing for his children. Or indeed that he would not have a son to break the entail on his estate. She did leave five hundred pounds to be divided among his offspring. Thinking, you see, that you would require nothing, but wanting to leave a token. And... and a choice of the current kittens, miss."

Euphie couldn't speak for a moment; then she said, "Aunt left us each a hundred and sixty pounds and a kitten?"

Gaines nodded. "More precisely, one hundred and sixty-six pounds—"

"Well, I don't want a beastly kitten! Let them stay here with their wealthy friends!" And Euphie got up and ran from the room.

The solicitor shook his head. "Outrageous," he murmured. "I said so." He looked around the room apologetically. "I must go on."

Aggie and Thalia nodded.

"Of course, please do," said Miss Hitchins.

Gaines cleared his throat a third time. "Yes, ah, where was... oh, yes, 'enumerated below. I appoint my good friend Eugenia Hitchins to administer this trust, knowing as I do that her feelings and mine are in harmony on the subject of animal nurture and protection.'" He read on, through a series of small bequests to the servants and the one to the girls themselves, but they scarcely heard. Miss Hitchins, who had started visibly at the mention of her name, seemed lost in a pleasant daydream. And Aggie and Thalia were stunned. They had been cared for by their aunt since they were children, and it had always been assumed that she would provide for their future. Finding that she had not, they were momentarily lost. What would they do?

Mr. Gaines finished reading and began to roll up the document. He looked at the two girls sympathetically. "I wish I could offer you some hope or consolation," he said to them. "But as I mentioned, this is a valid will. I do not think it can be broken."

They simply looked at him.

"Ah, yes, well, I must be going. Miss Hitchins, you will call on me at my office when convenient? Yes. Well, good day, ladies." The solicitor left the room hurriedly.

Aggie and Thalia turned to stare at each other.

"You are welcome to stay and help me here," said Miss Hitchins. "I will of course keep this house. The cats will prefer to stay in a familiar place. And there is so much room; we can add many more to our little family." She bent down and reached for a yellow cat who sat near the corner of the desk. "Can't we, Socrates? We will be ever so happy and free." The cat turned pointedly away and began to lick its front paw.

"No," said Thalia involuntarily. Then she stopped

and looked at her older sister. Their eyes held for a moment.

"No," agreed Aggie. "We thank you for your offer, Miss Hitchins, but… but I really think we must make other arrangements."

"But what can you do? I daresay your aunt meant you to stay. Otherwise, she would have changed the will."

Aggie's eyes widened. She looked both shocked and hurt.

But Thalia merely raised her eyebrows and said coolly, "I shall teach. And I daresay my sisters can find other occupations better suited to their talents and interests. You will, of course, allow us some time to pack our things and make arrangements."

This was not a question, and meeting Thalia's frosty green eyes, Miss Hitchins quickly agreed. "Of course, of course. As long as you like."

"Thank you. And now, if you will excuse us, we have much to talk over."

As if irresistibly drawn, Miss Hitchins rose to her feet "Yes, indeed. I must be going." She gathered up her shawl and reticule and turned, then paused and said, "I had nothing to do with this, you know. I knew nothing about it. I am terribly fond of the cats, of course, but otherwise…"

"It's all right, Miss Hitchins," said Aggie.

"Yes, well, it's what your aunt wanted, I suppose. But I didn't wish you to—"

"Not at all," interrupted Thalia. "Good day."

"Yes, good day. I will see you… well… good day." And she went out.

When she was gone, the two sisters sat down again. At first, there seemed to be nothing to say; they merely stared at each other, trying to adjust to this sudden change in their fortunes. Then Thalia said, "Mr. Gaines was right. It *is* outrageous."

"She meant to change the will," offered Aggie.

"I should hope so indeed. But she did not, Aggie. And that is outrageous. We have no training, few skills with which to support ourselves. And Aunt never gave us any hint that we would need them. Insupportable!"

"But you have, Thalia. You can teach, as you said. Any school would be lucky to get you."

"Possibly," replied her sister dryly. "Whether I would also be lucky is another question. My studies have always been a cherished recreation. I never thought to earn my bread with them."

"No." Aggie looked forlorn. "And I have no skills at all; you are right in that."

"You have the finest skill, a perfect character," retorted the other. "You are much nicer than I."

Aggie laughed briefly. "Even if that were so, one isn't paid for one's character." Her head drooped. "Oh, Thalia, what are we going to do?"

"Right now, we are going to find Euphie. Then, we are going to plot." She held out a hand and raised her sister to her feet. "Have no fear, Aggie. We will think of something!"

A month later, the Hartington sisters stood together in the early-spring sunshine in front of their aunt's imposing house. They were dressed for traveling, and each held a wicker basket over her arm. Three carriages also waited there, pointed in different directions. One, Aggie's, was to go into Hampshire, to the home of a wealthy couple with two small children, whose nursery governess she was to become. The second, Thalia's, would head north to Bath, where she had been offered a post at a very exclusive girls' school. Euphie's vehicle was pointed south, toward London. With great reluctance, the youngest girl had accepted a place as companion to an old lady there.

"I can't bear it," blurted Euphie. "I have been with you all my life. I shall miss you horribly." She gripped the two older girls' hands.

Tears started in Aggie's eyes. "I know, dear. I feel the same. But we shall write very often. And perhaps visit at holidays."

"We'll save every penny," added Thalia with an attempt at gaiety, "and travel together, a pack of curious spinsters."

But this only made Euphie's mouth droop the more. "I can't bear it," she said again.

"We must," replied her oldest sister, though tears now ran down her cheeks. "There is nothing else we can do."

"But it isn't fair!"

"Don't expect fairness, Euphie," said Thalia very seriously.

One of the coachmen leaned down to say, "We'd best be starting, miss. It's a long drive."

Aggie nodded, unable now to speak. And the three sisters cast themselves into one another's arms. "You will write to me every week, at the *least*," said Thalia fiercely. "Promise, Euphie. You are a terrible correspondent."

"Every day!" insisted the younger girl.

They stood back.

"G-good-bye," stammered Aggie.

Thalia turned and began to climb into her carriage. "We'd best get this over," she said. "It won't get easier."

Slowly the other two followed her example. The coachmen whipped up the horses, and the three vehicles moved off. Euphie leaned out to wave frantically for minutes after the others were out of sight.

I.
AGGIE

One

WHEN AGGIE ALIGHTED AFTER A JOURNEY OF A FULL day and a half, she felt very tired and dispirited. The Hampshire house she found herself facing was a pleasant one, of mellow red brick, surrounded by lovely gardens. And the butler who admitted her was kind. But she already missed her sisters very much, and she felt apprehensive and alone.

The butler took her to the housekeeper's room, on the ground floor at the back, and there she was introduced to Mrs. Dunkin, a large smiling woman in black bombazine.

"Come in, come in, my dear. Sit down," said this lady. "You must be tired out after your long ride. I'll order you some tea." As she talked and bustled about readying tea, the housekeeper eyed Aggie curiously, and the girl was immediately conscious of her sober gown, schoolgirl bonnet, and uncropped hair. But Mrs. Dunkin seemed rather to approve than to criticize her unfashionable appearance, and gradually Aggie relaxed. "Here we are," said the older woman, offering a cup. "Nice and hot and just what you need.

Drink it all, now." She sat down opposite and took her own cup. "The mistress was that sorry she couldn't be here to welcome you herself," she went on comfortably. "She promised to spend the day with her mother before we knew just when you would arrive. But Miss Anne, or Mrs. Wellfleet I should say, will be home to dinner. I was with her mother's household, you know, and I can't seem to get in the way of calling her by her married name. She seems a child to me still." Mrs. Dunkin smiled at Aggie, who responded rather shakily. "Your mother was a great friend of the Castels', I believe? Miss Anne's parents, that is."

"Yes," responded Aggie. "Yes, she was. She and Mrs. Castel were at school together. My family used to live nearby, you know."

Mrs. Dunkin nodded. "I do believe I recall your mother. It was years ago, of course, but I think she visited the Castels' house. A lovely woman, she was. You have the look of her."

"I have been told so. I hardly remember her. She died when I was very young."

"So she did, poor thing. And your father not many years after. Grief will do that to a man. Tch, tch."

Aggie, remembering her gay laughing father and his death on the hunting field, said only, "The memory of their friendship led me to write to Mrs. Castel when I was looking for a position."

"Indeed. So you and your sisters are thrown on yourselves?" Mrs. Dunkin's curiosity was clear, but not at all malicious. She was obviously a woman who enjoyed a good story.

"Yes. The… the recent death of our aunt has left

us… that is, has made it necessary for us to earn our own way."

"Tch, tch. And your father's great estate lying empty while the new baron gambles it away in London, or so we hear. Disgraceful, I call it."

"The estate was entailed to the male line." Aggie shrugged. She had never expected to inherit her father's property, and so she did not feel the loss of it. Her aunt's will had been a far greater blow.

Mrs. Dunkin nodded. "I never understood such things, and I never shall. A man's children should get what's his, not some distant relation no one's ever seen." Noticing that Aggie had finished her tea, she added, "You'll be wanting to see your room and all. I'll take you up."

She escorted Aggie to a large airy bedchamber on the third floor. Though clearly not one of the most elegant apartments in the house, it was comfortably furnished and had a lovely view out over the gardens from three dormer windows.

"Here we are. The children's nursery is down the hall there. They're out with their mother just now. Sarah, the nursery maid, will get you anything you need. You can ring for her there. She can help with your unpacking if you like. Mrs. Wellfleet will be home in an hour or two, I suppose, and she'll want to see you then. If there's anything you want, just tell me."

"Thank you. Thank you very much, Mrs. Dunkin. I can't imagine that I shall. This is a lovely room." Aggie realized that she was getting special treatment because her family had been friends with Mrs. Wellfleet's, and she wanted to show that she was properly grateful.

The housekeeper smiled. "Well, I am glad you like it. And I hope you'll be happy here with us, Miss Hartington. You'll want to rest now, and I'll leave you alone. Don't forget to ring if you want anything."

"Thank you," said Aggie again, and Mrs. Dunkin went out.

When she was gone, the girl walked over to one of the windows and sat down in the window seat. She looked out over the garden, where the first spring flowers were just visible, and the countryside beyond. It brought back vivid memories of her childhood, lived not far from this spot. Even the scents which rose from the grounds below seemed vaguely familiar. Aggie smiled slightly. This hint of familiarity somewhat eased her longing for her sisters. Perhaps it would not be so bad, living in this house alone.

Her thoughts were interrupted by a sudden vigorous scratching sound, followed by several sharp mews. Aggie started up and hurried over to her luggage, which had been piled in one corner of the room. On top sat a wicker basket, and it was from this that the protesting sounds emerged.

"Yes, yes, Brutus, I'm coming," said Aggie. She quickly opened the clasp on the basket, and a sandy kitten jumped out and rolled onto the floor. "I forgot you. How could I?" continued the girl. "Are you all right?"

Brutus, who had received his name from Aggie's aunt at his birth, got up, shook himself, and proceeded to ignore his mistress as he explored the boundaries of his new home. Satisfied that he had thus shown his disapproval of his treatment so far, he then returned to the girl and began to bite at her ankles playfully.

Aggie laughed. At that moment, she was very glad that she and her sisters had decided to take their aunt's bequest of kittens, in spite of their resentment over the rest of the will. "Stop that, sir," she said. "You will ruin my only pair of silk stockings. Go and sit down, and after I unpack my things, I will take you to the kitchen and see about some milk."

Brutus stared up at her briefly, then went back to his pursuit of her ankles. And it was only when she began to walk about the room, putting away her things, that Aggie was able to discourage this pastime. Then, disgusted, Brutus went to lie in the window, watching the movements of a family of sparrows with considerable interest.

At six o'clock Aggie was summoned to the drawing room to meet her employer and her charges. In the interval, she had arranged her small possessions to her satisfaction, successfully introduced Brutus in the kitchens, and taken a turn around the garden. She was very glad to be called downstairs; she was eager to see what sort of people the Wellfleets were.

But when she entered the drawing room, it at first appeared to be empty. Aggie looked from one side of the well-proportioned chamber to the other, but saw no one. Then, a charming giggle from the direction of the long front windows caused her to look more carefully and notice a pair of very small boots protruding from under the blue velvet hangings. "Hello," she said then. "Is anyone here?"

This produced a gasp from farther down the room, and suddenly a slender blond woman burst from another window embrasure, looking embarrassed.

"Oh, how silly you will think me," she said in a soft breathless voice. "We were playing hide-and-seek, you see, and I quite forgot the time."

Aggie surveyed her with interest. Mrs. Wellfleet, for this must be she, was a small and very pretty woman with pale golden hair and large blue eyes. Her clothes were in the first style of fashion, of a wispy green material that became her extremely.

Mrs. Wellfleet pushed at her profusion of curls and called, "George, Alice, come out. The game is over. Come and meet Miss Hartington."

There was a pause; then a tiny girl emerged from behind the sofa before the fireplace. She was dressed exquisitely in pink and was the image of her mother.

"George," repeated Mrs. Wellfleet.

There was no reaction.

Aggie smiled and cocked her head in the direction of the small boots visible under the curtain. Mrs. Wellfleet did not seem to understand at first; then she followed Aggie's gaze, dimpled, and nodded. Aggie walked quietly across the carpet and pulled back the hanging. "Found!" she called out.

A small boy of about five started, then gazed up at her indignantly. "You weren't even playing," he said. "Mummy and Alice would never have found me." George was also fair, like his mother and sister. But his eyes were a sparkling blue, and his chin had a much more decided set to it.

"It doesn't matter now, George," said Mrs. Wellfleet. "Come out. The game is over."

George put his hands on his hips. "It's not *fair*! She wasn't playing, and you didn't find me."

He looked so outraged that Aggie had to smile. "Perhaps we must count it that you won, then," she said. "Indeed, I did not mean to spoil your game."

The boy focused his bright blue eyes on her, considered a moment, then smiled angelically. "It doesn't matter. I always beat Mummy and Alice anyway." He came out of the window and stood eyeing her. "I am George Wellfleet," he said. "And you are our new governess. I know that. Pleased to make your acquaintance." He bowed carefully.

Aggie choked back a laugh. "Thank you."

Mrs. Wellfleet did laugh. "Oh, how well you did that, George. What a fine little gentleman you are. This is Alice, Miss Hartington. She is a bit shy at first, but I am sure you will all be great friends."

Alice, who looked about three years old and had been keeping close to her mother's skirts, looked up wide-eyed, dropped an inexpert curtsy, and retreated.

Mrs. Wellfleet laughed trillingly again. "Aren't they darlings? You children run along now and find Mrs. Dunkin. I want to talk to Miss Hartington. Go on."

George started out of the room, turned to look at Alice, then came back and took her hand. As they passed through the doorway, the boy turned his head and smiled at the two women.

"George is such a little man," laughed his mother. She turned to face Aggie, still smiling, and looked her up and down. "Oh, you *are* lovely," she exclaimed. "Mother said you would be, because *your* mother was. But she thinks it doesn't matter a fig, because Alex positively dotes on me." She laughed again.

Aggie, taken aback, did not know what to reply to this.

"Come and sit down. We must get acquainted as soon as may be, for I am convinced we shall be great friends." Mrs. Wellfleet sat on the sofa and patted the cushion beside her. Still uncertain, Aggie sat down.

"There, now tell me everything about yourself at once. Or, no, I shall begin. That is more polite, is it not? Well, you know who I am, of course. Our mothers were very close friends, and Mama recommended you to me. I have been married to Alex for seven years, and we are *blissfully* happy. I cannot tell you how nice it is. And there are Georgie and Alice; I spoil them dreadfully." She laughed. "How could I not? But Mama thinks that they need more discipline, even though they are babies yet, so she thought I should get a nursery governess. And when she got your letter, it seemed perfect! I am a heedless creature, I suppose. You will be just the thing to keep me from cosseting them to death. Alex says so, too. But you won't be one of those dreary stiff governesses who make the whole household miserable; you are far too young, and too pretty. Oh, I am sure we shall deal together admirably. And you must call me Anne. There. Now, you tell."

This had all come out in such a rush that Aggie hardly took it in. And now, facing her expectant employer, she felt breathlessly speechless.

Anne Wellfleet went off in peals of laughter. "You look so frightened, you silly goose."

Aggie smiled. "Not frightened. But a little overwhelmed, perhaps."

"Oh, I chatter like a magpie, I know. Everyone says so. But I can't help it, and you will become accustomed to it very soon, I daresay. Tell me whatever you like. Or nothing. It doesn't matter. Would you rather not?" Her large eyes showed disappointment at this prospect, but no inclination to press Aggie.

"Indeed no. I would like to tell you about myself." She took a breath. "You know my family, of course. My sisters and I have been living with our Aunt Hartington since my father's death eleven years ago. But Aunt died recently, and we needed to find positions, to earn our own way." She stopped, momentarily at a loss.

Anne bit her lower lip and leaned forward. "Is it really true," she whispered, "that your aunt left all her great fortune to her cats?"

She looked so eager that Aggie could not help but smile a little. She nodded.

"Truly? But how outrageous. Was she mad?"

"No. Merely eccentric. And I do not think she meant to leave all her money so. She did not change her will in time, however."

"And you, poor thing, left without a penny. Oh, it is wrong!"

Aggie shrugged. She was not ready to discuss this matter with anyone as yet, particularly not a woman she had just met.

"Well, we shall make it up to you. You must count yourself as one of the family here." She laughed suddenly and clapped her hands. "I know. We'll pretend that you are my sister, come to live with us. I never had a sister, and I so wanted one.

You will be my little sister." She smiled radiantly at the other girl.

Smiling back, Aggie thought to herself that she felt much more like an *older* sister, if anything, to this charmingly heedless lady.

"We'll have wonderful times," continued Anne. She eyed Aggie's clothes and braids. "First, we'll find you some new dresses, and then we'll have my woman cut your hair. How beautiful you will be!"

"Oh, no," said Aggie. "I couldn't let you do that. It… it wouldn't be right."

Mrs. Wellfleet's face crumpled. "But I *want* to. *Why* can't I?"

"Well, because I, I am your employee. And it isn't right that you should…"

The other brightened again. "Oh, fustian. I can do whatever I want, if you are my employee. What a stupid word! And I want to give you some dresses. I have hundreds I never wear." She dimpled. "You *must* take them. If you wear such stuff as you have on, you will depress my spirits until I fall into a decline. You don't want that."

Reluctantly Aggie smiled. "Well, no, of course not, but…"

"Good. Then it's all settled. Come upstairs, we'll look through my closet before dinner. I'm thinking of a dress that should just suit you; you can wear it tonight."

"But I thought I would take a tray in my room—"

"A tray! Nonsense. You will dine with Alex and me, of course." And taking Aggie's arm, she led her resolutely out of the room.

Two

IN THE NEXT FEW DAYS, AGGIE BEGAN TO FEEL MORE AT home in the Wellfleets' house. She met Mr. Wellfleet, a pleasant quiet man who clearly loved his little family very much. Large and genial, he was some years older than his wife, and often seemed tenderly amused by her chatter. Aggie herself was overwhelmed by her friendliness. Anne had Aggie's hair cropped and curled and almost forcibly bestowed various garments upon her. The girl also learned something of her new charges, George and Alice, charming children who could exhibit perfect manners when they remembered to. But their vivacious mother had obviously spoiled them, and they were wholly unused to following any schedule but their own inclination. Aggie found that she more often took them for walks or played games than taught any useful subject, for George became obstinate and Alice despondent if forced to study. But as they were so young, she did not much worry about this. With time, she felt, and a gradual change, they could be made to enjoy learning. At this point in her thoughts, Aggie always grimaced. If they did

indeed reach such a point, they would soon require a
new governess. She had little beyond the rudiments to
teach them, never having been bookish herself. As she
wrote to Thalia, "I am very fortunate in having pupils
who want only to explore the countryside and learn
new games, for at these things, at least, I am expert."

Aggie wrote both her sisters faithfully, describing
her situation and her gratitude for its pleasantness. The
letters made her smile, for she could imagine how
Euphie would laugh over some of the things that had
happened and the amusing remarks Thalia would find
to make. But they also made her sad, for she missed
her sisters cruelly.

On the sixth day after her arrival at the Wellfleets',
Aggie stood before the mirror in her bedchamber,
putting on her bonnet in preparation for a morning
walk with the children. As she did so, she was struck
yet again by the extraordinary change in her appearance. She wore a smart walking dress of blue-and-
white muslin, in narrow stripes, with long sleeves and
a high ruffled collar. This, like her straw hat and pale
blue sunshade, had until her arrival belonged to Anne.
But Aggie had to admit, as she surveyed her reflection,
that they became her very well. And the new haircut
changed her appearance so much that it was still
surprising to catch a glimpse of herself unexpectedly.
Anne's dresser had ruthlessly cut Aggie's long braids;
her auburn hair was now pulled up into a knot at
the top of her head, with wispy curls falling over her
forehead and ears, and she still felt rather a stranger to
herself in this new guise.

Aggie smiled, shook her head, and tied the blue

ribbons of her hat under her chin. How silly she was being. She needed Thalia to rally her on her pretensions, or Euphie to dance around her, laughing and teasing about her finery. This thought brought a sigh, but a timid knock at her door dispelled her gloom.

"Yes," called Aggie. "Who is it?"

There was no response, so she walked over to the door and pulled it open. Outside, looking a little scared, stood Alice Wellfleet, dressed for walking. "Hello, Alice," said Aggie warmly. "Are you ready to go out?"

The little girl nodded. "George said I should come to get you," she added, as if in excuse.

"Well, I am ready, too. Just let me get my sunshade, and we will go. Come in." Aggie held the door open, and Alice moved a few steps into the room. As she bent to pick up her sunshade, Brutus, who had been napping on a window ledge, suddenly raised his head and stared at the intruder. Suspicious, he jumped down and came over to walk slowly around the little girl.

"Oh, you have a kitten!" exclaimed Alice.

"Yes, didn't you know? His name is Brutus."

"Butus?"

"Brutus. It is an historical name. My aunt chose it; she named all her cats for historical personages."

This information seemed to puzzle Alice, and she ignored it. "May I pat his head?" she asked.

"Of course. Do you like kittens?"

Alice, who had squatted on her haunches and was trying to coax Brutus closer, nodded enthusiastically. "Mother says I may have one of my own next year. But I must take care of it all myself." Brutus came into grabbing range and was promptly scooped up into Alice's arms, an indignity he protested with voice and claw. "Oooh," cried Alice. "He scratched me." She held out a tiny hand for Aggie to inspect. Three small pink lines showed on it.

"I see that he did. Cats are not fond of being picked up, you know. They are very independent creatures, and you must be very polite to them."

Tears had been welling up in Alice's eyes, but at this interesting information, they receded. "Must you?"

"Oh, yes. You cannot treat them at all as you would a dog, for example. Imagine a cat on a lead."

The little girl frowned, evidently trying to picture such a thing. "But I was only trying to pat him," she said.

"I know. But you must do so carefully. Like this." Aggie walked over to the window, to which Brutus had returned, and ran a hand gently down his sandy fur. "You see? You cannot maul him about."

Brutus looked up at her disdainfully and wriggled away from her hand.

Aggie laughed. "And even when you are, cats sometimes prefer their own company to yours."

Alice stared at her, wide-eyed.

"Are we going for a walk?" asked an aggrieved voice from the doorway. And George came into the room. "I've been ready for ages."

Aggie laughed again. "We are. We're going right now. Come along."

"Let's bring Butus," suggested Alice.

The older girl considered. Brutus had not yet been outside, but he was a lively animal and needed more space than he had in the house. She was afraid, though, that he would scamper off and be lost. "I'll take him in his basket," she concluded. "We can let him run in the garden when we come back." And she accordingly put a reluctant kitten into his basket and set out with it on her arm.

They walked through the back garden and out into the fields beyond. The children's favorite route was over a hill and down to a small shallow stream that meandered through the next valley, punctuated by trees and a few great mossy stones, and they headed this way today. George ran on ahead, coming back occasionally to show Aggie something he had found. Alice moved between her brother and her governess, seeming to want to cling to both.

They climbed the hill and went down the other side, reaching the stream quickly. Aggie led them to a charming spot where an old willow overhung the water and a wide flat stone made a comfortable seat. This place also had the advantage of being very safe. In spots, the stream deepened to two or three feet, but here it ran over a gravel bar and reached no more than three inches. Alice and George were allowed to play at the edge, as long as they did not venture in and get wet, and George delighted in launching endless sticks, leaves, and pieces of bark as "ships of the line," watching them whirl away downriver with great interest. He settled happily to this game now, sending his sister out foraging for suitable ship material.

Aggie sat down on the rock and, after a moment's hesitation, opened Brutus's basket. Immediately his head appeared above the rim, and she lifted him out.

"Now, sir," she said, holding the kitten up to her face. "If I let you down, you must promise to stay close by and to avoid the water. Unless you mind your manners, I shall never bring you outside again. Do you understand me?"

"Yeoow," replied Brutus.

Aggie eyed him suspiciously. "Yes, very likely. Well, we shall try this experiment once." And she put him down on the ground.

Brutus bounded over to the stream, bent to sniff it, and backed abruptly away. Aggie laughed. "You have some sense." The kitten then proceeded to investigate the various plants and weeds growing nearby. He showed no signs of running away, and after a few minutes Aggie relaxed her vigilant watch over him.

Alice had unearthed a particularly large and flat piece of bark, and she and George were happily embellishing it with such amenities as leaf sails and twig oars before launching. Everything seemed tranquil. Aggie pulled some paper and a pencil from her basket and, keeping one eye on the children, began writing a letter to Thalia.

The sun moved up the morning sky, and the green shadows shifted. Aggie put down the news of the previous day, glancing up often to see that George was not getting wet. She heard him telling his sister, "There. That is the way it should be. Of course, a *real* ship would have a crew, and passengers, like… like that. They would stand on deck."

"Butus doesn't *want* to," replied Alice.

Aggie looked up sharply. George had set the kitten in the middle of his bark boat and was trying to get

Brutus to take a twig oar in his mouth. "George!" she exclaimed. "Stop that immediately."

The boy started, his hand jerking away from the bark. At once the lazy current took hold of the light vessel and carried it out of arm's reach. Brutus expressed his extreme indignation by hissing at the water, his fur all on end.

"Oh, no," said Aggie. "Now, look what you've done."

"I didn't *mean* to," retorted George passionately. "You scared me. I wasn't going to let go until I took him off. I was only showing Alice."

"Well, you should not have been showing her in that way. Accidents can always happen."

They had all risen and begun to walk along the bank, following Brutus and his "craft." The current was not particularly rapid, and there were no rocks or other hazards likely to tip the bark over, but the stream moved steadily along, carrying the kitten farther with each minute. Brutus yowled angrily, glaring at his mistress.

"I'll get him," said George, sitting down and beginning to take off his boots.

"You will do no such thing," responded Aggie decisively. "Put your boot back on. We don't know how deep the water is here, and I will not allow you to go into the stream in any case. Your mother would be very angry."

"Wouldn't," said George. "She'd laugh."

Aggie declined to dispute this highly likely assertion. Instead, she walked farther along the bank, looking anxiously ahead for a narrow place where she might reach Brutus. The children ran along behind her.

"Are you just going to leave him?" asked George.

"Butus'll drown," wailed Alice.

"He'll do no such thing. I'm only waiting for a good place, then I'm going to get him out," said Aggie. But she eyed the water doubtfully. She had no wish to ruin her new stockings and dress by wading in, and perhaps falling—the stones looked slippery.

They continued along the bank, but no likely rescue spot appeared. In fact, the stream was widening, and Brutus was farther away than ever. At last Aggie stopped and sat down on a large rock to take off her shoes. "I shall have to go in," she said. But before she could make the attempt, George began waving his arms and jumping up and down wildly.

"Sir, sir!" he shouted. "Over here."

Aggie, in stocking feet, turned to discover a gentleman riding a brown mare toward them. Hastily she redonned her shoes. The rider, a fresh-faced young man of about twenty, pulled up before them. "Is something wrong?" he asked pleasantly.

"Our kitten is in the water," replied George. "You know my father. I have seen you at our house." He added this as if to validate his summoning of the man.

He swung down from his horse. "Have you? But where is this kitten?"

"Oh, you needn't… that is, I was going to… it is quite our fault…" stammered Aggie. She had been mortified when George called this stranger to their aid. And now that it appeared he actually meant to go into the water, she was even more embarrassed.

The man turned to her and stopped dead, transfixed. His mouth fell a little open, and frank admiration showed in his eyes. Aggie turned redder yet.

George tugged at the man's coattail. "Come on," he said. "He's over here."

"What? Oh, oh, yes, of course." Together they hurried down the bank, and the man hastily removed his boots and waded in to retrieve the kitten. In a moment he was back, handing Brutus to Aggie with a flourish. "He's not hurt," he told her, "but this adventure hasn't helped his temper." The man sucked at a finger Brutus had gracelessly scratched during his rescue.

Indeed, Brutus was in a foul humor. He clawed at Aggie, too, and soon induced her to put him down. Once on the grass, he turned his back on all the humans and began to lick his foreleg ostentatiously.

Aggie and the gentleman laughed. "Oh, I do thank you," said the former. "I was just about to go in myself."

"Then I'm doubly glad I happened along."

"Well, I would have gotten him, but Miss Hartington wouldn't let me," put in George stoutly. "You *are* a friend of my father's, aren't you?" He asked this as if checking credentials.

The gentleman, who had been staring fixedly at Aggie, said, "What? I don't know, really. Who is…? Wait a minute, aren't you the Wellfleet boy? Of course, I know your father very well."

George nodded happily. "I knew I had seen you."

"I should introduce myself," he continued. "I am John Dudley. I live about five miles from here."

"John Dudley?" echoed Aggie. She stared up at the brown-haired man.

"Yes. Am I mistaken, or have we met? Your name sounds very familiar, though I can't imagine I would

have forgotten meeting *you*." His smile as he said this
was warm.

"I am Aglaia Hartington," answered the girl. "My
family used to live not far from here, and I think we—"

"Uglea!" exclaimed Mr. Dudley, and blushed bright
crimson all the way to his ears.

Aggie laughed. "You are Johnny Dudley, then! I
wasn't certain. It has been a long time."

"I am. The graceless Johnny Dudley."

"Yes. You used to make such a game of my silly
name. I have never forgotten."

"Alas," he groaned.

Aggie laughed again. "Well, I can't blame you.
It is hard to say. But I hope you will not call me
Uglea anymore."

Dudley's pleasant blue eyes sparkled. "Never! Even
I am not so doltish, or so blind."

Aggie colored a little, and looked down.

"Butus is going into the trees," commented Alice
dispassionately.

The older couple turned hastily. The kitten was
indeed disappearing in a small copse nearby. "Oh,
what a tiresome animal," said Aggie.

"I'll get him," cried George, and he ran after
Brutus, returning in a moment with the indignant
kitten under one arm.

"We must go back and fetch his basket at once,"
added Aggie. "Here, give him to me. I shan't let go
until he is safely shut up again." She looked down.
"You will stay in the house after this, sir."

"It wasn't Butus's fault," said Alice. "George put
him on the boat."

"That is true. Well, we shall see." Aggie turned to Mr. Dudley. "Thank you again. It really was kind of you to rescue Brutus as you·did."

"You are quite welcome. But can I not walk along with you a little? To… to see that he does not get in any more trouble?" He smiled down at her.

"Well, well I…" Aggie stopped. She had suddenly remembered her position in the Wellfleets' house and this man's ignorance of it. She felt that he must have a false impression of her, especially dressed as she was in Mrs. Wellfleet's gown. "I am the children's governess," she blurted.

"Really?" he replied, nothing but friendly interest in his voice. "How does that come about?"

Aggie blinked and began to walk back the way they had come, partly to conceal her confusion. She had expected some stronger reaction to her confession. Unable to think of anything else to say, she found herself telling John Dudley how she had come to be the Wellfleets' governess.

"Are you serious?" he said at one point. "Your aunt left a fortune to a pack of cats?"

Aggie nodded.

"But surely such a will could be set aside? It is outrageous."

"The solicitor said not. It was all very legal. And our aunt did not have any real obligation to us, you see."

"Nonsense. Of course she did. She took you in, didn't you say? That made her responsible."

Aggie shrugged.

They had reached the basket by this time, and Aggie deposited Brutus in it before picking it up to return to the house. Mr. Dudley's stockings had nearly dried, and he put his boots back on and prepared to mount his horse again.

"I do thank you," said Aggie, holding out her hand.

"My pleasure, I assure you. I hope I may call tomorrow, to see that Brutus has taken no lasting hurt." His blue eyes twinkled.

But the girl looked down. "I don't know… that is, I shall have to ask Mrs. Wellfleet if it is all right."

"Oh, it's all right with Anne. She's used to having me about the house. But what about you?" He bent his head, trying to catch her eye.

Aggie struggled with herself. She felt that it would be very pleasant to see this man again. But she was not sure it was right to receive callers when she was, after all, an employee in the house.

"Come, you could endure a little further conversation with your childhood tormentor, couldn't you?" he continued. "You must give me a chance to make up for my cloddishness. And I can tell you everything that has happened since you went away."

"Oh, I would like that," said Aggie.

"Capital. I'll come tomorrow, then."

"Come *on*, Miss Hartington," called George from ahead of them. "I'm *hungry*."

John Dudley laughed. "One cannot stand against that. Good day. I shall see you tomorrow."

"G-good day."

He mounted and rode off as Aggie stood watching. She didn't move for a moment; then George repeated, "Miss Hartington!" and she hurried after her charges.

Three

AT DINNER THAT EVENING, AGGIE TOLD THE WELLFLEETS about her morning encounter. She felt some slight embarrassment as she did so, though she could not have told just why. But they heard it calmly, Mr. Wellfleet merely remarking that John Dudley was a good fellow and his wife smiling silently. However, when Aggie had left the table to go upstairs, Anne Wellfleet turned to her husband triumphantly. "Didn't I say so?" she challenged him. "She is so pretty, every young man in the neighborhood will soon be hanging about. And a good thing, too! A proper husband is just the thing for her, poor girl." She laughed and clapped her hands together. "Why, I believe I shall marry her to John Dudley. He is charming, and with a tidy little estate as well."

Her husband laughed indulgently. "John may have something to say about it, you know. He is well able to decide for himself whom he wishes to marry."

"Nonsense! No mere man can do that."

Alex raised his eyebrows. "Indeed? And I thought that *I* had."

Mrs. Wellfleet rose and went to drop a kiss on the top of his head. "Poor goose. I decided to marry you months before you had the notion. John Dudley will be perfect. I must think." She started to drift out of the dining room, a pensive look on her face.

"You mustn't interfere, now, Anne."

"Interfere? I? Don't be silly." She went out, leaving her husband smiling ruefully at the doorway.

Mr. Dudley duly called the following afternoon. Aggie was sitting in the back garden with the children and Brutus. George and Alice were occupied with a hoop, the kitten was vainly pacing the garden wall looking for a means of escape, and Aggie was sketching desultorily when the man came out. "Good day," he said as he approached Aggie's bench. "You are looking very well."

And indeed, in her primrose muslin gown, Aggie looked splendid. She smiled uncertainly as she rose.

"No, don't get up. I was just about to join you. May I?"

"Oh, yes… that is, I will tell Mrs. Wellfleet you are here. She will want to—"

"No need. I spoke to Anne a moment ago. She is busy with something or other and sent me out here."

"Oh." Aggie looked around the garden; she was unsure what she should do. She had never received a male caller before in her life.

"You're not going to send me on my way again?"

"No, no. Please, ah, sit down."

They seated themselves side by side on the garden bench.

"You've been sketching?"

"A little. To amuse myself. I'm not very good."

"May I see?" He picked up her pad. "Why, I think that is a charming picture of young George. You have him to the life."

Aggie laughed. "The merest flattery, Mr. Dudley. I know my talent is small. I enjoy my drawing, but I have no pretensions."

The man looked at her appreciatively. "No, I don't believe you do."

"My younger sisters are both very talented, in scholarship and music. I am used to functioning as an audience."

"Unfair."

Aggie looked surprised. "Not at all. I loved it." She gazed up at him, her blue eyes wide.

"You weren't sometimes weary of these over-bearing sisters?"

"They are *not* overbearing! They are both wonderful. Thalia is brilliant, and Euphie is... is the most charming girl imaginable. How dare you say such a thing?"

"I beg pardon," he replied meekly. "My only excuse is that while I have never met *them*, I have you, and I regret that you should have had to spend so much time being their audience, however charming they may be."

"Well, if you did meet them, you would see how silly you are being. They are much more interesting than I."

"Impossible!"

Aggie looked at him, then laughed and shrugged.

"One of your sisters is called Euphie?" he asked, in an effort to turn the subject. "An unusual name."

The girl wrinkled her nose. "We all have unusual names. Hers is really Euphrosyne."

"Ah, the three Graces. Your parents were prophetic, at least in your case."

"Well, we think they were sadly heedless. They can't have realized how tiresome it would be to go through life with names like ours." She dimpled. "We have all been teased so about them."

"Cruel to remind me of my past sins. Let me admit that I was a beastly little boy and have done. I have tried my best to reform since then."

"And have you been successful?"

"That I must leave to others to decide, Miss Hartington. What say you?"

"Oh, I have not been acquainted with you long enough to say anything."

"Alas. I must remedy that as soon as may be."

Aggie, who was enjoying herself very much, was about to reply when Brutus returned from his explorations. Recognizing his rescuer from the previous day, the kitten went directly up to John Dudley's riding boot and began to scratch at its shining surface. "Brutus!" she said. "Stop that at once."

Dudley bent and picked him up. "Do," he agreed. "My valet will have an apoplexy." He held the indignant kitten up before him. "He seems to have taken no hurt from his sail yesterday."

"I don't think anything could hurt Brutus. He is the most obstinate animal I have ever seen."

"Why do you call him Brutus?"

"My aunt did. She named all her cats for historical persons. I don't know why."

"Perhaps to give them a sense of their own importance," laughed her companion, whose hand was being ferociously attacked by Brutus. "There, sir," he added, putting the kitten down, "go away."

Brutus, deeply offended, did so.

Aggie laughed too. "No, they never required any reminder of that. Perhaps it was to show how important she thought them. My aunt was very fond indeed of her cats."

"From what you told me yesterday, I would say too fond. You know, I have been thinking about your plight, and I am convinced that you should go to law over that will. No judge in the country could fail to have sympathy in the case. I am certain that it could be overturned."

"The solicitor did not think so."

"Well, did you not tell me that he wrote the will? Of course he would believe it perfect."

"Perhaps." Aggie frowned.

"Well, then? I would be happy to lend you any assistance you require, if you are reluctant to handle the business." He sounded very eager to be of help.

"It is not that so much," replied the girl slowly. She paused, still frowning.

"What, then?"

"Well, my sisters and I talked of this, of course. My aunt's will was a great shock, and we thought at first of doing as you suggest. But the more we considered it, the more it seemed wrong, or… or uncomfortable."

"Why?"

Aggie looked up at him anxiously. "I don't know if you will understand, or if I can explain it properly, but we felt that my aunt had a right to do as she pleased with her money. We had no claim on her, really, and if she did not choose to leave us anything—"

"Nonsense. In the first place, you are members of her family, so of course you have a claim on her. Secondly, you told me, did you not, that she had several times said she meant to provide for you. The fact that she did not literally do so seems irrelevant."

"Not to us. If she really wanted to, she would have."

"Nonsense," repeated Dudley. "Who put such ridiculous ideas in your head, that solicitor?" His voice was heated.

A bit offended, Aggie drew back. "Not at all. Actually, this was my own notion entirely. My sisters agreed with me, though, when I explained."

"Well, I think you are dead wrong," responded her companion bluntly.

The girl's chin came up. "You are entitled to your opinion, Mr. Dudley. But I mustn't go on about my affairs in this boring way. We are hardly well enough acquainted for you to have any *interest* in them." She rose. "Perhaps we should go in now and find Mrs. Wellfleet."

Dudley's response to this setdown was gratifying. "You are right. I have been pushing into matters that are none of my business. And rudely, too. Will you forgive me, please? I can plead my genuine concern for your welfare as a partial excuse, though I know that gives me no right to order you about."

Only partly mollified, Aggie said, "Why should you be so concerned about a stranger?"

"Oh, but I don't think of you as a stranger. How can I, when I remember teasing you so boorishly as a boy? And I remember some more pleasant meetings as well. A picnic, I think, and a children's party at some neighbors'."

"The Ellisons," responded Aggie, much struck.

"That's it. Surely you feel something of the same thing?"

She looked down at him, realizing that he was right. She did feel somehow that she had known John Dudley for a long time, as if they were old and familiar friends. She would never have told him the story of her aunt's will at all, she thought, if she had not felt this. She was not in the habit of blurting out her private concerns to strangers.

"You do," he added, rising to stand beside her. "Come, let us cry friends again. I sincerely beg your pardon, and I promise not to mention your aunt's eccentric will ever again." He held out a hand and smiled at her.

After a moment's hesitation, Aggie took it, smiling slightly in her turn.

"There. That is better. Am I forgiven?"

Aggie cocked her head. "Provisionally. I must see how you behave in future."

"Alas, I have proved myself a clod once again. How may I make amends?"

"Tell me about the neighborhood," responded Aggie, "and the people we used to know. Now that I am back here, I keep remembering more and more. How are the Ellisons? And that brown-haired girl I used to play with; what was her name? Edith? Emily?"

"Ellen Jennings?"

"That's it!"

"She married last season, in London. And the Ellisons moved out of the county some years ago. I had almost forgotten them until now. Come, let us sit down again, and I will tell you anything you like."

"No, I must see what George and Alice are up to." The children had been out of sight for some minutes, though their happy shouts could still be heard.

"I'll walk with you, then," he replied promptly, offering his arm.

They strolled down the garden, chatting contentedly about old neighbors and remembered outings from their first eight years. They found George and Alice near the back wall, trying the hoop along a gravel path. Eventually George coaxed John Dudley into trying his hand, and he proved surprisingly skillful with the hoop stick. By the time the children were called for tea, they were all breathless from running behind the hoop and catching it as it began to wobble.

"Oh, my," said Aggie, smoothing back her hair as the children ran to be tidied before eating. "I don't think I have ever run so much. I am thoroughly winded."

"You look wonderful," replied Dudley. Aggie's cheeks glowed with the exercise, and the little curls of auburn hair that had escaped around her forehead and ears were charming.

"Oh, undoubtedly. All blown about and untidy."

He merely smiled down at her. "I suppose I must go. I had no idea it had gotten so late."

"Yes, I must make tea for the children."

"I enjoyed our talk immensely. I hope I may come again and repeat it?"

Aggie looked down. "I am sure the Wellfleets are always glad to see you."

"And what about you? Will you be glad as well, in spite of my occasional lapses into boorishness?"

The girl laughed, and nodded.

"Splendid! I shall see you soon again, then." And he pressed her hand briefly before striding toward the house.

Aggie watched him go, thinking how odd it was to feel so easy and friendly with a man she had met only the previous day. It really must be true that they remembered one another from childhood. As she turned to go in herself, she nodded slightly. There was no other explanation.

Mrs. Wellfleet joined them for nursery tea, very ethereal and lovely in a gown of clinging pale blue muslin. The children, as usual, greeted her with shouts of joy and much jumping up and down. Their mother welcomed this display laughingly and danced around with them a moment before directing everyone to the table.

"How lovely this is," she said then. "I do so love this room."

Sunlight poured in through the broad windows of the nursery, touching the chintz sofa, the battered table where they sat, and the bright heads of all four occupants.

"Yes indeed," continued Anne Wellfleet, beginning to pour out the tea. "I am convinced that this is the most comfortable room in the house."

"But, Mother," answered George, shocked. "Our sofa is all bumpy, and the rug is not nearly so soft as the one in the drawing room."

Anne laughed. "Isn't it, lazy boy? Well, I still say this is a fine room."

George shrugged and addressed himself to his bread and jam.

They drank their tea in silence for a moment; then Mrs. Wellfleet said, "Did you have a nice afternoon, all of you?"

"Yes," said Alice. "We played with the hoop, and Mr. Dudley showed us how. And I patted Butus three times."

"Mr. Dudley is a bang-up runner," added George, his mouth full.

His mother shook a finger at him before turning to Aggie. "Did you have a pleasant time as well?" she asked.

Looking at her plate, Aggie nodded.

"John Dudley is such a pleasant young man, I think. And he told me that the two of you were acquainted years ago, as children?"

"Yes. We often played together."

"Isn't that the most amazing thing? That you should meet again after all this time." Anne watched the other girl from the corners of her eyes.

"Well, your house is very close to our old neighborhood, so I suppose it is not so amazing as all that. But it was strange to see him again."

"We like him so, don't you?" A twinkle danced in Mrs. Wellfleet's eyes.

"Oh, well, I... I hardly know him well enough to say."

"But you are old friends!"

"There is a great difference, meeting as adults. I really don't… that is…"

"Very well. I shan't tease you anymore." Anne laughed. "I shan't even ask about that difference, interesting as it sounds. But I *do* like John Dudley; I hope he means to call again soon."

"I… I think he does."

"Splendid." And Mrs. Wellfleet turned back to her children, exclaiming, "Oh, no, George, you have jam on your coat *again*. Mrs. Dunkin will be so angry."

Aggie watched her with some puzzlement as she scrubbed at George's coat with a moistened napkin. What had she been leading up to? And why teasing? Aggie shook her head and turned to help Alice spread another slice of bread with jam.

Four

THE DAYS PASSED QUIETLY BUT PLEASANTLY FOR AGGIE. As she spent more time with George and Alice, she grew to like them more and more. And as they gradually became accustomed to the schedule she set for them, both showed more interest in learning the things she had to teach. They began to spend mornings in the schoolroom reading aloud or talking, going for walks outdoors in the afternoons.

Aggie's liking for her employers also grew. She saw little of Mr. Wellfleet, except at dinner, but he was unfailingly polite and kind to her. And Anne would clearly have overwhelmed her with kindness if she had had her way. Her huge enthusiasms and childlike enjoyment of things often made Aggie laugh, but the girl also saw that there was real warmth behind them. The two women were rapidly becoming good friends.

Of the surrounding neighbors, Aggie saw little. She spent much of her time with the children, and this left small opportunity to encounter any guests the Wellfleets might have. Too, though Anne always urged her to join any entertainment in the house,

Aggie felt awkward about doing so and usually kept to her room. It did not seem right to her that she should push into social activities; she always remembered that she was the governess, even though Anne Wellfleet did not seem to. However, John Dudley called several times and made a point of seeking her out and chatting. Her growing acquaintance with him was pleasant.

She received frequent letters from her sisters, Thalia in Bath and Euphie in London, and these went far to prevent any loneliness she might otherwise have felt. Both wrote amusingly, and both seemed reasonably happy, which raised Aggie's spirits.

But though Aggie was content and rapidly settling to a routine in her new circumstances, her employer was by no means so reconciled. "It is impossible," said Anne Wellfleet to her husband one evening. "How am I to introduce Aggie to eligible young men if she refuses to come downstairs when I invite them? I am convinced that she could make a splendid marriage, with only the smallest of exertions, but she *won't*." Mrs. Wellfleet pouted very prettily. "I declare I cannot understand the girl."

Her husband smiled. "What, have you given up on John Dudley, then? I thought you had determined that he was the one to marry Miss Hartington."

"Well, of course. But she must have some choice, must she not? How can she see how very nice John is if she meets no other young men? Oh, how vexing it is. Last evening, I had young Lord Wrexham and Mr. Lewes on purpose to meet Aggie, and she *refused* to come down! What is the *matter* with her?"

"I suppose, my dear, that she feels her position awkward. Her modesty does her credit."

"Whatever can you mean, Alex? What position, how awkward?"

He smiled down at her again. "You did engage Miss Hartington as a nursery governess for the children, Anne. And it is not at all usual to try to marry off one's governess in the neighborhood." He looked reflective. "Or out of it, for that matter."

"Pooh," replied Mrs. Wellfleet "Usual. I shouldn't care to be 'usual' even if I could. And no one ever had a governess like Aggie. She is so lovely, Alex!"

"She is that."

"And you must see that it would be positively criminal for her not to marry and have a wonderful family." She went over to sit on the arm of his chair, and he put one arm around her waist. "Just like mine!"

"I'd be a fool to try to dispute that statement. But I do think you should try to see the girl's side of it, Anne. She is probably embarrassed."

"But I *am* trying. If I wished to be selfish, nothing would be easier than to keep her as governess and never ask her downstairs. But I want to *help* her!"

"I know that. I wasn't criticizing. How could I? I simply meant that Miss Hartington probably does not know how to act when you try to make her one of the family. I suppose she does not want to seem encroaching."

"Aggie? She couldn't be."

"Doubtless. But it is because she worries over the matter that she couldn't."

Anne Wellfleet laughed musically. "How witty you

are. Well, I must have a talk with her and explain, I suppose. I wanted to do the thing quietly, without letting her know what was in my mind, but it appears that will not do." She started to rise, but her husband held her back.

"I think you should consider one thing, Anne, before you raise the girl's hopes too high."

"What?"

"Miss Hartington is indeed very beautiful and amiable, but she is also penniless. Many men will consider that fact before they speak."

"Odious Alex! Do you mean to say that any man would allow money to influence his feelings when he had once seen Aggie?"

"I fear that I do."

"Well, such a man is not worth one hair of her head, and I hope I am given the opportunity to tell him so!"

Her husband smiled. "You would administer a thundering scold, would you?"

"To be sure I would."

"Poor fellow. And yet one must sometimes consider practical matters."

"Not in this." Anne looked down at him, her blue eyes glittering. "I see it all now. You would not have offered for me, I suppose, had I not had a reasonable portion. How horrid men are!"

"I should have married you if you had been a beggar in the streets," responded her husband promptly, pulling her closer and putting an end to all conversation for several minutes.

When she could speak again, Anne laughed. "Liar.

You would not have met me at all had I been a beggar, but I shall forgive you because you are so absurd. Now, you shall not divert me. I must decide what to do about Aggie."

"Decide tomorrow," suggested Mr. Wellfleet, drawing her close again.

"Impudence. I shall decide now, for I have just conceived the most famous plan. I shall give a dress party for Aggie. She must come if she is the guest of honor."

"But, my love, do you think—?"

Anne clapped her hands. "I don't know why I didn't think of it before. I must go and tell her at once." She dropped a kiss on the tip of her husband's nose and stood. "What fun it will be. We have not had a real party in weeks." And with an impish smile she skipped out of the room.

Her husband, shaking his head, went back to his newspaper with a rueful smile.

Thus it was that Anne burst in on her children's lessons and blurted, "Oh, Aggie, I must speak to you. I have just had the most famous notion."

George and Alice turned quickly to look up at her. Though more docile now, they still welcomed any interruption in their studies. "Hullo, Mother," said George. "Did you know that in France they call a window a 'fenet'? How stupid they are."

"Yes, dear," replied his mother absently, with little regard for her offspring's future prejudices. "You and Alice run along to Mrs. Dunkin now, and perhaps she will find you a sweet. I want to talk to Miss Hartington."

"But we are having our lessons," said George, trying to look virtuous.

"Well, you may have them later. Go along, now."

"May I take Butus?" asked Alice, who had become very attached to the kitten in his brief sojourn in the house.

Aggie nodded, and the little girl scooped Brutus from the window seat and turned to go out.

When the children were gone, Anne dropped into the chair beside Aggie. "I must tell you what I have decided," she said.

"Certainly. But you know, Mrs. Wellfleet, it is best for the children to have regular hours of study. They become accustomed to it then, you see, and—"

"Oh, never mind that. And why won't you call me 'Anne'? I have told you and told you."

"I'm sorry." Aggie sighed and looked down.

"Well, that doesn't matter. Only listen. I have determined to hold a dress party for you, in three weeks' time, to introduce you to the neighborhood. Is that not a marvelous notion?" She smiled at Aggie expectantly.

The girl stared at her. "A dress party? For me?"

"Yes."

"But… but… why?"

"Why? So that you can begin to make your way in society, of course. You meet no one up here, and you won't come down when I ask you to. So I thought of this scheme."

"Mrs. Wellfleet, Anne, you can't, or rather, I can't. That is, one cannot give a party for one's children's governess. Think how odd it would seem."

"Pooh, I don't care for that." Aggie started to speak, but Mrs. Wellfleet forestalled her. "Alex said you might feel this way, so I came to explain everything to you. Aggie, you must marry. It isn't right that you should spend your days with George and Alice and have no beaus. My children are charming, but you should be thinking of children of your own, not tending other people's. So I have determined to act for you in this, as your mother would." She giggled at this idea. "We have heaps of suitable young men in our neighborhood here, and I shall see that you meet them all so that you can make your choice." She smiled blindingly. "There, now you see that it is all right."

Aggie gazed at her, her eyes very wide. She couldn't seem to find anything to say to this preposterous scheme.

"We must have a new dress made for you," continued her employer gaily. "White, I think, or perhaps pale primrose. We must study the patterns. And naturally—"

"Mrs. Wellfleet, you *cannot*," blurted Aggie.

Anne raised her eyebrows. "You don't want a new dress? But, Aggie, it would be such fun to—"

"You cannot give a party for me. It is wholly unsuitable. I have no thought of marrying. I am quite happy doing my work here. Please, let us not talk of this anymore." The mention of new dresses had evoked a vision of dancing and lighthearted gaiety that Aggie found hard to bear.

"But, Aggie," began the other.

"Please!"

Seeing that the girl was really upset, Mrs. Wellfleet

rose. "Very well. We shan't talk of it any more now. But I am not giving up. I still think it a grand scheme."

Aggie turned a little away from her, struggling with her feelings. She felt immensely grateful to her kind employer, but she also felt very much like crying.

Anne watched her with concern. "I didn't mean to worry you," she added, perplexed.

"I know. I'm sorry."

Mrs. Wellfleet laid a hand on her arm. "Aggie…"

"I'm quite all right. It was nothing. I really should get back to the children's lessons now, Mrs. Wellfleet. I do want them to learn everything that I can teach them."

The other woman frowned at her for a moment, then looked down. After a moment, she rose. "I'll send them back in," she said.

Aggie jumped to her feet. "I can fetch them."

"No, no, I have to walk past Mrs. Dunkin's room." She half turned to go, started to speak, then changed her mind and went out. Aggie spent the short time before George and Alice reappeared composing herself and trying to forget the feelings that their conversation had raised.

She did not wholly succeed. The children distracted her through the morning, but when they set out on a walk later in the day, her thoughts turned back to what Mrs. Wellfleet had suggested, and she was forced to ponder her own reaction.

Because of her aunt's eccentric views on marriage and the male sex in general, Aggie had experienced few of the diversions common to girls of her age and position. She had never been to a ball, or even an evening's dancing. Though she had once or twice attended the theater and often met her aunt's friends at home, she had never been to a gathering that included young people. She had felt the lack, less perhaps than her youngest sister, but more than Thalia seemed to. But as there was apparently no remedy, she had calmly shrugged off regrets. Now Mrs. Wellfleet had offered her something of what she had missed. Aggie had felt a part of her respond eagerly at the idea. But the offer came in a way that seemed to her to make it impossible. She had been engaged as a governess, and a governess she must be. Such did not dance at evening parties.

She concluded this as she seated herself on the rock beside the stream where Brutus had taken his epic sail. The children were playing happily by the water. Aggie sighed as she watched them.

"Whatever is the matter?" asked a voice from behind. "You look as if the cares of the whole world had been put on your shoulders."

Aggie turned quickly to find John Dudley coming up to them. "Oh," she said.

"Anne said you were outdoors, and I took the liberty of coming to search for you. But what is wrong? You really did look dejected."

"Nothing."

Dudley sat down beside her and looked into her face. "I can't believe that. But perhaps I am intruding; I won't press you."

He sounded so kind and so genuinely concerned, that Aggie could not help answering, "It isn't anything important. Mrs. Wellfleet wants to give a party for me."

He paused a moment, seeming surprised, then began to laugh.

"*You* see how improper it is, don't you?"

"Improper? Not at all. I was just imagining Anne hatching the scheme. It is so like her."

"She is very kind, but I can't seem to make her understand how ridiculous it would be to give a party for her nursery governess."

"Ridiculous? Why? I think it is a capital idea."

Aggie looked at him despairingly. "How can you say so? You must see what I mean. Only think a moment!"

"Oh, I understand that in most cases it would be extremely odd, even eccentric. But you are hardly the usual nursery governess, Miss Hartington. You are a special case."

"I took the position, and I will fulfill its requirements," replied the girl stiffly. "I do not want special treatment; a party is out of the question." She turned a little away from him.

He nodded slowly. "That is what you feel, is it?"

"Of course it is. How could I feel anything else?"

"Perhaps *you* couldn't, though I can imagine a good many other reactions to an offer like Anne's. But don't you think you are being a bit overnice?"

She frowned at him.

"You *are* a special case, you know, whether you wish to be or not. Anne must know the story of your aunt's will?"

Reluctantly Aggie nodded.

"There you are, then. Your being forced to seek employment was a sad accident, and you are obviously destined for finer things than governessing."

Still frowning, she looked down.

"Have you ever considered, Miss Hartington, what you will do when George and Alice are older? George will be off to school in a few years, and you have told me that you do not feel qualified to take complete charge of Alice's education."

"No, I'm not. I shall, ah, find another position."

"Indeed. And another, and another. Most of them much less pleasant than this one, I wager. Is this the way you wish to spend your life?"

"My wishes don't signify," she retorted. "I haven't any choice!"

"Ah, but you do. Now."

Aggie looked up at him, perplexed. "You are telling me that I should accept her offer, take advantage of her kindness?"

"It is not taking advantage. In some cases it might be, but in yours, never."

The girl leaned back a little and stared out over the stream, considering the situation.

"I admit I have a selfish reason for urging you to accept as well," added Dudley, smiling.

"What?"

"I should very much like to dance with you at an evening party."

Aggie's lips curved slightly upward. "You do not even know if I *can* dance. Perhaps I should tread on your feet and give you a miserable half hour."

"Impossible. I feel somehow that you were born knowing how to dance."

"How absurd." For some reason, Aggie felt much better than she had only a few minutes past.

"You will accept, then?"

"I don't know. It still seems... wrong somehow."

"You know what you might do to convince yourself that it is not?"

"What?"

"Speak to Alex."

"Mr. Wellfleet?"

"Yes. He's a sensible, levelheaded chap. And he knows Anne better than any of us. Why not ask his opinion?"

"I... I hardly know him," faltered Aggie, a bit daunted at this prospect.

"Oh, well... he is your employer, though. He's bound to give you aid and advice."

Aggie laughed. "Indeed?"

"Well... but you know, he's a good fellow. Always glad to help."

"Perhaps I could speak to him," she mused. "I might at least convince him that this whole idea is preposterous."

"Do," urged her companion.

She looked at him, then nodded once. "I will."

"Splendid. You'll see; he'll be a great help." Dudley rose to his feet. "I must go."

"Oh." Aggie stood also, a bit surprised at his haste.

"Yes. Just remembered an engagement, actually. I'm sorry to rush off."

"Not at all. Good-bye."

"Good-bye." And John Dudley turned to hurry back to the house, to see whether, as he hoped, his friend Alex Wellfleet was still sitting in his study. If he weren't, thought Dudley, he would dashed well find him wherever he was.

Five

AGGIE THOUGHT OVER WHAT JOHN DUDLEY HAD
advised for the best part of a day. There was no
opportunity, in any case, to speak to Mr. Wellfleet that
evening, and the following morning she was occupied
with the children, as usual. But later, when George
and Alice went to sleep after luncheon, she resolved
to carry through with the idea and went downstairs to
look for her employer.

She knocked on the closed door of his study rather
timidly. And when a deep voice bade her enter, she
took a breath before turning the knob and stepping
into the room. Mr. Wellfleet sat behind the desk,
some papers spread before him, but he nodded pleasantly when Aggie appeared. Indeed, John Dudley had
prepared him to receive the girl, so he was not at all
surprised at her visit.

But Aggie knew nothing of this. "You are busy,"
she stammered. "I can come back another time."

"Not at all, Miss Hartington. How may I assist you?
Please. Sit down."

Aggie nervously took the armchair before the desk,

folded her hands, and looked at the floor. It was more difficult than she had expected to begin.

Mr. Wellfleet watched her with curiosity and more interest than he had felt heretofore. His conversation with his friend Dudley had been eye-opening, and he had felt that there must be more to Miss Hartington than he had suspected. Until then, she had seemed to him excessively quiet and perhaps even a bit dull, though certainly very lovely. He frankly preferred a livelier woman, as his choice of Anne demonstrated. Now he wondered if he should revise this opinion. John Dudley had been very persuasive. "Can I be of assistance?" he repeated finally. "Is something wrong?"

"Oh, no. Not at all. It is just that… that I have been concerned about something, and I thought perhaps you could advise me. Or, that is, I know that I haven't any… I mean…" Aggie stumbled awkwardly to a halt.

"I should be delighted to advise you as best I can. What is worrying you?"

"It is not worry exactly. But, well, perhaps Mrs. Wellfleet has mentioned to you that she wishes to hold an evening party for me?" Aggie looked at him anxiously.

Wellfleet nodded.

"Yes. Well, I feel that it would be wrong for me to accept such a great kindness. I came here to be nursery governess, Mr. Wellfleet, and I mean to fulfill my bargain. Mrs. Wellfleet has been wonderful to me, but I feel this is too much. It is quite unsuitable, do you not think so?"

He looked at her. The girl seemed to feel this intensely, and he began to understand something of what Dudley admired in her. "Unsuitable? I don't know that I would call it that."

"I meant no criticism of Mrs. Wellfleet," added Aggie hurriedly, suddenly horrified that he might construe her question in that way. "I simply feel that it would be wrong in *me* to accept."

"Your only objection to the scheme, then, is that? You would not shrink from a party on any other grounds?"

"Why, no."

"Well, then, I will tell you what I think, Miss Hartington. I think you should give in and allow it. We know something of your history here, naturally, and it makes your case unique, I believe, in the annals of nursery governesses. My wife is right in thinking you belong in a different sphere. I think you should take this opportunity to enter it." He smiled at her. "Of course, I must plead some self-interest in this matter. Anne has set her heart on this party, and I am not accustomed to denying her wishes."

Aggie looked anxious.

"Of course, I would do so if I thought her idea wrong or improper, but I confess I do not."

The girl took a breath. "Everyone seems to feel that way, except me."

His smile broadened. "Don't you think, then, that you should reconsider your position?"

"I'm not sure. Perhaps."

"After all, Miss Hartington, this is not such a great matter, is it? What real harm can one small party do anyone?"

Aggie raised large blue eyes to his. "I am afraid it

might do harm to me, sir. I fear I might enjoy it far too much."

Mr. Wellfleet's opinion of her went up another notch. The girl was not stupid. She saw the same danger in her situation that he did. It was all very well for Anne to talk of marrying her off, and probably right, too. But the risk the girl foresaw of that not happening might have been very real. However, a conversation he had had the day before had changed his opinion on this subject. "I won't pretend not to understand what you mean," he replied. "But I do not think you need to be concerned."

Aggie looked at him. He seemed so sure, but how could he *know*? She rose. "I will think about what you say. Thank you for listening to me."

"Of course." Mr. Wellfleet had a sudden impulse to tell her what he had learned yesterday from John Dudley, but as quickly as it came, he denied it. He could not violate his friend's confidence.

Aggie turned and went out; she still felt uncertain, but as she walked back upstairs, her step was lighter, and a small smile played about her lips.

It required three days' struggle with herself, but at last, Aggie gave in. Her longing to taste the gaieties of society, reinforced by the urgings of everyone around her, finally overcame her doubts, and the next time Mrs. Wellfleet broached the subject, she agreed. This threw Anne into transports and loosed a perfect deluge of party plans on Aggie's head. The invitations were sent that very day, and Aggie was forcibly pulled into consultation about the dress she would wear. When she objected that she must get back to the children,

Anne scoffed. "Pooh. They are perfectly fine with Mrs. Dunkin. And she loves having them to herself again. Come look at this pattern, Aggie. It is the most cunning thing; there are tiny tucks all down the front." She held out the latest number of the *Fashion Gazette*, and the other girl took it absently. "I cannot decide," continued Anne, "whether you should wear white or primrose. Pink is clearly wrong, with your lovely hair. What do you think?"

"I have always wanted a pale blue gown," responded Aggie involuntarily.

Mrs. Wellfleet was transfixed. "Pale blue," she repeated in the voice of one who has had a revelation. "Of course!" She clapped her hands together. "The perfect thing! How clever you are, Aggie. We shall find the cloth this very afternoon. My dressmaker can make it up in whatever pattern you like."

Aggie nodded. "And I have some money from my aunt's will. I insist upon paying for the dress."

Anne's lower lip jutted out. "But I wanted to get it for you." Her pretty face creased in a pout.

"You have been far too kind to me already." Aggie met her eyes resolutely.

Mrs. Wellfleet held her gaze for a moment, then shrugged. "Oh, very well, but I think you are a deal too nice." She reached for the fashion periodical once again. "Did you see a pattern you like?"

❧

The following days flew by in a whirl of activity. They found a lovely pale blue gauze and the dressmaker was set to work on it. Anne persisted in consulting

Aggie on every detail of the party, and gradually Aggie felt herself being caught up in the excitement of it. Despite her situation, it was wonderful to be looking forward to her first real party—her come-out, as it were. She found it harder and harder to concentrate on the children's lessons in the mornings, a fact which they did not appear to mind in the least.

Three days before the event, Aggie suspended them entirely, confining her time with George and Alice to walks and games. That morning, they went again to their favorite spot, beside the stream, and she lapsed into a pleasant reverie as they played on the bank. As before, John Dudley found them there. This time he rode up from the opposite side of the water, jumping his horse over it and dismounting to join Aggie on the sun-warmed rock.

"How are you?" he said then.

"Very well, thank you. And you?"

"In prime twig. Looking forward to Anne's party, as I hope you are as well."

Aggie dimpled. "I admit I am."

"No more doubts?"

"Oh, I have thrown prudence to the winds and am bent on dissipation."

He laughed. "Splendid. And I particularly want to claim the honor of the first dance. You cannot deny that to such a staunch advocate of the thing."

Aggie smiled again. "No, indeed."

"Splendid," he said again. "Now I know I shall have a fine time."

George called to them to show them a snail he had found on the verge of the stream. When they had admired it sufficiently, he turned away again, and Dudley said, "And so, have you been very busy preparing?"

Aggie nodded. "Anne is half distracted. But we always talk of me and what I am doing, Mr. Dudley. I suddenly realize how rude I have been; I seem to be always pouring out my troubles to you, yet I have asked you almost nothing about yourself. Tell me."

He looked a bit nonplussed. "Tell you what?"

"About yourself. Your interests."

"There's very little to say on that head, I'm afraid. I'm not a very interesting chap."

"I don't believe it. Very well, I will begin then. You like to ride, I think?"

He shrugged. "Well enough. What makes you say so?"

Aggie looked at him from under lowered lashes. "You ride this way so often. I thought it must be one of your favorite pastimes."

Dudley started and looked down at her. Catching a twinkle in her eye, he smiled. "The ride is not the primary attraction," he replied.

Aggie lowered her eyes. "What do you like, then? I should really like to know."

He leaned forward, putting his elbows on his knees, "Well, I fear my interests are prosaic. My estate is nearby, you know, and it occupies most of my time. Since my father died, I have managed it, and I frankly enjoy that a great deal." He smiled ruefully at her. "Very dull, you see."

"Not at all. I think it would be very interesting to care for land. You are alone there now?"

"Yes, as you know, my mother died some years ago. And my sisters are both married and living in other parts of the country."

"It's strange; I hardly remember them. Yet we must have met."

"Well, both of them are a good deal older than I. I never saw much of them myself, so it's not surprising that you didn't. Eliza was making her come-out when you left."

Aggie nodded. "What do you do on your land? Is there a farm?"

"Yes. There is quite a large home farm, besides the leased land. Actually, I have recently become quite interested in some experiments we are doing. We are ditching some of the fields and will be trying a special new seed this year. They say that it yields twice as much as the old type."

"How is that possible?"

Dudley's eyes lit. "That is the amazing thing. They are working with the different varieties of seed, you see, crossing one type with another, and they are producing some revolutionary new sorts." He gestured expansively. "I wouldn't be surprised to see crop yields increasing by several times in the next few years. And you see what that means, of course. More food, more livestock, and generally a better living standard for everyone."

Aggie watched his excitement with a slight smile, interest and admiration in her eyes.

"It will take time, of course, especially to convince landholders to change their methods. So many of them resist any new thing. Why, even the small farmers don't want to change, even when you tell them they can grow more with less work. On my own land..." He stopped abruptly and flushed. "But you don't care for this. I am being what my sisters call a prosy bore. Forgive me."

"But you are not. I think it is fascinating. If we had more food, perhaps we should have fewer hungry people. My sisters and I visited London once, with my aunt, and I was frightened by the people in the streets."

"Exactly so," agreed Dudley eagerly. "There is great need, and it seems to me that improving our production might be more useful even than political change."

Aggie gazed at him. "Indeed. How wonderful to have thought of all this."

He flushed again. "Well, I didn't really think of it myself, you know. There are several men around the country working and writing about such things."

"But you have found them out and understood, applied their methods practically. That is admirable."

"Are you roasting me, Miss Hartington? I know my particular hobbyhorse seems ridiculous when one goes on and on about it."

"Not at all! I am perfectly sincere."

He looked into her eyes. "I believe you are. I hope I may show you my estate one day. Mainly the house, of course, but—"

"I should like to see it *all*," asserted Aggie.

The two young people gazed into one another's eyes, in perfect harmony, until George, with a yell he later explained was meant to imitate a wild Indian, managed to drench his little sister by hurling a large stone into the stream. They were forced to hurry

Alice home to dry clothes and a fire, and there was no further opportunity for conversation. John Dudley did manage to say, as he was going, "Don't forget, you have promised me the first dance."

And Aggie replied, "I shan't," as she urged Alice up the stairs. But no other remark was possible in the bustle.

However, as he mounted his horse in front of the house, John Dudley did not look particularly put out. His mind, which had been pretty well made up before, was now completely so. He would speak at the party, in that romantic setting, near the end perhaps, perhaps in the garden.

Aggie, having delivered Alice to the nursery maid amid much tutting and clucking, went over to the front hallway window on her way to her bedchamber. She could just see Dudley, riding along the lane to the road. She gazed at his blue-coated back with a pensive smile and remained at the window until he was well out of sight.

Six

ON THE EVENING OF THE WELLFLEETS' PARTY, AGGIE stood before a full-length mirror that had been brought up to her room some days before and looked at herself with amazed approval. Her reflection was a stranger, but one she thought she might like very well, given the opportunity. Her glowing auburn hair was dressed in a cloud of curls, and the pale blue gown was unquestionably a success. It fell straight from the high waist to a series of flounces at the hem, and the dressmaker had embellished these with lacy trim until they reminded an observer of sea foam. Blue ribbons fluttered from the waist of the dress, and the bodice and sleeves were simple and elegant.

"What do you say, Brutus?" asked Aggie gaily. "Do you still know me now?"

The kitten, who was perched on the back of an armchair in the corner, watching his mistress suspiciously, mewed sharply once.

"Surely not," laughed Aggie. "I think I look very fine." She went over and picked him up, holding him near her face. "You are the most exasperating, dearest animal, Brutus, and I am very glad I brought you from home after all."

She had just set him down again and turned back to the mirror when there was a flurried knock at her door and Mrs. Wellfleet burst in. This lady looked enchanting in sea-green gauze draped over satin, with an emerald necklace. "I couldn't wait to see how you looked," she exclaimed. "Oh, beautiful!" She pushed Aggie up to the mirror, then took her shoulders and turned her around. "Yes indeed, the dress is perfect. I knew it would be."

"I love it," admitted Aggie. "I am so grateful to you, I can't even say how much."

"Pooh," said the other. "Anyone would have done the same, after seeing you. You belong in such gowns."

"On the contrary, I think no one else in the world would have done so. Only the most generous, kindest person I have ever met." Aggie held out a hand, and Mrs. Wellfleet squeezed it.

"Well, I am glad you are happy," she replied ingenuously, "for I am having such fun that I should be quite cast down if it should end too soon. Come, let us go downstairs. Our guests will be arriving in half an hour."

Aggie obediently followed her out, shutting the door on Brutus to make certain that he would not wander away.

"By the by," continued Anne Wellfleet airily as they walked down the staircase, "I have not thought it necessary to explain your exact circumstances to everyone coming tonight. So fatiguing. Some of them

knew your parents, of course, and I have put it about
that you are visiting us."

Aggie frowned. "That seems like deception."

"Oh, well, of course you will tell anyone who
comes to know you well. But I did not see the necessity of spreading the story throughout the neighborhood. Some of them are *such* gossips; they would
never be done talking."

"Still—" began the other girl.

"And besides," interrupted Mrs. Wellfleet, "it
won't matter a particle after tonight." She smiled
as she thought complacently of the information her
husband had passed along to her.

"What do you mean?"

Turning startled eyes on Aggie, the other said, "Oh,
nothing. Nothing at all. Just that it doesn't signify.
Come, we should hurry." And she practically ran
down the hall to the drawing room, leaving Aggie
to follow more slowly, trying to puzzle out what she
had meant.

❦

The entire neighborhood came to the Wellfleets'
drawing room that evening. Aggie had never even
seen most of them, though several remembered her
parents. She stood beside Anne, greeting each guest
and being introduced, and tried to keep all the names
straight in her head. Long before everyone had
arrived, she had given up in despair. It was, apparently,
a very populous county. By nine, fully thirty people
stood about the room, and the buzz of conversation
was overwhelming.

"I believe everyone has come," said Anne. "I must see about the dancing. You will start, dear Aggie. Shall I find you a splendid partner?"

A little color showed in Aggie's cheeks. "I promised the first dance to Mr. Dudley," she answered. "And I admit I am glad now. He is almost the only gentleman I know."

"Did you? How nice. Let us go and find him."

They discovered John Dudley, who had arrived sometime earlier, in a corner, deep in a discussion of livestock with several of his male neighbors. "Come, John," said Anne Wellfleet. "I want to start the dancing, and Aggie says she is promised to you for the first."

"She is indeed," he replied promptly. "Gentlemen, if you will excuse me."

"Bound to," said one of his burly companions, eyeing Aggie appreciatively. "But mind you, John, if I were twenty years younger, you shouldn't walk off with such a prize so easily."

Dudley laughed and offered Aggie his arm. "I can only thank Providence, Sir Charles, that you are not."

The burly man's guffaw followed them out onto the floor. Mrs. Wellfleet went to speak to the musicians she had hired for the evening.

"You have scored a coup," said Dudley as they waited for the music to begin and the others to choose partners, "Sir Charles is counted quite a connoisseur."

"He is funny."

"Oh, yes, though I admit that I do not always appreciate his wit. He is one of those in the neighborhood who mocks my efforts at experimental farming."

"Oh, no."

"Oh, yes. He believes that the ways of his grand-fathers are good enough for his grandsons as well. He finds much to amuse himself, and anyone else who will listen, in my changes."

"Too bad. I shan't speak to him."

Dudley laughed. "This is punishment indeed. He will think himself cruelly used."

Several couples had joined them on the floor by this time, and the music started up. It was a country dance and offered few opportunities for conversation, so Aggie and John had to content themselves with smiles and nods in one another's direction.

By the start of the second set, Mrs. Wellfleet was surrounded by young men begging for an introduction to her charming guest. She laughingly chose one and presented him to Aggie. This process was repeated several times before supper, and Aggie soon met most of the eligible gentlemen of the neighborhood in this way. She received a great many compliments, and there was no mistaking the frank admiration in her partners' eyes, but somehow she was captivated by none. This one seemed very young and frivolous; that one awkward and tongue-tied; and another, who fancied himself a budding beau, quite embarrassed her with his fulsome flattery. All in all, Aggie found that she felt a vast relief when John Dudley came up to her as the final set before supper was forming and begged for another dance. Seeing Mrs. Wellfleet approaching with yet another stranger, she consented quickly and took his arm to walk onto the floor.

"What is it?" he asked, amused. "You looked hunted."

Aggie sighed. "It is hard, I find, to dance with so many strangers. I have often imagined how wonderful a ball would be, but I see now that it is a great work. One must chat and laugh and look as if she were having a splendid time, even when the exact opposite is the case."

"Alas, which of our poor young men has left you with this feeling? I take for granted, you see, that it is not I, for I at least am not a stranger, however prosy I may be."

"You aren't. I enjoy talking to you. You always talk of such sensible things."

Dudley grimaced, but she did not notice.

"Some of these gentlemen seem to have nothing in their heads but empty compliments." Aggie dimpled. "And hackneyed ones, too, my sister Thalia would say. Not one vestige of originality."

"You inspire in me a wish to meet your sister, tempered with a healthy dread. Is she very severe on us?"

"Not unless you deserve it," laughed Aggie.

"Ah. In that case, I will take care to avoid her."

"No, she is really very charming. She is simply so intelligent, you see, that many people seem a trifle dull to her." They had begun to dance by this time, and Aggie looked up at him. "Thalia is the *most* intelligent person I have ever met."

"Admirable," murmured Dudley, seemingly unable to tear his gaze from her face.

"Yes, she is."

"And your other sister, er, Euphie was it? She is also a paragon?"

Aggie laughed. "Oh, Euphie is the most delightful girl imaginable, but she is not precisely a blue-stocking." She laughed again, seeming much amused by her own remark.

"You are an amazing family."

"Why?"

"So much beauty, grace, and intelligence combined. Your father was truly a prophet when he named you, thought I cannot imagine that your sisters are as lovely as you."

Aggie's gratification at the compliment was tempered by a protest. "To be sure they are! They are much prettier."

"Impossible." He laughed a little.

"It isn't. And you cannot know how lovely they are, after all, never having seen them."

"True. I bow to your more expert opinion. But I reserve the right to form my own someday."

"Oh, yes. I wish you could meet them. I think they would like you."

"I hope they may," he replied, gazing into her eyes.

Aggie flushed a little and returned his look steadfastly.

They went in to supper together soon after. John found them places at a table filled with young people, and the meal was very lively, full of jokes and chatter. Aggie, with John beside her, enjoyed herself immensely. And afterward, she found it somehow easier to dance with the new partners her hostess presented to her.

Several sets went by, and it began to grow late. At eleven, there was a pause, and Aggie stood near one of the windows fanning herself and trying to cool her hot cheeks. The spring night was warm, and the room had become stifling as the evening went on. John Dudley came up to her and said, "Very stuffy, isn't it?"

"Yes, terribly."

"Would you consent to take a brief stroll with me in the garden? There is something I particularly wish to discuss with you." He faltered only slightly over his request, but the hesitation made Aggie look up quickly.

"Well, I, I suppose I could," she answered.

Dudley breathed a deep sigh of relief. "Splendid. Shall I fetch your shawl?"

"I'm so warm, I hardly feel I want it, but I suppose I must take it." Aggie started across the room, and the man walked with her. They said nothing, each preoccupied with the conversation to come.

They had just reached the chair where Aggie's shawl lay and were picking it up, when Mr. Wellfleet came through a nearby archway, followed by a man in riding clothes liberally spattered with mud. "Miss Hartington," said the former. "This man has just arrived; the butler brought him to me. But he insists upon seeing you. He says he has a message."

"I was to give it to the lady herself," said the other man, "and as soon as may be, as it's very important." He spoke stubbornly, as if rehearsing something he had said often before.

"What is it?" said Aggie. "Not my sisters? Has something happened?" She put out a hand, and John Dudley grasped it firmly.

"I don't know nothing about sisters," answered the

messenger. He pulled an envelope from his coat. "This is from Mr. Gaines, the solicitor. He told me it was terrible important, and you should see it at once. So here it is." He looked very pleased with himself.

Aggie took the letter mechanically. "Mr. Gaines? But what can he have to say to me?"

"You'd best open it and see," responded Mr. Wellfleet.

Absently pulling her hand free, Aggie tore open the envelope and spread out the single sheet it contained. The note was short, and she read quickly. "They have found a new will," she said then, seeming a bit dazed. "Mr. Gaines says I am a very rich woman now and that I must return home immediately to consult with him." She stared up at Mr. Wellfleet.

"Congratulations, my dear Miss Hartington. So your aunt was not so irresponsible as we thought her. Splendid."

"Yes, but I… I don't know just what…"

"It is a surprise, certainly. Perhaps you should sit down, I'll fetch Anne. She *will* be pleased."

"I'll get her," put in John Dudley quickly, and before anyone could reply, he strode away, a grim look about his mouth.

The party did not go on much longer, for which Aggie was grateful. She could not make trivial conversation when her mind was wholly occupied with this new development. By the time she had gathered her wits again, most of the guests had departed. She looked around for Mr. Dudley, but he was nowhere to be seen, and she assumed that he had left her alone to become accustomed to her news. No doubt she would see him tomorrow, and they could continue their very interesting conversation.

As predicted, Anne Wellfleet was delighted. The only thing that clouded her happiness was the fact that Aggie would be leaving them. "You will go to London, of course," she mused. "You *must*. What a come-out it will be. The town will be bowled out. Oh, how I wish I could see it!" She turned cajolingly to her husband. "Alex, might we go up to town, for just a tiny time?"

Mr. Wellfleet laughed. "Perhaps, if you wish to abandon your children, madam."

"Oh, no, but, well, Mrs. Dunkin *does* take splendid care of them."

He laughed again. "So she does."

Anne clapped her hands. "It is settled, then. We shall come up to town to watch you dazzle the ton."

"But I am not at all sure I shall go to London," protested Aggie. "I don't know just what I'll do." She thought again of John Dudley.

"Not go? Of course you will. You must have a season. And your sisters, too."

Much struck by this idea, Aggie paused. "Euphie would love a season," she said to herself. "I must write them."

"And so will you," urged Anne. "Wait and see."

The last guests departed, and Aggie went up to bed without having finally settled this matter in her mind. It seemed to her that there were more important issues to decide first. But one thing was clear. She would have to go home for a time and consult with Mr. Gaines.

She said as much to the Wellfleets the following

day, and they agreed, putting their traveling carriage at her disposal. As Aggie thanked them for this courtesy, Anne added, "You must go at once, much as I should wish to keep you. But if you are to reach London before the season ends, all must be done quickly. Why not leave tomorrow?"

"Don't thrust her out of the house, Anne," said her husband.

"Of course not! But you agree, do you not, that she should go soon?"

"I do. Business matters should be settled with dispatch."

"Well, I mean to go soon," responded Aggie. "Perhaps tomorrow." But there was doubt in her voice. She did not really care when she went home, as long as she might see John Dudley beforehand.

With this in mind, she sat all morning in the drawing room. But no callers appeared. After luncheon, she walked out to the stream, remembering as she went all the occasions she had met Mr. Dudley there. But though she sat and tried to read for quite an hour, he did not come. Anxiously she hurried back to the house, thinking he must have called in her absence. But the butler told her that no one had come.

Puzzled, and a little hurt, Aggie climbed the stairs to her bedchamber and sat down in the window seat. Where could he be? He had been so eager to speak last night.

Brutus came over and began to claw his way up her skirts. Absently she picked him up and set him beside her. Then she looked down. "I shall send a note," she told him positively.

"Rrroww," answered Brutus, as Aggie got up and went to her writing desk.

The note was duly dispatched. Aggie had her valise brought up and began slowly to pack her things. She would have to go soon. She was just finishing her packing before changing for dinner when one of the maids brought in an envelope from Dudley.

Aggie tore it open and scanned the contents; then her face fell. The note said:

> *I regret that an unusual press of business prevents me from calling on you just now.*
>
> *Be sure that I congratulate you heartily on your recent good fortune and wish you all the best for the future.*
>
> *Sincerely,*
> *John Dudley*

Aggie read it again, frowning. What had happened to make him so stiff and cold? Why should he treat her this way?

She refolded the note and put it back in its envelope, slipping it into her valise. There was nothing to wait for now. She had stooped to summon him and been humiliated. She would leave for home tomorrow.

II.
THALIA

Seven

THALIA ARRIVED IN BATH AFTER A FULL DAY ON THE road. The school at which she was to teach was on the outskirts of the town, and her carriage took her past the Pump Room and the fashionable shops on the way. She looked at them with interest, but without regret at the idea that she was unlikely ever to enter them. Since her childhood, Thalia had been more interested in books than in anything else, and she rather looked forward to trying to teach other girls this love.

The Chadbourne School was a large red brick building situated in its own extensive gardens near the edge of Bath. Thalia leaned out of the coach window to survey it as they drove up the drive. This would be her home for an unknown number of years. She had already heard a good deal about it, for Chadbourne was one of the most exclusive and best-known of the Bath seminaries. Here the girls were said to get the finest education available to them in England. Thalia's green eyes were bright as she looked it over. She had no fears of failure, for she knew her abilities were great; she wondered only what sort of people she would meet and whether they would be pleasant companions and colleagues.

A footman opened the carriage door for her and helped her down. She saw her luggage unloaded, then walked up four steps and through the wide double doors of the entrance. In the hallway, a diminutive maid awaited her. She curtsied slightly and said, "Miss Chadbourne will see you now, miss. If you'll come with me."

Thalia followed her up one flight of stairs and down a corridor to an oak door. "Here we are, miss," said the girl, and she opened the door onto a large, pleasant office/study, shutting it behind Thalia without coming in. The room was painted blue, and broad windows gave onto the front of the building and the side garden. Books covered the other two walls, even in shelves over the doorway, and there was a large table set before one of the windows with two blue velvet armchairs before it. Thalia liked the room immediately; she felt comfortable in it. And this disposed her to like the woman at the desk, who was now rising to greet her. This must be Miss Aurelia Chadbourne, the headmistress and descendant of the founder of the school.

The two women looked at one another frankly for a moment. Thalia saw a tall, slender, commanding woman with light gray eyes and brown hair. Miss Chadbourne was dressed quietly, but with an elegance that made Thalia the more aware of her own drab traveling dress and the braids wrapped around her head. "Good day, Miss Hartington," said the older woman then. She did not smile. "Sit down, please."

Thalia moved to one of the armchairs, and Miss Chadbourne sat down behind her desk once more.

"I want to welcome you to our school," continued the headmistress. "I hope you will be comfortable here."

Thalia looked around the room, her eyes lingering on the leather-bound books on the walls. "I think I shall," she replied in a voice as cool and cultivated as her companion's.

A slight smile curved Miss Chadbourne's lips. "You must not take this room as typical, I fear. Here I receive our parents and guardians. It is furnished for them. Your own quarters will not be so luxurious, Miss Hartington." She watched Thalia closely.

"I don't care for luxury."

"Doubtless." The other's voice was dry. She hesitated, then continued. "I wanted to speak to you immediately, Miss Hartington, even before you were taken to your room, because I have some misgivings about our association. Frankly, I am not at all certain that you *will* like it here."

"I am perfectly capable of doing the job," replied Thalia stiffly.

"Oh, indeed. I am not concerned about your skills. They are, in fact, far above anything we usually require. From the list of your studies and the reports of your quite impressive tutors, I should say you are an exemplary scholar. No, I am more worried about your reaction to the day-to-day living situation here. You are used to something quite different, I know, and can have no idea of what you face. I think you will have difficulty adjusting."

Thalia frowned at her. "I cannot, of course, dispute

that, for as you say, I have no definite idea of the conditions you refer to. But I can say that I am ready to make any adjustments necessary."

Miss Chadbourne, who had continued to watch her closely throughout this exchange, smiled genuinely for the first time. "I think you mean that."

"Of course I do."

The other's smile broadened. "I am not insulting you, Miss Hartington. Women who are *forced* to take employment such as this, as you have been, are not often so ready to change their way of living. I have had trouble of that sort before. But perhaps I will not with you. I am glad. And if I can be of any assistance to you, at any time, you need only ask."

"Thank you."

It seemed that Miss Chadbourne almost laughed, though Thalia could see nothing amusing in her response. Then she added, "Let us just discuss your duties briefly, before I summon Mary to show you your room. As I said, I fear your learning is far broader than we really require. Our girls study music, dancing, and languages chiefly. We have recently added some instruction in household economy. But I must admit that our literature classes are quite rudimentary. Our oldest girls study it a bit, chiefly poetry, but we make no attempt to give them more than a passing acquaintance with it. I hope you understood this when you accepted the position."

"I did. But I was given the impression that you wished to expand this course."

"A bit, perhaps. But the scope will be limited, Miss Hartington. You will be fairly free to choose your subject matter, but I must tell you that none of our pupils have any real knowledge of the classics. I understand that your chief interests are there."

"Yes. But I have read widely in modern literature as well."

"Of course. Well, I fear your Latin and Greek will be useless here. I hope that does not disappoint you."

"Not at all."

"Good." Miss Chadbourne rose and went to pull the bell. "I'll let you go to your room now and begin to settle in. Then you will want to speak to Mrs. Jennings, our housekeeper, about the daily routine and so on."

Thalia rose. "Yes, thank you."

The headmistress's pleasant smile appeared again. "You needn't thank me, Miss Hartington. We are very fortunate to acquire a teacher with your intelligence and skills. I hope our association may be a long and happy one."

"As do I."

The maid came in, and Thalia took her leave, following the girl up more stairs to a room on the second floor. "Here we are, miss," she said. "This is your room. The bath is at the end of the hall. If you need anything, you can ring." And with that, she went away again.

Thalia stepped into the bedchamber. It was very high and narrow, with only one small window looking directly out onto the drive. There was a small bed, a writing desk and chair, and a battered washstand in the corner. The wallpaper and hangings were drab. Thalia looked around with some bewilderment. This was wholly unlike Miss Chadbourne's study, or the communal rooms she had glimpsed as she came in. It was rather dispiriting, in fact.

A sudden noise broke into her thoughts. It came from the wicker basket on the top of her pile of luggage, which someone had brought up while she talked to Miss Chadbourne. Thalia went quickly and opened it. A black kitten with great golden eyes poked his head out and surveyed his surroundings slowly. He then transferred his steady gaze to Thalia.

"I know, Juvenal," she said. "It is not what you are used to. Well, it is not what I am used to either. But we must accustom ourselves to it as soon as may be."

The cat made no reply. He looked toward the window.

Thalia lifted him down and put him on the bed, from which Juvenal leaped onto the windowsill and began to examine the landscape below.

"I suppose I should have asked Miss Chadbourne if I can keep a cat here," continued Thalia. "I quite forgot. I shall ask the housekeeper."

Juvenal, his curiosity satisfied, turned from the window and jumped back to the bed. There he curled into a neat ball and rapidly went to sleep.

Thalia laughed. "Well, I needn't worry about you, apparently. You seem quite at home already. I wish I felt the same."

Juvenal opened one golden eye, looked at his mistress, then went back to sleep.

Thalia laughed again. "Indeed. It is not so bad as that, is it? I must not fall into a decline. I shall wash and go in search of Mrs. Jennings, and perhaps I may find something for you to eat."

This she soon did. And hot water and a fresh gown made a great difference in her mood. By the time she went downstairs again, Thalia felt much better, and her interview with the housekeeper was very amiable. Mrs. Jennings, a massive, motherly woman of about fifty, told her the hours of meals and gave her a general plan of the building, saying that she would know the place in a trice. She explained what services the maids provided to the mistresses and told Thalia what instruction room had been set aside for her. "I hope you'll be happy here, miss," she finished. "We've done what we can to make you so, and you must let me know if anything is not to your liking."

"I'm sure I will be. There is one other thing, Mrs. Jennings. I have a kitten. I hope that's all right?"

"A kitten, is it?" The older woman frowned. "Well, we don't usually hold with animals. The girls aren't permitted to keep them."

"He is very quiet and well-mannered. He won't disturb anyone. And I'll see to it that he stays in my room if you like."

"Oh, well now, he won't like that, will he? I suppose it's all right. I shall have to ask Miss Chadbourne. Come to think of it, Miss Leveret had a dog years ago. It died, and she never got another. But he was no trouble at all."

"Nor will Juvenal be, I promise you."

"Juvenal?"

"My kitten."

Mrs. Jennings frowned. "What an odd name you've given him."

"My aunt named him. She left him to me in her will."

"Indeed. Well, in that case I'm sure it will be all right. You just take him down to the kitchens and tell Mrs. Fife that I said it was allowed."

"Thank you, Mrs. Jennings."

"That's perfectly all right."

Thalia stood. "Well, I must get settled in. Thank you for all your help."

"Glad to oblige. You have only to ask, and we will do everything possible to make you comfortable."

At this renewed offer, Thalia took a breath and said, "I did want to ask… that is… I was wondering. My room is rather small and close. Is there any other I might have?"

Mrs. Jennings drew back a little. "All the rooms are the same, miss. Except Miss Chadbourne's, of course, and some of the senior mistresses'. But all the rest have the same, Miss Hartington. We try to keep them as cheerful and clean as possible."

"Of course." Thalia moved toward the door.

"It's not easy," continued the housekeeper, "looking after more than a hundred girls, all used to the best, and the mistresses as well. No one is ever satisfied."

"Indeed, Mrs. Jennings, the room is quite all right. Good day, thank you again."

"Dinner is at six," was the housekeeper's only reply.

Thalia hurried back upstairs. She spent the hours before dinner unpacking her things and trying to arrange such personal possessions as she had brought to make her room more pleasant. She found that this helped a great deal. The sight of some of her books lined up along the back of the writing desk, and her Dresden figurine on the mantel over the fireplace, made the room seem much more her own. She vowed to use some of the small sum her aunt had left her to purchase new curtains and a new counterpane for her bed. Then, she thought, the room might be very nice, though still small.

Before she went to dinner, she introduced Juvenal to the kitchen staff. To her relief, the cook liked cats, and it seemed there would be no trouble over his meals. This established, Thalia walked toward the large dining room on the ground floor. A buzz of conversation already came from that direction. The whole school took its meals together.

In the dining-room doorway, Thalia halted, taken aback by its size and by the seemingly countless number of females in it. The room seemed huge at first glance, and it was filled with long narrow tables, now populated by a horde of chattering girls. The noise alone was daunting. Thalia hesitated, but then she saw the housekeeper beckoning her from the front of the room and walked quickly toward her. She was conscious, as she did so, of many pairs of eyes turning to follow her progress, and of conversations stopping abruptly, to be replaced by interested whispers. Only natural, she told herself. In such a closed community, any new arrival must excite comment, and that of a new teacher even more.

Mrs. Jennings took Thalia to a table at the front of the dining room, where a number of older women stood at their places waiting for the meal. "This is the mistresses' table," she told her. "You sit there, Miss Hartington."

Thalia obediently went to a chair near the foot of the board. She nodded to the others.

"This is our new teacher, ladies," continued Mrs. Jennings. "Miss Hartington. And these are Mlle. Reynaud, the French mistress; Mlle. Benzoni, the Italian mistress; Miss Hendricks, who teaches painting and drawing and use of the globes; Miss Allen and Miss Reynolds, the music teachers; Miss Eliot, manners and deportment; Miss Jones, mistress of the third form; Miss Anderson, second form; and Miss Jacobs, first form."

The housekeeper had started at the top of the table and worked her way past Thalia to the foot, but the names and labels were so many and so rapid that the girl retained few of them. The other teachers nodded and smiled at her, and she greeted them collectively, but she knew it would be a while before she could identify them all as individuals.

At this moment, Miss Chadbourne entered the dining room, and the noise died down. She walked majestically to the head of the mistresses' table, paused, and sat down. Mrs. Jennings followed suit, at the foot of the table, and then the rest of the teachers. This was the signal for the students to sit down, which they did, with much giggling and scraping of chairs. The kitchen staff began to serve at once.

"You have all met Miss Hartington, I hope?" said Miss Chadbourne. "She arrived this afternoon."

There was an affirmative murmur.

"Good. I know you will all make every effort to welcome her to our little community." And with this Miss Chadbourne turned to her soup.

The table ate in silence for a while; then Mlle.

Reynaud addressed some remark to Mlle. Benzoni opposite her, and others began to talk quietly as well. Thalia turned to the woman on her left, a lively-looking dark girl of about thirty or thirty-five, she guessed. "I am sorry, I have forgotten all the names already," she said. "Did Mrs. Jennings say you teach music?"

The other smiled. "Yes. And I am surprised you can remember even that. It is so difficult when names are thrown at one in that way. I am Miss Reynolds; I instruct the girls on the pianoforte and harp, while Julia, Miss Allen, teaches them voice."

"Miss Allen is…?"

"Second down opposite," replied the other promptly, "I shouldn't worry about getting all the names at once, you know. In a few days you'll find you know everyone."

"I suppose so. But it seems rude to forget."

Miss Reynolds shrugged good-naturedly. "Everyone is the same at first. I know I was."

"Have you been here long?"

"Long enough. Three years."

"And do you like it?"

The older woman grimaced. "Oh, like it! As much as can be expected, I suppose."

"What do you mean?"

"Well, one doesn't *really* wish to be a teacher in a girls' school, no matter how exclusive, does one? But as schools go, this is certainly one of the most pleasant."

"It seems so to me."

"Is this your first post?"

"Yes. I was… living with my aunt until her recent death."

"I thought you looked very young. Well, I will ask you again in several weeks' time, and then we can discuss schools." Miss Reynolds smiled ironically at her.

Before Thalia could reply, her companion's attention was diverted by the woman on the other side. Thalia returned to her dinner briefly, then looked to her right. The teacher on that side was much younger than Miss Reynolds. She seemed, in fact, nearer Thalia's own age. She was a blond, rather plump, and looked good-natured. Catching Thalia's eye, she said, "I am Miss Anderson, in charge of the second form. Welcome to Chadbourne."

"Thank you."

"I hope you'll like it. But you're far too pretty to be stuck here with us. I daresay Mlle. Reynaud will have it in for you because of it."

Thalia flushed a little. She started to speak, but Miss Anderson forestalled her.

"Oh, I should not have said that, I suppose. But it's the truth, and why shouldn't you know it? You will be teaching literature, I understand?"

"Yes. I am not certain just what works."

"Whatever you can cajole the girls into reading," laughed the other. "I wonder if you have any idea what lies before you?"

Thalia smiled. "I am not so naive as to believe that every student will love poetry, or any such thing. I realize that teaching is hard work."

"Do you? Well, that's to the good. My girls are so obstinate sometimes that I wish I could beat them, as they do boys."

"You are in charge of the second form?"

"Yes. The first three forms, the younger girls, are kept with one mistress for everything. It is only the last two who are taught by our 'experts.'" She gestured toward the top of the table with amusement. "And of course, we occasionally encounter a particularly talented younger girl, and she is given special tutoring."

"I see."

"Perhaps. I'll ask you again in three weeks. *Then* you'll see."

"Miss Reynolds said something very like that just now. I do realize I have a lot to learn."

"Did she?" Miss Anderson nodded as if satisfied.

"Would you be so kind as to repeat the names for me?" asked Thalia then. "I want to learn them as soon as possible."

The other girl grinned. "Certainly. You know Miss Chadbourne, of course. You will have been to the inner sanctum already. Well, the lady to her right is Mlle. Reynaud. She's been here forever. She claims she left France during the troubles, trying to imply that she is an aristocratic refugee, but no one believes it. She teaches French, of course. Then opposite her, on Miss Chadbourne's left, is Mlle. Benzoni. She's simply mad. She screams and yells something awful when she teaches. Italian. I can't blame her, considering how stupid some of the girls are with languages. Beside her is Miss Allen, the voice teacher. She's a sweet, quiet little mouse, has a lovely singing voice herself. Are you taking all this in?"

"Yes, thank you," replied Thalia, trying not to laugh. Miss Anderson's characterizations were amusing.

Hearing the enjoyment in her voice, Miss Anderson grinned. "Just so. Opposite Julia Allen is Miss Hendricks—drawing and painting. She's quiet too, but she has a fine wit when you get to know her. You've spoken to Miss Reynolds. Opposite her is Miss Eliot, in charge of manners and deportment. She teaches the girls how to make a court curtsy and that sort of thing. I should hate it, but she seems not to. I don't know her well; she keeps to herself. And that leaves only us plebs, the lower-forms mistresses. Ellen Jones, across from you, has the third, and Georgina Jacobs, opposite me, the first. We're a jolly lot, rather separate from the others."

Miss Jones and Miss Jacobs, being close enough to hear these remarks, smiled indulgently at Miss Anderson. "Some of the time we are," added Ellen Jones across the table.

"And there you are," finished Miss Anderson. "My first name is Lucy, by the by. What's yours?"

"Thalia," she answered, grimacing slightly.

"Thalia? How strange. It sounds Greek or something."

"It is. My mother was, ah, fond of classical poetry."

"Indeed? That is just like Miss Chadbourne; her first name is Aurelia." The servant came to clear away the main course, depositing shallow bowls before each diner as she did so. "Oooh," exclaimed Miss Anderson. "Pudding!" And she subsided into her dessert.

After dinner, the students had a free hour, and most of the teachers went quickly up to their bedchambers, eager for a little solitude after a busy day. After a few minutes, Thalia followed suit. She knew none of the pupils, and though they examined her curiously, none seemed eager to introduce herself.

Thalia read for a while in her small room, then made ready for bed. She had been told that her corridor was also inhabited by other teachers, but she saw no one when she went down to the bath. At last, she got into bed early, thinking over the events of the day. Tomorrow she would teach her first class. The thought was both exciting and a little frightening. She fell asleep wondering what Miss Reynolds and Miss Anderson had meant by saying that they would ask her in three weeks what she thought of the school.

Eight

WHEN THALIA OPENED HER EYES EARLY THE NEXT morning, they met the golden ones of Juvenal, who was sitting on the windowsill at the head of her bed. He stared at her inscrutably as she blinked and woke up fully, then turned his back and looked out over the dew-covered lawn. Thalia laughed a little. "Is it a fine day, Juvenal?" she asked, throwing off the bedclothes and sitting up. The kitten did not reply, but looking over his black-furred shoulder, she saw that it was. The sun was just rising behind some trees to the east, throwing long shadows across the gardens below.

Thalia dressed hastily but carefully, wrapping her braids into a coronet at the back of her head and putting on the least dowdy of the dresses her aunt had thought suitable for a young girl. She then sat down at her writing desk and looked over the thin sheaf of papers she had left there last night. When she had first learned that she had gotten a position as teacher at Chadbourne, she had set down her ideas on what literature she would teach. And when she had submitted these to Miss Chadbourne some weeks past, there had been no objection. She scanned them again. Shakespeare; some of Milton's sonnets; Pope and Dryden; Gray and Scott and Cowper; Dr. Johnson; and daringly, a novel lately published, *Pride and Prejudice*. She drew a deep breath. This was an ambitious program for the sort of classes she would face, she knew. Folding the sheaf in two, she rose and went down to breakfast, taking Juvenal to the kitchen on her way.

The dining room was noticeably quieter this morning, and many of its occupants looked sleepy. The meal was eaten with dispatch, and students and mistresses went out as soon as they finished. Thalia, done eating, looked around uncertainly. Should she go directly to her classroom, or wait until she was sure all the pupils were there before her?

She had not decided this question when Miss Chadbourne spoke to her. "Miss Hartington? I will go with you to your classroom today, and present you to the fifth-form girls. We will wait a moment."

"Thank you, Miss Chadbourne."

"Not at all. Will you move up here?" The table was nearly empty now, and she indicated the chair beside her. Thalia rose and took it. "Another cup of tea?" continued the headmistress.

"No, thank you."

Miss Chadbourne sipped her own tea. "Are you uneasy?" she asked then.

Thalia smiled. "A little, perhaps. I have never faced a class before."

The other nodded. "You are very young. But you will get in the way of it in no time. And today you needn't keep them long. You need only introduce your program. We have procured copies of most of the works you mentioned, or seen that the girls did so. I think you will find them prepared."

"Thank you," said Thalia again. As she waited, she was feeling more and more restless.

Miss Chadbourne rose. "Let us go, then."

Thalia followed her down a corridor to the room where her class waited. Miss Chadbourne walked firmly in and stood behind the desk at the front, leaving Thalia to trail behind. The sounds of conversation audible from the hall ceased immediately, and the young ladies in the rows of smaller desks straightened. "Good morning, girls," said Miss Chadbourne. "I want to introduce our new literature mistress, Miss Hartington. She is here to teach you about poetry and prose, and I know you will be very attentive." Miss Chadbourne nodded slightly to Thalia, turned, and left the room, shutting the door with a click behind her.

Thalia moved up to stand behind the desk. She put her papers down on it and looked out over her class. When she had first entered the room, it had seemed to her that she faced a veritable sea of faces. Now, these resolved themselves into perhaps twenty young girls of sixteen or seventeen. All wore the school's compulsory buff gowns and had their hair dressed much as Thalia's, but in that moment, she was very conscious of the fact that she was no older than they.

"Good morning," she said, a tiny quiver in her voice. "I am pleased to be here, and I hope we will all learn a great deal together in our sessions. I have planned a progression of studies—"

At this moment, in an audible whisper, someone in the back of the room said, "She is much too pretty to be a schoolteacher."

Titters spread across the room and then back.

Thalia looked around sharply as every student assumed an expression of bland innocence. She realized then that her first impression had been superficial. Despite their identical costumes, there were obvious differences among her pupils. And in particular, a group in the back-right corner was conspicuous. These young ladies clearly chafed against the limits of buff gowns and braids. Most had coaxed a few curls over their ears, and all wore some ornament, several quite expensive. The whisper had come from here.

Thalia looked them over, her nervousness evaporating. "Did someone speak?" she asked blandly. "I am always ready to answer any question." She pretended to look over the class, but kept one eye on the group in the corner.

"Do you dye your hair that lovely color?" piped up someone.

There was a collective gasp.

But Thalia smiled. She had the culprit now. It was a pretty blond girl in the farthest corner, one of the group she suspected. "What is your name?" Thalia said to her quickly.

The girl was clearly taken aback. A tall statuesque creature, with more curls and finer ornaments than any other pupil, she had the direct eyes and petulant mouth of one used to her own way and conscious of her own superiority. After a moment, her natural arrogance asserted itself. "I am *Lady* Agnes Crewe," she replied haughtily, tossing her blond head. She did not rise, and her tone held contempt.

"Ah," responded Thalia. "Well, to answer your rather tactless question, no. I do not dye my hair. It quite comes this color. And I fear I must add, Lady Agnes, that you should pay more attention in Miss Eliot's classroom. I am convinced that she has told you that such personal questions are not at all the thing. Quite hoydenish, in fact."

Lady Agnes flushed a dull red, and there was another wave of giggles.

"Now," continued Thalia, "to get on with our lesson. I am going to read you a poem this morning. It is one of Cowper's. And I want you all to listen closely, for we will discuss it after." She picked up a sheet on which she had copied out the poem, one of her favorites, and began to read. There were no further whispers.

The rest of the time went as well as a first class can. The discussion was halting and reluctant, and Thalia often had to lecture a bit. But her confidence increased as she went, and by the time she dismissed them with an assignment, she felt wholly in control.

"And please," she finished, "will you each come and tell me your names as you go out. I want to learn them as soon as I can."

Accordingly, the students filed past her, saying their names shyly or stoutly according to their various natures. Lady Agnes was one of the last to go. She started to walk past without speaking, but Thalia said, "I *know* your name, at least, Lady Agnes, so I have made a beginning." And she smiled warmly. Thalia did not think she would come to like this impertinent young lady, but she had no wish to be on bad terms with any of her pupils.

Lady Agnes merely stared a moment, her lips pressed together, then stalked out.

"Oh, how awful she is!" exclaimed a soft voice behind Thalia. Turning, she saw that one pupil remained in the room, a slight girl with pale skin and brown hair. She did not remember noticing her earlier. The girl flushed painfully red. "I shouldn't say so, I know," she added. "But she *is*."

Thalia suppressed a smile. "What is your name?"

The girl's flush, impossibly, deepened. "Oh, I beg pardon, ma'am. I am Mary Deming." She hesitated, then went on in a rush. "I waited until last because I wanted to tell you how *wonderful* the poem was! You read it so beautifully. How I wish I could do so."

"I daresay you could."

"I? Oh, no. I would trip over my tongue, or make some blunder so that everyone laughed. I always do, when I try to speak before strangers."

"But you will get over that. It is a matter of practice."

The girl hung her head, looking unconvinced. "Will we be reading more poems like that one?" she asked then.

"Yes indeed. And I have a volume of Cowper I could lend you, if you like."

"W-would you?"

"Of course. I will bring it tomorrow."

Mary smiled beautifully and turned to leave. At the door, she stopped abruptly. "Oh! Oh, thank you, Miss Hartington. Good day."

Nearly laughing, Thalia replied, "Good day, Mary," and the girl left.

Thalia's second class, with the fourth form later that day, was less challenging than this one. It seemed to her that the younger girls were much more docile. As she dismissed them at one and prepared to go in to luncheon, she thought to herself that she would have no problems here, at least, which was fortunate, for she had a feeling that the fifth-formers were going to demand a good deal of her energy.

After the meal, Miss Chadbourne paused to speak to the teachers at the foot of the dining table. "Miss Hartington, you will want to speak to Miss Jones, Miss Anderson, and Miss Jacobs about special pupils. No doubt there are several lower-form girls who would benefit from extra study in your field. You can tutor them in the afternoons."

"Of course, Miss Chadbourne," responded Thalia, and the headmistress moved away.

Lucy Anderson giggled. "I wish I might give you Lydia Appelton. She is an absolute terror."

"Yes," said Ellen Jones, "and I should like to be rid of that new girl, Louisa Ferncliff. She does nothing but look doleful or cry quietly into her handkerchief. It is past bearing."

Thalia laughed. "Please! I can teach literature, but those girls sound as if they need something quite different. Give them to Eliot, I beg."

"Oh, she won't take them," replied Lucy. "And even if she did, she couldn't do anything. All she knows is curtsying and how one addresses the King and that sort of twaddle."

"Lucy!" exclaimed Miss Jacobs. "Mind your tongue."

"Why? There's no one to hear. Miss Hartington won't tell, will you?"

Bemused, Thalia shook her head.

Georgina Jacobs turned a shoulder on the other. "I will prepare a list for you, Miss Hartington, and you can arrange the times with my girls. It will be a small group, I fear. The little girls are really not ready for literature, except in a few exceptional cases."

"I have three, I think," said Ellen Jones. "I will send them to you later this afternoon."

"As will I," added Miss Anderson. "I believe I have two."

"Thank you. I shall be in my classroom from two till four; they may come anytime."

The others nodded and drifted out of the dining room. Thalia went to collect Juvenal and took him back upstairs. In her bedchamber, she sat down and took a deep breath. She was tired. Apparently, teaching was a more exhausting task than she had ever realized.

In the next few days, Thalia gradually became accustomed to her new life. Her classes went better and better as she gained confidence in talking to the older girls, and her tutoring sessions with the younger ones were almost fun. Juvenal adjusted even more rapidly, seeming in his element in the school. He spent a great deal of time sitting in high places, a bookshelf or windowsill most often, and simply watching the people go about their routine.

Mary Deming showed more and more interest in Thalia's subject, particularly the poetry, and Thalia lent her books and talked with her after class with enthusiasm. Here, at least, was a student who truly loved learning, as Thalia herself did. Indeed, Mary often reminded the older girl of her childhood self, and she guided her progress lovingly.

With Lady Agnes Crewe, however, relations did not improve. Apparently, once offended, this young lady did not forgive. She treated Thalia with cold contempt and was as impertinent as she dared be in the classroom. After a week of this, Thalia was at her wits' end. She could manage the girl, of course, but it was not pleasant to have to do so. She preferred thinking about the subject matter and how best to communicate it. She wondered if she should go to Miss Chadbourne with the problem, but she hesitated. She did not wish to seem to be complaining, or to appear to require help with her job.

Then, one afternoon just before tea, she came upon Miss Hendricks, the drawing mistress, in one of the downstairs parlors. No one else was near, and Thalia took the opportunity to put the question to her, for she seemed like a sensible woman.

"Lady Agnes?" replied the other, not seeming surprised. "Oh, there is nothing to be done there. That girl likes only those who toady to her, and I'm certain that you would never do that." She smiled ironically.

Thalia looked at the slight Miss Hendricks, somewhat taken aback. The painting teacher was very plain, with sandy hair and brows and thousands of freckles, but her voice was acidly mocking. "Surely no teacher would do so?" replied Thalia.

"Would they not? It depends upon what they think

they can get out of it." Seeing Thalia's astonishment, Miss Hendricks laughed. "You'll see, if you stay here long enough. You are not really meant to be a teacher, you know, Miss Hartington. Oh, I'm certain you can *teach* well enough, but you have no understanding of schools and the plotting and nastiness that go on behind our demure facades."

Thalia frowned at her.

"But as for Lady Agnes, I'd advise that you ignore her. She can make trouble, there's no question about that. Her father is an earl and very powerful. But fortunately, she's leaving us very soon. She's to 'come out' this season, and London is welcome to her."

"I thought perhaps if I talked to her…" began Thalia.

"It would do no good. In fact, it might even do harm. She would interpret it as a sign of weakness, see you as giving in to her. Really, I would ignore her if I were you."

"That is what you do?"

"Generally. Unless she becomes too exasperating. Then I set her down. The amusing thing is that she is never sure if that is what I am doing. She is not very intelligent, really."

"But this seems so cold. She is hardly more than a child."

Miss Hendricks fastened her pale eyes on Thalia's face. "That may be true of others here, but not Lady Agnes. She has never been a child. She was an overbearing arrogant girl when she arrived here, and she remains so. We have barely managed to force a few facts into her mind and make her understand that certain polite forms must be observed in public. There will be a general sigh of relief when she goes."

Unsatisfied, Thalia thanked the other woman and turned away. It seemed wrong, somehow, to dismiss a young girl as intractable. But she did not know how one would go about changing a pupil who had defied the efforts of a whole school of more experienced teachers.

In the days that followed, she thought further on this subject, but found no answers. She also explored the gardens, which were very pleasant, and wrote her sisters amusing, anecdotal letters describing her new life.

In these pastimes, several weeks went by, and Thalia felt generally content with her lot.

Nine

THURSDAYS WERE HALF-HOLIDAYS AT THE CHADBOURNE School, though some of the teachers were usually required to oversee outings for the girls. When her fourth such holiday came around, Thalia felt a great urge to get away by herself, and she determined to take a long solitary walk through the countryside near the school.

Accordingly, she set off directly after luncheon, taking only a book and Juvenal, who seemed nearly as pleased as she to get away.

They moved quickly across the school gardens, greeting several girls on the way, and out the great gate at the front. A road here ran into Bath on the left and into country the other way, soon degenerating into a mere lane. Thalia went right, stepping briskly along. She wore a walking dress and stout shoes, for she intended to leave the road as soon as possible. Juvenal paced beside her with his usual gravity.

They soon left the school wall behind, coming to cultivated fields on either side of the road. Several prosperous-looking farms were visible, as was a sizable copse, and Thalia headed for the latter.

It was a fine spring day. The sun was bright but not hot, and a breeze stirred the air, carrying the scent of sun-warmed grass and budding leaves. Thalia took deep breaths and walked with increasing pleasure. She had not tramped in the country since before her aunt died, and she realized now how she had missed it.

At the first opportunity, she left the road for a footpath which wandered in the general direction of the trees. Here Juvenal showed more liveliness, bounding ahead to attack grass hummocks and then returning, proud of himself, for Thalia's approval. He even flushed a rabbit, though this startled him quite as much as it did his prey, and he fell back on his haunches dumbfounded instead of chasing it.

They reached the edge of the trees well before midafternoon. The footpath continued through the copse, and Thalia enjoyed the sudden quiet that came when they walked under the first trees. She sighed with happiness. "Where shall we go, Juvenal?" she said. "Shall we stay on this path and see where it leads? Or shall we strike off into the forest? I want to find a lovely comfortable place and read for a while, out here where everything smells so fresh and wonderful."

Juvenal, a patch of black against the green shoots, looked up at her for a moment, then, as if in answer to her questions, bounded off to the left, away from the path.

Thalia smiled. "Are you sure you know where you're going?" she called. But she followed him, pushing aside branches and stepping over an occasional fallen log.

These obstacles made the going slower, and Thalia

twice lost sight of the kitten as he ran ahead. But when she called him, he immediately reappeared, staring inquiringly from his golden eyes, as if to ask why she did not go faster.

At last Thalia heard the sound of water ahead, and saw brighter sunlight through gaps in the trees. "Is it a stream?" she asked Juvenal, but he ignored her.

The sound indeed came from a stream, she found a moment later, stepping from the trees into a wide clear area. But the tiny brook ran into a pond, overhung with willow and moss, in the midst of the copse. Thalia was delighted. "Juvenal, you splendid animal. Did you know this was here?" she exclaimed. "This is a perfect spot. I shall settle under that willow right there and idle away the afternoon." As she spoke, she walked around the edge of the pond toward the tree. She sank down on the moss under it, after spreading an old shawl she had brought for just this purpose, and looked happily about. The pond was small and closely shrouded by trees and underbrush, giving it the feeling of a secret place. Thalia could easily imagine that fairies gathered here on moonlit nights, or that Pan might visit on his northern journeys. She smiled at her own silliness. But at that very moment, a strange sound came to her ears. She cocked her head, listening, and her eyes gradually widened. It couldn't be, but it was; yes, it was unmistakably ancient Greek. Someone was declaiming here in this secret spot. Astonished, she looked around.

There was no one to be seen, but the voice seemed to be coming from the edge of the pond a bit farther along. The trailing branches of the willow hid the bank from her. Very slowly Thalia rose and peered through the leaves. There was nothing there. She hesitated, then began to walk along the shore. As she moved, the voice became clearer. It positively was Greek, and it was being practically shouted across the water. She had thought the speaker closer than he was because of this.

At last, rounding a bramble bush, Thalia discovered the source of the sound. Under another willow tree stood a young man; he was facing the pond and declaiming Greek poetry passionately.

Fascinated, Thalia shrank back a little to watch. The man was above middle height and rather thin, but he had a fine head, thickly covered with curling blond hair, and his hands, which were continually gesturing as he recited, were those of an artist, long and chiseled. Clearly he was aware of nothing and no one but the verse.

And as she listened, Thalia was also caught up. She had studied Greek for two years, and though she knew her knowledge was meager, she thought she recognized this as Euripides. But whatever it was, the sounds were wonderful. One of her tutors had read aloud to her from Greek poetry, and she had been enthralled then. But that had been nothing like *this*. The young man before her spoke with passion, his head thrown back and no sign of a book anywhere near.

She stood spellbound until he paused, and then she stepped forward, saying eagerly, "That was Euripides, was it not? Oh, how beautifully you did it!"

The man started violently and whirled about. He stared at her as if she were a phantom, and Thalia flushed a little. But she also noticed that his eyes were a clear sparkling gray.

"I beg your pardon," she went on. "I came upon this pond quite by accident and sat down to read. I couldn't help but hear you. I don't mean to intrude."

The man found his voice again with some difficulty. "N-not at all. That is… I didn't realize there was anyone about. I wouldn't have shouted so if I… mean…" he stopped helplessly, still staring.

"Oh, it was wonderful. I'm glad you shouted. *Was* it Euripides?"

Bemused, he nodded slowly.

"It was! I thought so. And now I am very pleased with myself for identifying it, for you must know that my knowledge of Greek is of the slightest."

"Are you real?" asked the man dazedly. "Or are you some strange northern wood nymph I have called up with my poetry?"

Thalia laughed. "I am quite real, so you needn't expect me to behave like a nymph, some of whom were *quite* improper." She smiled at him.

"But where do you come from? How did you appear here? Did you really recognize the Euripides? I cannot believe you are real."

"Well, I came from the Chadbourne School, and I appeared by thrusting my way through all sorts of thorns and brambles, which should testify to my paltry reality. And as for Euripides, I have studied Greek a little—very little—and so I managed to guess."

With this mundane information, the man seemed to recall himself. "I see. Admirable. But in my aston-ishment, I forgot my manners. I am James Elguard." He bowed.

"How do you do? And how did you appear here,

Mr. Elguard? For I declare it is just as unusual for me to find a man reciting Greek in the forest as for you to meet me here. Odder!"

He laughed. "I came out from Bath in search of some solitude to indulge my penchant for reciting, as you call it. I am staying in town."

"Ah."

"Will you not tell me your name?"

"I am Thalia Hartington."

"Thalia! And you say you are not a nymph?"

"Indeed not. Only the daughter of another lover of Greek poetry."

"I see. Then you don't have two sisters, equally lovely, who preside over all human graces?"

"Of course we don't," laughed Thalia.

"You *do* have sisters?"

She dimpled. "Oh, yes."

"Aglaia and Euphrosyne, without doubt."

"Well, my father began the conceit, and then was forced to go on with it, you see."

"I see that your claim to reality was nothing but a sham. You are a goddess."

"On the contrary, I am a schoolteacher, Mr. Elguard."

He burst out laughing and was about to speak again when Juvenal trotted out of the bushes and sat down at Thalia's feet, beginning at once to lick his black fur energetically.

"Your familiar?" asked James Elguard.

"Am I a witch now? For if I am a nymph, I cannot have a familiar."

"Alas, I have mixed my conceits woefully. I give it up. He is merely a schoolteacher's cat. What is his name?"

Thalia dimpled. "Juvenal. But I didn't give it to him, so you needn't be *satirical*."

He gave another shout of laughter. "I am afraid to try. But do you like Juvenal's *Satires*? I do, immensely."

"I have not read enough to say, really. My studies were the simplest things only, for I started with Latin very late."

"Ah. Who named him, then? Your teacher?"

"No, my aunt. And if she knew anything of Juvenal beyond his name, I should be greatly surprised. She named all her cats for classical persons."

"Chiefly Romans?"

"Oh, yes. I have an idea she didn't *really* approve of the Greeks."

Mr. Elguard's eyes sparkled with amusement. "All, you said? She had a great many cats, then?"

"Oh, yes. Twenty-six. Or perhaps twenty-four. I'm not certain."

He laughed again. "You are the most original, delightful girl I have ever met. Why have I not come across you before this? You said your name was Hartington? Are you connected with the Hampshire Hartingtons?"

"Yes, that is my family. But my father died years ago, and we went to live with my aunt, until she too died, recently."

"And now you are a schoolteacher? You weren't bamming me?"

"No. I am at the Chadbourne School. It is nearby."

"Yes. I've heard of it."

"In fact," continued Thalia, looking up at the sun, which was now lowering in the west, "I must be starting back there now. It is a two-mile walk, and I must be in for tea."

"Let me drive you,' said Elguard quickly. "I have a gig tied at the edge of the trees. Please."

Thalia hesitated.

"Please. I do so want to talk a bit more."

The girl, realizing that she too would find this very pleasant, gave in.

"Splendid. And now we needn't start immediately, need we? The journey will be much quicker in a gig."

Thalia laughed. "I really should go."

"Oh, very well. But I shall drive slowly. And you will tell me everything about yourself as we go."

"Shall I?"

"I hope so."

"And what of you?"

"Oh, I mean to tell you everything as well. I shall begin at once, in fact." And as they walked through the trees to his carriage, he did. Thalia discovered that he was the second son of Sir George Elguard and destined for the church. He was in his last year at Oxford and very much enjoying his studies there. Next year, he would be ordained, and a modest living being held for him would be his. "It is in the country near York," he told her. "The stipend isn't large, but it will do. And I hope, of course, to move on to greater things someday. There are several books I would like to write, and I hope to be of some help to my parish as well."

"I'm sure you will be," responded Thalia. "What sort of books?"

He laughed. "No, no, I mustn't begin on that. You mean to get me started on my pet theories, I see, to avoid telling me about yourself. But I shall merely finish by saying that I am in Bath for a few days to prepare the way for my mother. She comes next week to drink the waters. Or so she says. I think she comes to gossip and play whist all the day long, out of my father's sight." He grinned to show that this was a joke. "I get frightfully bored, so I come out here and recite poetry, as you discovered. There. Now you know all my secrets. It is your turn."

They had by this time mounted the gig and were, with Juvenal between them, driving slowly back along the road. Thalia looked sidelong at him, smiling slightly. "Secrets?"

"Every one!"

She laughed. "Well, I haven't any. And I have told you most of it already. My parents died when I was very young and my sisters and I were reared by our aunt. She died recently, and we found positions to support ourselves."

"Too bad!"

"Not at all." Thalia's tone was not encouraging. She liked this man very much, but she was not inclined to tell him the whole story of her aunt's will on such short acquaintance.

"You like being a teacher, then?"

"Is that so surprising?"

"Oh, no, not at all. I have always thought I should like it myself. I mean to have some pupils when I am settled in Yorkshire. For languages; preparing them for university, you know. But I had thought that girls' schools were beastly places; that is the impression my sisters gave me, at least."

"Sisters? Aha! And you claimed you had told all about yourself. You never mentioned sisters."

He laughed. "I must have forgotten. I have three older sisters, two married now. I scarcely ever see them."

"And so of course, you forget them," finished Thalia agreeably. "One can quite easily see how it might happen."

"Only for a moment," he laughed. "But I refuse to talk about my family any longer. I am finding out about you. Your school is not beastly?"

"Oh, no. There are all sorts of people there, naturally, and some are more pleasant than others, but I have not found it beastly." She thought suddenly of Lady Agnes Crewe and her veiled impudence. "At least, not any more beastly than any other profession," she added.

"But it is a pity you must work."

"I don't agree. I think it is a pity my sisters must do so, for they are not at all suited for it. But I am glad to have something worthwhile to do with my time. I always loved my studies, and now I have the chance to help other girls, a few at least, feel that love as well."

James Elguard looked down at her admiringly. "I think that's splendid!" he exclaimed. "And I'm sure you are a splendid teacher, too."

Thalia smiled and shrugged.

They had by this time come to the high wall of the Chadbourne School and were driving along it, approaching the gate. Thalia abruptly realized that it might cause a good deal of comment if she drove up to the door in the company of a handsome young man. "I'll get down here," she said, as they reached the gateposts.

"Nonsense. I mean to drive you to your threshold."

"Please don't. I mean, I wish you wouldn't."

"But I could not be so discourteous." He frowned at her; then a thought seemed to strike him. "You think it might look odd?"

A bit embarrassed, Thalia nodded.

"Yes, I see. I am unknown here. Very well." He pulled up before the gates. "But I warn you I mean to bring about a proper introduction, and to take you to call on my mother and sister when they arrive. Will you come?"

Thalia, climbing down from the gig, looked up at him. His gray eyes smiled in response, and he looked altogether charming. "I should like that."

"Good. And in the meantime, do you always go walking on your holidays?"

She cocked her head, dimpling. "Invariably."

"Splendid. That pond is a fine place to spend one's leisure hours."

"So peaceful," agreed Thalia.

He laughed. "Indeed. I shall hope to see you soon, then, Miss Hartington."

Thalia nodded and went to open the gates and slip through; she stood on the other side, looking back at him and smiling.

"You look shut away from the world." He laughed. "I am still not altogether convinced that you are not a wood nymph who will disappear when I turn my back and never be found again."

"Oh, no," replied the girl, setting Juvenal on the

ground beside her feet. "I shall be here, boringly real, reading Pope to my students and trying to convince them he is admirable."

He laughed again. "Good luck! I shall see you soon again. Good-bye."

"Good-bye."

Thalia started up the drive, and Elguard turned the gig toward Bath. Neither of them noticed a small group of schoolgirls among the shrubbery near the gate, but one of that group, a tall sturdy blond, quite obviously noticed them.

Ten

A WEEK PASSED IN THE USUAL ROUTINES. THALIA taught her classes, met with individual pupils in the afternoons, and chatted with the other teachers at meals. But through it, she felt a new lightness and happiness which she did not attempt to define. Everything simply seemed better. Even Lady Agnes was less trouble. She stayed generally silent in the classroom, merely staring at Thalia with a faint smile on her face. This new tactic rather amused the older girl. If Lady Agnes thought to outface her so, she would be disappointed.

Toward the end of the week, she heard that Lady Agnes had been given special permission to go into Bath on Thursday, to visit some family friends. This was a rare treat, and Thalia believed this fact accounted for the girl's silent superiority. No doubt she felt that she was somehow triumphing over Thalia by going into society. Thalia smiled to herself and went on with her work.

Thursday, the half-holiday, came round again more quickly than she had expected. Lady Agnes was absent from her class that morning, making it easier for everyone, Thalia thought. Even the girl's particular friends were pleasanter when she was not there to urge them on.

After lunch, Thalia fetched Juvenal and a heavy shawl from her room and went outside. A chilly breeze was stirring the foliage in the garden, making the day cool despite bright sun. With Juvenal following, she went across the lawn and down the drive to the gate. There she found Lucy Anderson and the other two lower-form teachers just setting out for town.

"Hullo, Thalia," said Lucy. "We're going shopping. Come along."

Thalia flushed a bit. "Thank you, but I am going the other way. I want a walk in the fields."

Lucy grimaced. "Whatever for? You'll only get damp feet and inflammation of the lungs. Don't you want to see Milsom Street and all the fine Bath shops?"

"Another day."

Lucy shrugged, and she and her friends set off at a brisk pace toward town. Thalia watched them for a moment before turning right herself. Oddly enough, she really had no desire to go with them.

She walked down the lane and off on the footpath that led to the copse. The wind pulled at her shawl and tightly pinned braids and made her long to run and take great lungfuls of air. She did skip a few steps now and then, startling Juvenal and causing him to leap ahead of her, fur bristling.

Reaching the trees, she walked surely to the little pond. It was warmer in the copse, and when she reached the water, the hush was in marked contrast to the wind outside. At first glance, the clearing appeared deserted, but then she saw James Elguard, waiting in the same place as before and looking eager. He noticed her at nearly the same instant and hurried forward. "You did come!" he exclaimed. "I am glad. I was afraid the wind might keep you at home."

"What, this feeble breeze?" mocked Thalia. "I am not so frail."

"I'm glad," he said again, looking down at her with a warm smile.

All at once, Thalia felt uncertain. She had looked forward to this outing the whole week, but now that she was here, a certain awkwardness threatened to descend upon it. What would they do? What would they find to say to one another, standing here beside the quiet pond? She wondered suddenly whether she should have come.

Seeming to sense her feelings, Elguard said, "I have a scheme for the afternoon, if you like."

"What?"

"I have the gig once again. And I brought a flask of tea and some sandwiches. I thought we might drive over to a place near here and have tea—a sort of picnic tea—and then come back. It is a kind of ruin, an old abbey." He shrugged sheepishly. "It has always reminded me of Greece, silly as that sounds. We used sometimes to stay near here when I was a boy, and I explored it then."

"It sounds wonderful—a delightful plan."

"Do you think so? It will be a little cold, I fear, but I have several lap robes."

"Nonsense. There is bright sun. I shan't be at all cold."

He smiled. "A woman of spirit. Let us go, then."

Accordingly, they made their way to the gig and climbed up. Elguard insisted that Thalia take two robes and wrap up securely, and once they were under way, she admitted to herself that he had been right. In a moving vehicle, the air was indeed cold. Juvenal was soon burrowing into the robe around her ankles and expressing his disapproval of the temperature sharply.

"Clearly a cat made for warmer climes," laughed Elguard. "Your aunt was wise in naming him."

"Yes, he is very lazy. He likes nothing better than to curl up before a good fire."

"Unlike his mistress, who is impervious to cold."

"Oh, I am fond of fires too. But I do like to get out, especially after being kept indoors all week."

"Ah, that is too bad."

"Well, I can walk in the garden, of course, but that is not the same."

"No, indeed. I like walking immensely. During the last long vacation I did a walking tour of the Alps. I have never had such fun."

"I should think so. How I envy you!"

"I mean to do the same in Greece as soon as I can, to see all the ancient sites."

"Wouldn't that be splendid—to come upon them just as one must have centuries ago, along the ancient roads."

"That is what I hope to do. It won't be just the same, of course, for they would not have been ruins then. But I think it will be wonderful."

"Oh, yes."

He smiled down at her. "How did you come to

study Greek, Miss Hartington? It is so unusual for a girl."

"It is, I know. I simply wanted to. And my aunt kindly engaged a special tutor for me. Our old governess sat by and knitted, as a chaperon, you see."

"I begin to. It is quite a picture."

Thalia laughed. "It was. Miss Lewes—that was our governess—always used to fall asleep after a few minutes, and she snored amazingly. And then, of course, I would begin to giggle. I couldn't help it; it was so absurd. And my poor tutor would shake his head and sigh. He despaired of me at first, but then I began to improve."

"I envy him."

"Oh, you shouldn't. I don't believe he cared for his job at all. He didn't think women *ought* to study Latin and Greek, but he needed the fees my aunt paid him to teach me." She paused, then added, "And even so, I think he tried to discourage my aunt from letting me learn. What a peal she must have rung over him for that!"

"Your aunt sounds like an unusual woman. Was she in favor of female education?"

Thalia wrinkled her nose. "Well, no, not exactly that. She was certainly unusual, but insofar as we could tell, she wasn't *in favor of* anything. There were a great many things she *didn't* favor, however."

"Such as?"

"Oh, well. Dogs. Port wine. The vicar."

He laughed ringingly. "And she liked…?"

"Cats. Claret. And, uh…"

"And her nieces, I hope. Did she really drink claret?"

"Oh, yes. But not to excess, you understand."

"Of course not."

"And as for liking us—I suppose she did. It was difficult to tell. She was always very kind about material things, my lessons and Euphie's and so on, but she rarely said anything kind, and of course she…" Thalia broke off; she had almost told him about her aunt's will.

He waited a moment, to see if she meant to go on, then asked, "What made you want to learn, then, Miss Hartington?"

She cocked her head. "Made me? What do you mean?"

"Well, you say you learned because you wanted to, and your aunt was kind enough to provide a teacher. But why did you want to? It is not a common desire."

"No, I suppose it isn't," replied Thalia, frowning. "It's not like Euphie wanting to study music, because lots of girls do that." She considered the question.

"Perhaps your father encouraged you? He must have known and loved the classics, if your name is any indication."

"Oh, I don't think so," said Thalia involuntarily. She added, "I mean, he may have done. I can't remember very clearly; he died when I was only seven. He never read to me or anything like that." Her frown deepened. "It is odd. I have wondered before why I wanted to study. I simply *did*, you know."

"You had a natural bent, I suppose. I was the same."

"Were you?"

"Oh, yes. I was always plaguing my father for books. He never knew quite what to make of me. He cares for little beyond his estate and the hunting field himself, and my older brother is the same. There's no accounting for such things."

"I suppose not."

"Look," he added, "that's where we're going."

Thalia looked up. Ahead of them, off to the right of the road, was a massive pile of fallen masonry, all grown over with ivy and creepers. Two perfect arches still stood near the edge, but otherwise all was tumbled rock and cracked pavement. "Oh," she said.

"Do you like it?"

"It looks like one of Mr. Gray's poems."

He laughed. "A bit. His landscapes are rather neater, I think."

"You're right. But I do like it. And I can see how it might remind you of Greece."

"Not ancient ruins, but old ones, at any rate." He pulled the gig off the road and urged the horse a little way toward the pile. "We can't go farther, too many stones."

"We can walk," responded Thalia gaily, throwing off her lap robes and preparing to climb down. Juvenal, revealed by this action in a huddle on the floor, protested.

"Wait," said Elguard. "I'll help you."

"No need." Thalia sprang lightly down and reached to set Juvenal on the grass.

"Rrrooww," said Juvenal, swatting at her skirt with one tiny paw.

"No sir," she replied. "You *shall* walk around a little. Try to live up to your name."

The kitten stared up at her with his great golden

eyes, then turned haughtily and stalked off toward the ruin.

"You have been finely set down," laughed Elguard, coming around the gig with a basket on his arm.

"Odious cat."

They walked side by side up a slight incline to the pile of stone. Elguard led the way around to the right. "There is a place that should be out of the wind," he said.

They went toward the two standing arches. Just beyond, through one of them, was a spot where three walls remained up to shoulder height. The fourth had fallen outward, leaving the shell of a small room intact and a fine prospect to the south.

"Oh, but this is lovely," cried Thalia.

"I thought you would like it." Elguard spread one of the lap robes on the dry stone paving and gestured grandly. "My lady's tea awaits."

Thalia dropped a tiny curtsy. "My thanks." She seated herself on the robe. "What a good idea this was."

"You should wait and see if the tea has kept any heat at all before you judge it."

"Of course it has."

He took a metal flask from the basket and felt the side. "I believe you're right. What luck."

He poured tea into two mugs from the basket and got out a packet of sandwiches. "There. No cakes, I fear."

"We don't want them. Juvenal? Have you recovered your manners? If so, I will give you a bit of tongue." She held it out.

The kitten, relinquishing his pique in the face of this inducement, came and took it daintily. Thalia drank her tea and watched him, smiling.

"My mother arrived in Bath yesterday," said Mr. Elguard after a moment. "I want you to meet her."

"I hope to."

"Could I ask you to call at her hotel? I will escort you. I would bring her to the school, but…"

"Of course. You have only to let me know when. I have little free time, I fear, however."

"Oh, that's all right. We'll arrange something." He leaned back against the rock wall and sighed happily. "How Mother will like you."

"You think so?"

"Oh, of course."

Thalia watched him for a moment, as he looked out over the countryside. His blond curls were tumbled by the wind, and his face reddened. He looked content, and she suddenly felt a great contentment descend on her as well. It was exceedingly pleasant to sit here in this way.

They sat thus for some time, until Thalia reluctantly said it was time she was getting back. Then they gathered up the picnic and Juvenal and set off the way they had come. The sun was halfway down the western sky, and it was getting colder, so Elguard urged the horse to greater speed. In half an hour they were approaching the copse again, and a little while later, the wall of the Chadbourne School came into view.

"I very much enjoyed this outing," said Mr. Elguard then.

"I too."

"I hope we may repeat it."

She nodded.

"But first you must meet Mother, and my sister as well. Perhaps on Sunday?"

"I am free on Sunday afternoons."

"Splendid. I will arrange it and send a note round to you."

She nodded again.

"Perhaps once you have met her, she could do something... that is... she might be able to help..."

"Help what?"

He hesitated, then burst out, "It is damnable that you are shut up in that school day after day. You should be out dancing and, and that sort of thing."

"But I have said—"

"Yes, yes, I know what you say. But I am convinced that you are too noble a creature to tell me how it really is."

Thalia stared at him, and he looked down, flushing slightly.

"I suppose I must let you down at the gate again," he continued.

"I think it would be best."

"Best!"

"What *is* the matter?"

"Oh, nothing. Nothing at all." He pulled up beside the front gate, and Thalia started to climb down. "Wait. I'll help you."

"Who will hold your horse, then? I can manage perfectly well." And she jumped down and reached for Juvenal.

"You always manage perfectly well, don't you, Miss Hartington?"

Puzzled by his peculiar tone, she smiled. "Not at all. Rarely, in fact."

He met her eyes and, after a moment, smiled ruefully back. "Of course. I beg your pardon. I will write to you very soon."

"I look forward to meeting your family."

"Thank you."

Thalia turned to open the gate. "Good-bye."

"Good-bye." And as she shut the gate behind her, he drove off.

Walking back to the school building, Thalia wondered about his odd remarks. What had he meant? She was far too engrossed in her own concerns to notice a little group of pupils loitering in the front hall when she entered. She went directly to the stairs and up to her bedchamber, but they lingered to whisper eagerly together, then moved en masse to one of the parlors. There a tall blond girl sat down at the writing desk and began avidly to compose a note. When she had finished and read it over, she laughed. "I shall have John take it into town first thing tomorrow," she told the others. "I'll give him a shilling, and he'll deliver it by hand. Then we'll see something." She laughed again, and one by one her friends joined her, but most of them sounded more nervous than amused.

Eleven

WHEN THALIA CAME DOWN TO BREAKFAST THE NEXT morning, she noticed Lady Agnes Crewe in the front hallway, in earnest conference with John, the school's footman and general message carrier. As she looked, Lady Agnes gave him an envelope and some coins, saying, "You'll hurry, won't you?"

"Yes indeed, miss," replied John, fingering the money appreciatively. "It'll be there before the cat can lick her ear."

"Good." Turning, Lady Agnes caught sight of Thalia on the stairway. She started a little, then recovered and began to turn away.

"Good morning, Lady Agnes," said Thalia with some amusement.

The girl looked sharply up at her, then returned the greeting before walking hurriedly away in the direction of the dining room. As Thalia followed more slowly, she wondered what kind of mischief the other was up to. For there was no doubt that she was plotting something; Lady Agnes was never so intent as she had been just now unless she was up to something devious.

Breakfast was a pleasant meal. Thalia was in a happy mood, and she had an interesting conversation with Miss Reynolds, on her left, about the pianoforte and its origins. Euphie's interest in music had meant that her sisters also learned a great deal about it, and Miss Reynolds was pleased to find such a knowledgeable party beside her. Their talk lasted through the meal, until Miss Chadbourne rose to go out. As Thalia followed her, she saw Lady Agnes stop before Miss Chadbourne and drop a small curtsy. This was so unusual that she increased her pace slightly and came up with them in time to hear the girl say, "I wondered if I might see you today, Miss Chadbourne? There is something I want to talk over with you."

The headmistress showed no signs of surprise. "Certainly, Lady Agnes. You may come up at two, after luncheon."

"Thank you, ma'am." The girl dropped another curtsy and walked away.

"Odd," murmured a voice near Thalia's ear, and she turned to find Miss Hendricks, the painting teacher, next to her. "I would wager that our Lady Agnes is going to tell tales on someone. It is one of her favorite little nastinesses, though she has never gone so high as Miss Chadbourne before. I sincerely pity her victim. Miss Chadbourne has very rigid ideas of propriety."

"We should do something," replied Thalia. "Perhaps I should speak to Lady Agnes and find out what it is. We don't want any of the girls wrongly accused."

"Oh, I doubt it will be wrongly. The little Crewe is usually careful to be sure. But you stay clear of it. You'll only be pulled into the row yourself if you interfere."

"And what does that matter, if I can help?"

Miss Reynolds merely looked at her for a moment, then shrugged. "You're a kind person, Miss Hartington," she said as she turned away. "Do as you like. But I warned you."

Thalia went to her classroom somewhat troubled as a result of these incidents. She was not sure what she should do. Lady Agnes sat in her customary place in the back of the room and smiled complacently through the session. Thalia felt a growing urge to wipe the smug look from her face, but she could think of no way to do so.

The morning passed placidly, with no untoward event marring Thalia's classes. Indeed, Mary Deming came up after the first to tell her how much she had enjoyed the poetry they read. In Thalia's weeks at Chadbourne, Mary had devoured every book she possessed and was well on her way to becoming a fine student of literature.

"Those last three lines," she said to Thalia when the rest of the fifth form had filed out, "they are so beautiful I thought I should burst into tears when you read them aloud."

"They are fine," agreed Thalia.

"And you read them so well. How I wish I could do so."

"I have told you that it is merely a matter of practice, Mary. Why not try some reading by yourself, in your room?"

The younger girl flushed. "Actually, I... I have. Once or twice. But it sounded so foolish."

"It does, at first. But if you keep at it, you will soon be declaiming like an orator."

Mary laughed. "I? But I shall keep trying, Miss Hartington. Perhaps I can improve, at least."

"I'm sure you will."

Mary turned to go, but at the doorway she paused. "I wanted to tell you that I... I love your class. It is the best in the school, and I am so glad you came here."

"Why, thank you, Mary."

The girl ducked her head shyly, blushed, and left the room.

Thalia smiled to herself as she readied her papers for the next class. Mary was a sweet child; it was hard to believe that she and Lady Agnes Crewe were of the same universe, let alone the same age. Thalia wondered what had happened to each to make them so different.

When her morning classes were over, Thalia went up to her room to fetch Juvenal and take him down to the kitchen for his meal. She had just deposited him there and was walking back toward the dining room when one of the maids stopped her. "Here you are, miss. I've been looking everywhere. A lady has called for you. She's outside in her carriage."

"Outside? But it's chilly."

"I know, miss. But she wouldn't come in. She asked that you come out and speak to her. Here's the card."

Thalia took the small square of pasteboard and read it. "Lady Constance Elguard." Her cheeks flushed a bit and she caught her breath. "Oh." She turned quickly back toward the stairs. "I'll get my shawl."

In three minutes Thalia was at the front door, her shawl wrapped around her. The school was going in to luncheon, but she ignored them. She would go without her meal, since Lady Elguard had been so kind as to call.

A luxurious private chaise stood outside, and Thalia went directly up to it. As she reached the gravel of the drive, the window was put down and a woman of about fifty looked out. "Miss Hartington?" she said.

"Yes, ma'am. And you are Lady Elguard. It is very kind—"

"One moment," interrupted the other, and put the window back up with a snap.

Thalia blinked, but at once the door of the chaise opened and Lady Elguard stepped down. Thalia caught a glimpse of a younger woman inside the vehicle, pale and sitting very straight, before she turned her attention to James's mother. Lady Elguard was a tall woman, with prominent bones in her face and gray hair dressed in fashionable ringlets. Her clothes were good, but somber, and her eyes a piercing light gray. At the moment, she was looking Thalia up and down appraisingly.

"Pretty," she said finally. "But that was to be expected."

Thalia stared at her.

"Come," said the older woman. "It is too cool to stand about here. Let us walk up and down."

"But won't you come in for a moment?" replied Thalia. "You must be chilled after your drive."

"I won't," snapped Lady Elguard. "I told the maid so already." She began to walk, and Thalia went with her perforce.

There was a short silence. Thalia, more and more

puzzled, did not know what to say. But she was about to venture a commonplace remark on the weather when Lady Elguard snapped, "I have heard all about my son's entanglement with you."

Thalia stopped dead and stared at her.

The other faced her grimly. "I believe in plain talk, Miss Hartington. And I see no reason to mince words. You needn't play the innocent, either; you know very well what I mean."

Thalia shook her head slightly and started to speak.

"Oh, stuff, of course you do. Don't playact with me. I have come to tell you that you won't succeed. You may have fooled my son, but you won't me. He'll never marry you, and you may as well give it up."

"M-marry," stammered Thalia. In her astonishment, she couldn't seem to put three words together.

"Of course marry. My son is destined for a great career in the church, Miss Hartington, and he must have a wife who can forward that career. No penniless little schoolmistress is going to stand in the way." Lady Elguard looked her up and down again. "However pretty," she added.

Thalia drew herself up. "You have made a mistake," she said tightly. "There is no question of marriage."

"Indeed? And I suppose you will say next that you did not entice my son into clandestine meetings, or spend hours alone in his company?"

The word "entice" made Thalia's green eyes flash. "I did *not*."

"I see you are a liar as well as an adventuress, Miss Hartington," answered Lady Elguard coldly. "I have nothing more to say to you. You understand my position." And she turned and went back to her carriage, leaving Thalia standing rigid in the drive.

The chaise drove smartly away, and after a moment, Thalia shuddered slightly and turned toward the school, walking automatically, as if in a daze. She went through the front door and toward the stairs. Suddenly noticing the babble of voices from the dining room, she stopped, put a hand to her mouth, and then ran up the stairway as quickly as she could. The idea of seeing anyone now was insupportable.

In her room, she threw off her shawl and sank onto the bed. She could still hear Lady Elguard's harsh words ringing in her ears. Who could have given her such a mistaken impression of Thalia's friendship with her son? Surely not Mr. Elguard himself; he could not.

And as she went over the scene once again in her mind, Thalia suddenly blushed crimson. Perhaps she had been a bit heedless to meet Elguard all alone. Not the first time, of course; she had not planned that. But the second—it had been perhaps a bit unconventional. Then her chin came up. Had she been living elsewhere, she might at any time have driven out with a young man in an open carriage, and stopped for tea, too. She had seen nothing wrong with the outing at the time, and she did not now. There hadn't *been* anything. And she had certainly not been "setting her cap" at Mr. Elguard. No such thought had entered her mind!

With this, Thalia's embarrassment dissolved in outrage. How dared that woman come here and talk to her in such a way? What right did she think she had? She got up and began to pace the room. Nothing seemed more important at that moment than that Lady Elguard should see what a monstrous mistake she had made, and be sorry!

A sharp rap on the door halted Thalia in mid-stride. She went over and pulled it open, revealing one of the maids outside.

"Miss Hartington, Miss Chadbourne wants to see you in her study as soon as possible," said this girl.

Thalia heaved an angry sigh. She did not feel at all like speaking to Miss Chadbourne. But there was no avoiding it. "Very well," she answered. "I shall be there directly."

"Yes, miss. She said at once, miss," added the maid with relish.

"Thank you," snapped Thalia.

The girl left reluctantly; Thalia resisted an impulse to kick the door shut behind her. She went to the small mirror on the wall, smoothed her hair, and started off to Miss Chadbourne's study downstairs.

Thalia was admitted immediately, to find the headmistress seated behind her broad desk looking very grave. She indicated a chair, and Thalia took it.

Miss Chadbourne's fingers drummed briefly on the desktop. "There is no pleasant way to approach the subject I wish to talk about," she began, "so I shall simply tell you that reports have reached me that you have been spending your holidays in the company of a young man. I do not, of course, put any faith in gossip. I have summoned you to ask if this is in fact true." She looked at Thalia steadily.

Thalia's mouth tightened. Someone had been very

thorough. "It is not," she snapped. "I went walking on Thursday afternoon two weeks ago and happened to encounter Mr. James Elguard in the countryside near here. Last Thursday, we went for a drive. That is all." She looked at Miss Chadbourne defiantly.

The older woman sighed. "I see."

There was a pause; then Thalia added, "I have done nothing wrong."

The headmistress looked at her. "Do you remember the talk we had when you arrived, Miss Hartington? I expressed some concern then about your adjustment to our life here at Chadbourne."

"I remember, but—"

"Well, I think we face here an example of what I meant. Certainly in terms of your upbringing and the circles in which you might have moved, you did nothing wrong." She looked up. "Though it was perhaps unwise to begin an acquaintance with a young man in such an unconventional way. But my staff here at Chadbourne cannot behave as young ladies in society might, surrounded as they are by the protections of family and custom. They, all of us, must hold to a higher standard. And by that standard, I judge you behaved wrongly."

"But it was nothing. It meant nothing."

"I believe you. But you see, we are set up here as guides to a group of very young ladies. We are in a sense models for them. And if they knew that you met a young man, alone, they might feel that they can do so as well. And we could not have *that*, could we, Miss Hartington?"

A sort of generalized despair settled over Thalia.

Though she knew she had done nothing wrong, she could foresee endless petty indignities arising from this event. For a few hours of pleasure, she was being outrageously punished, and there seemed to be nothing she could do about it, for she was dependent upon Miss Chadbourne's goodwill for her living. Choking on the words, she murmured, "I suppose I was unwise."

"I'm glad you see that. And I know the meetings will not recur. We will not talk of them again."

This was clearly a dismissal, and Thalia rose. "Who told you?" she asked.

"I think it best not to say, Miss Hartington. It might cause ill feeling."

So it was someone at school, concluded Thalia, and then, in a flash, it came to her. Lady Agnes, of course. This explained her behavior yesterday. She turned back to the headmistress. "But if it was someone here, and I assume it was, will there not be talk among the pupils?"

Miss Chadbourne looked grave again. "That is one of the reasons such conduct *is* so unwise. Girls do talk; we can't stop them."

Thalia nodded. She would get no help here, she saw. She turned and left the room, closing the door carefully behind her. She must steel herself to whispers and sneers, she realized. Lady Agnes would waste no time in spreading this story. The next few days would undoubtedly be very horrid indeed.

Thalia stiffened. She would at least be sure the girl did not get the satisfaction of seeing how very much she cared. She would act as if nothing had happened and ignore any remarks others dared make. But as she walked back toward her room, tears threatened. How very uncomfortable this place would be for her now. She longed for her sisters, and even, briefly, for her aunt. Things had seemed so much simpler only a few days ago.

Twelve

THALIA PASSED A MISERABLE EVENING. SHE HAD returned to her bedchamber after her interview with Miss Chadbourne and sat there through the afternoon with only Juvenal for company. She began a letter to Aggie, but could not go on with it. The events of the day were too fresh and painful to relate, and she was incapable of commonplaces. She nearly did not go down to dinner, but her hunger after missing luncheon and her conviction that not going would show everyone that something was indeed wrong forced her downstairs. She went in at the last possible moment, just before Miss Chadbourne, and kept her eyes on her plate throughout the meal. She imagined that she heard some whispers, but it seemed that the story had not yet made the rounds of the school, and she slipped away later without comment.

Upstairs again, she tried to read, and returned to her letter without success. Finally, despondent, she put down her pen. "Oh, Juvenal," she said to the kitten, who was curled comfortably before the fireplace, "what a wretched tangle this is. What am I going to do? I cannot stay in my room forever."

Juvenal looked up and fixed his golden eyes on her face. Then he rose and came over to rub against her ankle.

Thalia laughed a little. "Yes, that's all very well, but it does not answer my question, does it?"

"Rrrroww," responded Juvenal.

The girl sighed. "I may as well go to bed. Perhaps in the morning I can think what I should do. Should I start to look for a new post? I was just getting accustomed to this one."

The cat made no reply, and Thalia rose and began to get ready for bed. She lay down soon after, but she did not sleep for hours. Instead, she went over and over the events of the day and tried to find some solution to the problems they had created.

As soon as she entered the dining room the next morning, heavy-eyed from lack of sleep, Thalia knew that Lady Agnes had done her work. There was a hush when she came through the doorway, then a few giggles, and finally murmurings from all sides. None was audible, and no one offered to accost her, but it was clear that nearly everyone in the room was discussing her affairs.

Thalia faltered only briefly; then she put up her chin and walked proudly to her place, trying to show by her bearing that she was utterly unconcerned with what they might think. As she took her place, it was immediately clear that the teachers had also heard the story. Mlle. Benzoni turned her head away in a marked manner; Miss Allen looked at her plate; and

Miss Eliot stared at her with severe disapproval, as if to show that she, as teacher of deportment, had the best right to condemn Thalia.

Miss Chadbourne came in and signaled the beginning of the meal. As they sat down, Thalia caught a sympathetic glance from Miss Hendricks and an embarrassed one from Miss Reynolds beside her, and she seated herself quickly, avoiding other eyes.

When the food came, she ate quickly. Miss Chadbourne initiated a very dull discussion of expenditures for supplies at the top of the table, for which she was very grateful. Under cover of this, Lucy Anderson squeezed her hand under the table. "I think they are all beastly," she whispered, "and so do some of the others. What a tempest in a teacup!"

Thalia nodded, not daring to look at her for fear she would show something of what she felt at this open sympathy.

At a pause in the conversation, Mlle. Reynaud, the French mistress, leaned forward from her seat beside Miss Chadbourne and addressed Thalia down the table, a thing she had never done before. "Ah, Miss Hartington, I did not expect you would come down this morning. So brave of you." Her tone was acid, and her faded eyes showed an avid curiosity.

"Why not?" answered Thalia, with as much nonchalance as she could muster. "I do so every day."

"Naturally," added Miss Chadbourne, in accents that let everyone know there was to be no talk of what had happened.

Mlle. Reynaud subsided, and a little while later, breakfast ended. Thalia rose with relief and turned to leave. How she would face her classes, she did not know, but it could not be any harder than this meal had been.

Lady Agnes and her group were gathered near the doorway. As she passed them, Thalia braced herself. "Good morning, Miss Hartington," said Lady Agnes in a poisonously sweet voice.

"Good morning," she replied, and raising her eyes, she met the younger girl's squarely, trying to put all the contempt she felt for her in one glance.

But Lady Agnes was not so easily affected. She held the gaze for a moment, then laughed falsely and looked away.

Thalia was about to move on when a breathless voice behind her said, "Oh, Miss Hartington, there is something I particularly wanted to ask you." She turned to find Mary Deming standing there, spots of red burning in her thin cheeks. "Would you care to come into Bath with me this Sunday afternoon?" continued Mary in a burst. "My mother is coming for a visit, and I should so like to introduce you to her. I have written her all about you and how much I like your class."

Thalia, realizing that the girl had successfully vanquished her shyness and made this public offer to show that she set no store by the gossip, was touched. "Thank you very much, Mary," she answered. "I should be honored to meet your mother."

Lady Agnes tittered. "I daresay," she whispered quite audibly.

Mary gasped, the red fading from her face.

But Thalia turned calmly to look at Lady Agnes,

then turned back to add, "It would be a privilege to meet the woman who instilled in you such consideration for others and true good manners. Would that we could see such more often." And with this, she swept out.

But the satisfaction of having set down Lady Agnes was short-lived. By the time she reached her room once more, Thalia was at once crushed and blazingly angry. What a petty, mean place the Chadbourne School turned out to be. All these women with nothing better to do than talk scandal. Yes, and fabricate it, she added to herself. "I have done nothing improper, Juvenal. Nothing. Whatever story that spiteful little creature is spreading."

Reluctantly she gathered up the books and papers containing the lessons for the day and started back downstairs. There was nothing to do but face this unpleasantness and get it over as soon as possible. But at the head of the stairs, she paused. Sounds of unusual commotion drifted up the stairwell. Someone was shouting—a man. This was so odd that she almost forgot her own dilemma; she walked down, listening closely. She had reached the landing when she realized with a shock that she knew the voice. It couldn't be, but it was, Mr. Elguard.

"I most certainly shall see her," he was saying. "And if you do not go and fetch her straightaway, I shall go myself."

"You wouldn't!" responded a maid's voice, sounding dumbfounded.

"Try me!" was the response.

Thalia nearly ran down the remaining stairs. "Mr.

Elguard," she said when she reached the hall. "What are you doing here? You must go away at once."

The man turned quickly at the sound of her voice. "Ah, there you are. You can run along now, girl," he told the maid.

The servitor threw him one wide-eyed glance and fled in the direction of Miss Chadbourne's quarters.

"I came as soon as I discovered what my mother had done," continued Elguard. "I cannot tell you how mortified I feel. I want to apologize for her."

"There is no need. Please, you must go." Thalia looked around anxiously. She thought there were some students listening in the corridor, but she could not be sure.

"Nonsense. I have something to say to you. Let us go somewhere where we can talk privately."

"We cannot. And we have nothing to say. It is kind of you to have come, Mr. Elguard, but there was really no need. Please do go."

Ignoring this, he went to a door leading off the hall and flung it open, revealing one of the parlors. "Here, this will do. Come along."

"No. I cannot. I was on my way—"

But he grasped her wrist firmly and pulled her into the room, closing the door behind.

"There. Gods, what a noise they make over nothing in this place. How can you endure it?"

This echoing of her own thoughts might have drawn Thalia at any other time, but just now she was too concerned over his presence in the school and the effect it was likely to have on her position. "That is quite true," she retorted, "but the noise you have heard thus far is nothing to what will arise if you do not leave at once. You needn't say anything to me. Just go."

"Oh, no, I have a great deal to say."

"It doesn't matter. I am not angry with your mother. She—"

"Well, I *am*. And now will you hold your tongue for one moment and let me speak?"

Startled, Thalia fell silent.

"Thank you. Now, first, my mother somehow got quite the wrong idea about you and our meetings. Before I even had the chance to mention it, she was flying up into the boughs."

"One of the students told her."

"Indeed? Well, that explains it, then. A vicious little cat, I suppose. At any rate, my mother spoke to you with quite the wrong view of the situation, and I apologize for her. I shall talk her round, and when she has the chance to know you, to see what you are like, everything will be well."

"That seems unlikely," responded Thalia dryly, "either that she will know me better or that things will be well. She prefers that you spend your time with ladies more socially and financially acceptable than I. It is very reasonable. I understand."

"It is not reasonable! Don't you begin, now. It is odiously starched-up and grasping and… and despicable."

But Thalia hardly seemed to hear him. "A bishop's daughter would be just the thing, I think. Yes. You must be on the lookout for a bishop's daughter."

"Stop it!"

She blinked.

"I am the one to decide whom I shall 'look out for.' And it will not be a bishop's daughter. I have an income of my own and no need of a rich wife. I shall be perfectly comfortable with my living."

"Comfortable," echoed Thalia mockingly. "Poor stuff." Even as she said it, she wondered at herself. Why was she speaking to him so coldly? He had not been the one to hurt her.

Mr. Elguard seemed of the same opinion. "Will you stop? Why do you answer me so contemptuously? I have done nothing."

Thalia looked at him. His handsome countenance was flushed with emotion, and his gray eyes burned.

"I disagree completely with my mother, as I have told her. I also told her I was coming here today, whatever she may think, to ask you to be my wife."

Thalia's eyes widened, and she stared at him in astonishment. She opened her mouth to speak, but nothing came out. And at just this moment, the door of the parlor opened again, and Miss Chadbourne sailed grimly in.

The headmistress looked from one flushed face to the other. "This is highly irregular," she said, "highly irregular. I must ask you, young man, to leave at once. We do not allow male visitors here at Chadbourne."

"Respectfully, ma'am, I don't care a straw what you allow. I came here today to ask Miss Hartington to marry me, and I don't intend to leave until she gives me her answer."

"Indeed?" Miss Chadbourne looked at Thalia, then back to Mr. Elguard. "Well, well." She sighed.

"Things weren't done so when I was a girl," she added, and she turned to leave the room. At the door, she paused. "I give you ten minutes, no more. This *is*, after all, a girls' school." And she was gone.

James Elguard laughed. "An impressive woman."

But Thalia was too preoccupied with her own inner turmoil to heed this. "Mr. Elguard..." she began, and stopped.

"Yes? Will you marry me, Miss Hartington?"

She took a breath. "Of course I will not. This is the most ridiculous thing I have ever heard of. If you are offering for me out of some mistaken notion that I was... was compromised by one afternoon ride in an open carriage, I tell you now that—"

"—that that is idiotic," finished the man. "I couldn't agree more. And naturally my motives are very different. I have already told you that I have never before met a girl like you, so intelligent and interested in the things that interest me. I think we should suit admirably, and I want you for my wife. I have never enjoyed a day more than the one we spent together."

Thalia bit her lower lip. It was hard to maintain her composure in the face of statements like this. "It... it is impossible," she faltered. "You must see that it is. I will not marry you against your family's express wishes. I will not be called a scheming—"

"No one will dare say any such thing," he snapped. "My mother put this in your mind, I know, but she will be brought to see her mistake. And she is not all my family, you know. You must meet my father and uncles and... and everyone. They will all like you immensely."

Thalia shrugged. "I think not. They want a good match for you, and they are very right." He started to speak, but she held up a hand. "And in any case, this is all beside the point, Mr. Elguard. I hardly know you. We have spent perhaps four hours together in our lives. I could not marry a stranger. I... I..."

"Do you feel that I am a stranger?" he asked in a quieter voice. "Odd. I feel I have known you forever."

Thalia looked at the ground.

"Well, if that is all," he went on, "I can wait until we are better acquainted."

"We won't become better acquainted," Thalia burst out. "Please go now, Mr. Elguard, and don't come here again. It is impossible, wrong. Please."

"I don't see that at all. If we could see each other—"

"We cannot. I have a position here, and—"

"If you are trying to tell me that you would rather be a schoolteacher than marry me, you may give it up. I don't believe you. I may not be a nonpareil, but I can offer you more than this." He gestured at the room around them. "Come, we both know what a place this is, after what has happened in the last few days."

"I would never marry simply to escape the school," said Thalia.

He came closer and looked down at her. "You speak so positively. Does it truly not matter to you whether you meet me again? Is the interest all on my side?"

Thalia hesitated. This sort of question was not only new to her, it was for some reason very difficult to answer. She started to reply that indeed it did not matter to her, but then she met his eyes and paused again. That was not precisely true, and she had an idea that he knew it. She had never met a young man she liked more. But the memory of her encounter with his mother made her straighten. She would not be put in such a position, to be judged and condemned by all his friends. "That's right," she said, trying to keep looking him in the eye. "It doesn't matter. Now, will you please go?"

"Certainly not." He reached for her hand. "Do you expect me to believe that?"

But before he could go on, the door opened again, and Miss Chadbourne looked in. "All right. That is enough. If you have not settled your affairs by now, you must do so somewhere else. Mr. Elguard." She held the door, her meaning unmistakable.

"Yes, please go," cried Thalia, and before anyone could speak again, she ran out of the room and upstairs to her bedchamber.

The rest of the day was agony. Thalia carried out her duties mechanically and sat stony-eyed through meals, knowing that the whispering was more wide-spread than ever. She did not see how she could endure day after day of this, surrounded by people who did not really care about her. And an even sharper disappointment hovered at the edges of her mind, to be resolutely pushed away whenever it intruded: she would never see Mr. Elguard again. She would never enjoy the kind of talk they had had together, or feel so free and happy.

When evening finally came, Thalia retired to her bedchamber gratefully. Juvenal, seeming to sense her oppression, rubbed against her ankles and purred.

She was just about to undress and get into bed, when there was a rap at the door. Thalia froze. What now? Would this day never end? Fearing another summons to Miss Chadbourne's study, she opened the door very slowly, but the maid standing outside merely handed her an envelope, saying, "This just came for you, miss. The man had been riding all day, and he said it was important, so I brought it right up."

"Thank you," replied Thalia, taking the letter.

The maid nodded. "Hope it isn't bad news, miss," she added as the other shut the door again.

Thalia turned the envelope over in her hands. It was from Aggie, but why would she send it by special messenger? Thalia's heart pounded as she thought of accidents, illnesses, and other disasters, and she tore the letter open with trembling fingers. But as she began to read, her expression shifted to incredulity and, finally, dazed relief. "Can it be true?" she wondered aloud at one point. And as she finished the missive, she added, "Thank God!"

III.
Euphie

Thirteen

EUPHIE'S JOURNEY WAS THE SHORTEST OF THE THREE, and she arrived in London late in the afternoon of the same day she set out. She had never seen the city before, and some of her low spirits dissolved as she stared out the coach window at the crowds in the streets. There were more people together here than she had seen in her whole life.

The driver threaded their way through increasingly elegant thoroughfares to the house of Lady Arabella Fanshawe, Countess of Westdeane, whose companion Euphie was to be. And the closer they came, the more nervous the girl was. She had never met a countess, but she had been told that this one was "difficult." She wondered uneasily if she would get on with her, and she wished for the fifteenth time at least for her sisters.

They pulled up before an imposing mansion in Berkeley Square at a little after five o'clock. The driver rapped smartly on the front door as Euphie climbed down and stood on the top step. The door opened at once, and a tall butler ushered her into the most magnificent hall she had ever seen, or imagined. A great marble staircase rose at the back, and huge gilded mirrors reflected her slender, large-eyed figure from both sides. Euphie looked around her with a mixture of awe and fright.

"Shall I take your basket, miss?" asked the butler kindly. And when she turned to gaze up at him, he smiled.

"Oh… oh, no, it's quite all right." From within the wicker basket came the sound of small claws scrabbling for purchase.

"Perhaps you'd like to go upstairs, then, and see your room," he replied.

"Yes, thank you."

The butler smiled again and walked over to ring for a maid to take her up, but as he passed a partly open doorway on the left, an imperious voice said, "Jenkins, is that the girl? Bring her to me immediately."

The butler went to the door and stepped inside. "I thought, ma'am, that she might wish to rest after her journey," Euphie heard him say.

"And so she may," was the reply, "when I have had a look at her."

There was a pause; then Jenkins returned. He smiled at Euphie reassuringly. "Lady Fanshawe wishes to welcome you," he said.

Euphie doubted that this was exactly what her new employer wanted, but she stepped forward with all the assurance she could muster. The butler held the door for her, and she entered a very elegant library, carpeted in crimson, with tall mahogany bookshelves reaching to the high ceiling and several comfortable-looking velvet armchairs. In one of these, before the fire, sat an elderly lady looking toward the door. To Euphie's surprise, she was small—well below her own height, and slender to the point of emaciation. Her hair was silver and dressed in fashionable curls about her head. She wore a lavender gown that was clearly, even to Euphie's inexperienced eyes, the height of fashion, and her features still held an echo of great beauty. Her eyes were a sharp and critical blue, and at this moment they were examining Euphie with at least as much interest as she had shown in the countess.

Lady Fanshawe smiled thinly. "So. You are Miss Hartington, are you? Very pretty. That red hair is stunning, though you dress it abominably. What have you to say for yourself?"

Euphie, nonplussed, opened her mouth to reply that she had nothing to say, but before she could form words, a dreadful uproar broke out around her feet. She had not at first noticed that the countess kept a lapdog; Pug had been lingering among her ladyship's skirts. But now he erupted in furious barking and ran at her, snapping in a way that made her want to aim a kick at his hideous little face.

"Pug!" exclaimed Lady Fanshawe in outrage. "What do you think you are doing? Stop it this instant!"

But the dog was beyond the call of reason, and he continued to jump up Euphie's legs, groveling and snapping.

Annoyed, Euphie bent down and, awaiting her chance, seized his collar with her free hand, holding him up off the ground so that he could not reach her. Pug, nearly apoplectic, continued to try to lunge, and it now became clear that his object was not Euphie herself, but the basket she carried.

"Give him to me," said the countess commandingly.

Pulling the dog by its collar, Euphie did so.

The older woman gathered the small animal in her arms, effectively stifling movement, and then turned back to Euphie. "What have you got in that basket?" she asked. "Beefsteak?"

Euphie blushed scarlet. "No, it's... it's my kitten. I had forgotten he was there... or, that is, I didn't know..."

"Of course you didn't. And you handled Pug very well, too. He is the most frightful nuisance. My daughter gave him to me. For company! Can you imagine? Let us see him."

It took Euphie a moment to realize that she meant the kitten. "But won't your dog...? That is..."

"I shall hold Pug. Take him out."

Slowly the girl opened the basket and reached inside to draw out a pure white kitten, a little ruffled from recent events.

She held him up for the countess to see, and the two eyed one another interestedly. Pug growled fiercely.

"A pretty animal. Put him down; he must be wanting some exercise."

Doubtfully Euphie did so. The kitten paused a moment, then began to explore the room.

"Very pretty indeed. What is his name?"

Euphie blushed again. "Ah, Nero, ma'am. My aunt named him."

"Did she?" replied Lady Fanshawe, raising her eyebrows and smiling. "Well, by all accounts, your aunt was an odd creature. I understand you have an unusual name, too."

"Yes, ma'am. Euphrosyne. But everyone calls me Euphie."

"Sensible. I hope I may do so as well. And you will please stop addressing me as 'ma'am.' It makes me feel even older than I am."

"Yes, Lady Fanshawe."

The older woman smiled again. "I think you may do very well, Euphie. Run along now and see your room. We will talk at dinner."

Euphie went to scoop up Nero and started for the door.

"And, child…" added the countess.

She turned back inquiringly.

"I bid you welcome to my house."

Euphie smiled uncertainly for the first time. "Thank you, ma… ah, Lady Fanshawe." She dropped a sketch of a curtsy and went out.

Dinner that evening was very grand, and Euphie felt younger and more countrified than ever in her old white evening dress and braided hair. She and Lady Fanshawe sat alone at a large table in an opulent dining room, her ladyship at the head of it and Euphie beside her. The countess saw her gazing dazedly about as the soup was being served and chuckled. "Oh, yes, it is quite ridiculous for two people to dine in such state. But I like it, and I have reached the age where I can do as I like. It is my one remaining pleasure."

"It is a beautiful room," responded Euphie. "The

whole house is beautiful. And, my room is wonderful. Thank you."

Her employer looked at her interestedly for a long moment. "You are rather out of the common way, are you not?"

"I am?"

"Oh, yes. I have had companions before, you know." She chuckled again. "Three of 'em. My family insists on it, though I cannot imagine why. But never one like you. Usually they are either intolerable managing women who call me 'we' and think they can dictate my every move, or they are mousy timorous creatures who tremble at my least glance."

At these vivid pictures, Euphie could not help laughing.

"Precisely," continued the countess. "You are not at all like either type, and yet you are not like the young ladies of my acquaintance. I occasionally meet the daughters, or granddaughters, of my friends. I have some idea of the modern miss. You are not the least like them."

Euphie looked down. "I have never had the opportunity of going into society, ma'am."

"Yes, I know. I have heard something of your history, but you must tell me more. Not now." She gestured toward the kitchen, from whence Jenkins was just coming with the main course. "Later, in the drawing room. And I shall tell you the rules of my household. Then we may both be easy."

The girl looked at her apprehensively, but Lady Fanshawe was examining the roast with a very critical air and did not notice.

❧

Coffee was brought to the drawing room, and Jenkins left them alone. When she had sipped a little, the countess began to speak again. "I shall tell you something about myself. It is not my usual habit, but in this case..." She did not explain what she meant by this, but instead, after a meditative pause, continued, "My husband has been dead for six years now. We were very happy, and I still miss him a good deal. Since I have been alone, I have gone out less and less. My family began to worry, and finally insisted that I needed company." Lady Fanshawe smiled ruefully. "So they provided me with a succession of perfectly frightful 'companions,' until I revolted and declared that I should choose my own." She paused again, looking into space with a smile.

Euphie watched her. "You have a large family?" she asked finally, feeling that she should say something.

The countess turned to look at her, rather as if she had forgotten Euphie was present. "Large? Not really, though it often seems quite large enough. I have three children, two daughters and a son. Dora and Jane are married and have families of their own." Her mouth quirked again. "Indeed, one of my granddaughters will be making her come-out in three or four years. My son, Giles, the youngest, remains single in spite of the dogged efforts of his sisters to marry him off. He is very like his father." This time, the countess's smile was warm and reminiscent; then she looked at Euphie sharply. "Do not misunderstand me, young lady, I am not telling you a sad story. I am quite content with my life, except for missing my husband. I might go out continually in the season, and I am invited to friends' houses, too, as well as my daughters'. But somehow, as I get older, I find I don't enjoy visiting as I did." She chuckled. "I like directing a household too much, and I've gotten used to having things done my way, I suppose. At any rate, my only complaint nowadays is occasional boredom. People seem less clever than they were when I was younger. The ton parties are so dull."

Euphie stared at her, trying to imagine how anyone could find a party dull.

Lady Fanshawe caught her gaze and laughed. "You cannot imagine that, eh? Well, you have not been to so many."

Euphie shook her head.

"So," the older woman went on, "now you understand me a little better. Tell me about yourself."

"Well," began the girl uncertainly, "you know about my family and that I grew up in my aunt's house with my sisters."

"And a very eccentric house it was, I gather," murmured Lady Fanshawe.

Euphie nodded. "I suppose it was. I often wished Aunt would allow us to go out more; she kept us very close. But she also let us do as we pleased in the house. We studied as we wished and didn't have to work very hard."

"You studied music?"

"Yes. I always loved it. And then, when Aunt died—"

"Disgraceful," interrupted the other. "I have heard that story, and I think it is disgraceful. It ought not to be allowed."

There was a short pause. Euphie looked as if she agreed.

"And so you and your sisters found positions, and you came to me here," finished the countess. "How do you feel about that?"

"Ma'am?"

"How do you feel? Are you angry? I should be, I think."

The girl frowned. "I was, at first. It seemed very heartless of Aunt to treat us this way. But now…" She considered. "Well, perhaps I am resigned."

Lady Fanshawe laughed. "I doubt it. You don't seem the type. But I am glad you will not be raging about the house and hating everyone because you are forced to live here."

At this picture, Euphie laughed. "Oh, I should never do that. The one thing that I do feel is that I shall miss my sisters terribly. Indeed, I do already. I have never been away from them before."

"Well, we shall see if we can find you some other amusements." The countess watched the suddenly forlorn figure opposite for a moment, then said, "I should tell you about our daily routine, so that you will know what to expect. I don't come down in the mornings, so you will have that time to yourself. We will meet at luncheon, and afterward we may take a drive or I might ask you to read to me before tea. After, I go upstairs to lie down for a while. You may wish to go out walking; I know you are used to more activity than you will find here. If you can bring yourself to take Pug along, he can always stand a run. Then, we have dinner and perhaps cards or reading in the evening. I retire early. Occasionally my son or some friend will visit, but I admit I do not encourage them. I am not interested in gossip any longer, and people seem to have little else to talk about. What do you think?"

"A-about gossip, Lady Fanshawe? I don't—"

"No, of course not. About the schedule I have outlined."

"Oh. It sounds as if you give me very little to do."

The countess laughed. "I do not think you will find it so. I will send you on all manner of errands and even ask you to write letters for me on occasion. You will be busy enough."

"I hope so. I do want to be a help to you."

"I believe you mean that," replied the other, smiling.

Euphie nodded.

"Well, I think we shall deal together well enough. And now, would you ring the bell, please? I am tired and ready to go up to my room."

Euphie rose to do so.

"Oh, and one other thing," said the countess. "I must get my maid to do something about your hair. Shall you mind having it cut? I can't abide dowdiness."

The girl flushed, putting one hand to her wrapped braids.

"You would look lovely with ringlets, you know, and we must buy you a dress or two. Your aunt's taste was quite gothic."

"I... you needn't do so, Lady Fanshawe. I am perfectly content with the clothes I have," answered Euphie untruthfully.

"Then you're a ninny, my girl," was the reply,

softened with a smile. "And I don't believe you. But even if you were, *I* am not. I insist upon something easier on the eye. After all, I am the one who must look at you, am I not?"

Euphie eyed her doubtfully; then a reluctant smile curved her lips. "Yes, ma'am," she replied meekly.

"Good. That's settled, then."

Jenkins came in response to the bell, and Lady Fanshawe went upstairs to bed. Euphie followed soon after, tired out from her journey and the new experiences of the day. But before she fell asleep, she lay for a while in her bed, wondering whether she would indeed like this place and the life she would lead here. Lady Fanshawe seemed kind, if a little intimidating, and the house was certainly luxurious. Moreover, she was to have a fashionable haircut and some new dresses, things she had wished for for years. Euphie sighed and snuggled down in her covers. Whatever happened, it would be wonderful to look smart for the first time in her life.

Fourteen

THE FOLLOWING MORNING, EUPHIE'S HAIR WAS CUT by Lady Fanshawe's dresser, under the countess's close supervision. Euphie watched wide-eyed as her braids were unwound and snipped off, to be replaced by a cloud of auburn ringlets all around her face. "Much better," pronounced her employer in a self-satisfied tone, and before the girl could take a breath, she had summoned her own dressmaker to supplement Euphie's wardrobe.

"We shall want several gowns," she told the woman when she arrived. "Two for evening, I suppose, and a walking dress, and two morning dresses. That will do to start, at least. Let us look at your patterns."

They proceeded to do so, the countess clearly in charge.

"That one is pretty," said Euphie hesitantly after a while, pointing at one of the models in the dressmaker's booklet.

"Oh, my dear, not pink!" was Lady Fanshawe's reply. "You must never wear pink, with your hair.

Pale green, blue, buff, perhaps brown, and of course, white—but never pink."

"That's what Aggie always says," answered Euphie a little wistfully.

"Aggie? Oh, your sister. Well, she is quite right. I think we will have one of these, and a simple white evening dress, and…" She went on with complete certainty, while Euphie wondered whether the treat of getting new dresses was quite the same when one was allowed no choice in the matter.

But another concern was more pressing. "Lady Fanshawe, you cannot buy me so many new things," said Euphie. "You mustn't."

"And why not?"

"Well… well, because I am only—"

"You were engaged to be my companion, and I require the people around me make a good appearance. The clothes you have are not suitable."

She said this very coolly, but Euphie could not help but realize that true kindness lay beneath her tone. There was no necessity for her to clothe her hired companion.

"Besides," continued the older woman, "I am enjoying myself immensely. I had forgotten how much fun it is to outfit a young girl; my daughters came out years ago, and they have never wanted much help. Only think, I haven't felt bored this whole day, and it is nearly teatime. You cannot deny me this pleasure, Euphie."

When she put the matter this way, Euphie could do nothing but bow her head in assent.

"Let us go and have our tea, and then we shall look

through my closets and see what we can find for you. I have dozens of shawls and gloves and that sort of nonsense, none of which I ever wear."

Euphie started to protest again, but the countess waved her words aside.

"I will not listen. Haven't you realized yet that I am a disagreeable old woman who always gets her way? And I don't mean to change for you."

Smiling, Euphie followed her into the drawing room, where tea was already laid out, and they sat down behind the teapot. The girl vowed that she would be as helpful as possible to Lady Fanshawe, to make some return for her kindness.

In the next few days, Euphie learned the routines of her new home and recovered most of her customary gaiety, dampened since her parting from her sisters. Her new dresses arrived, and she spent a blissful few hours trying them one by one and admiring the effect in the mirror. She learned to deal with her new haircut and became accustomed to the vast increase in her wardrobe. Nero was introduced to the staff below-stairs, and received with great cordiality. For the sake of Pug, Euphie endeavored to confine him to her own bedchamber, but this was very difficult, since Nero was a playful, lively animal.

In the afternoons and evenings, she helped Lady Fanshawe with her correspondence or, sometimes, read aloud to her. But the countess seemed to get more pleasure from simply listening to Euphie's chatter and her opinions on the new things she saw in London when she went walking.

In a surprisingly short time, they were getting on

famously, and Euphie felt that if only she might see her sisters once in a while, she would be very happy indeed. She wrote them long letters, full of under-lining, detailing her good fortune.

❧

On the fourth evening after her arrival, Euphie and Lady Fanshawe sat in the drawing room after dinner, the countess reclining on a chaise longue and Euphie reading aloud. But after only ten minutes, the older woman made an impatient noise and said, "Leave off, my dear. This is the stupidest book I have ever come across. I don't care a whit whether this mawkish heroine manages to find her mother or not. Indeed, I hope she won't. Perhaps then she will be forced to show some initiative instead of moaning and sobbing like a hired mourner."

Euphie giggled. "The woman at the circulating library promised this was a very edifying work."

"I daresay. I shall turn to it the next time I require edification. For now, let us abandon it."

"Certainly," replied Euphie, shutting the volume without any sign of regret. "What shall we do then?"

"I haven't any idea," began the countess petulantly. Then she added, "Yes I do, though. You shall play for me. You see, I have not forgotten that you are supposed to be musical."

"Have you an instrument?" asked the girl eagerly, half rising from her chair.

"Of course. Weren't you told? How heedless of me. I'm sorry. We have a pianoforte in the back parlor. It was a fine instrument at one time, though I daresay it is monstrously out of tune now."

They walked together down the corridor to the back of the house, and Lady Fanshawe opened a door on the right. "Here we are. Just ring for candles, Euphie. And we must have them kindle a fire. I use this room so seldom, it feels quite damp."

But Euphie did not appear to hear her. All of her attention was focused on the pianoforte in the corner of the room. She walked up to it and sat down, running her fingers over the keys, trying one here, one there. The countess watched her with interest for a while, then went to ring the bell herself, a small smile playing about her lips.

The servants brought candles and lit the fire, making the room much more comfortable than before. But Euphie still seemed oblivious; she was trying snatches of melody and listening.

"It is out of tune, isn't it?" said Lady Fanshawe. "No one has played it since my daughters left home. I never had any skill myself, though I love music."

When she had repeated her question, Euphie finally replied, "Yes, it is a bit, but not so much that one can't play."

"We'll have someone in tomorrow to see to it. But now, if you would oblige me, I should love to hear you play."

"Of course."

"Shall I send someone for your music?"

"Oh, I don't need it. I'll do something I know."

"Splendid." The countess went to sit down in a capacious armchair near the fire, from which she had a good view of the instrument and Euphie's profile. The room was dim despite the candles, and the flames cast moving shadows over the deep half turned blue walls.

Euphie sat very still for a moment, then leaned forward and began a Mozart sonata which she particularly loved. She played with utter concentration, and her eyes gradually grew rapt as the music rose and fell. She moved with it, her hands delicate on the keys and then passionate. It was clear that she was aware of nothing else.

As she played, Lady Fanshawe's expression grew more and more arrested. She watched the girl with growing interest and respect, and when the last notes died away, she said softly, "Beautiful. You have great talent, my dear. That was wonderful."

Euphie started and turned around. "Th-thank you. That is one of my favorite pieces. I love it."

"Indeed. And have you always been fond of music?"

"Always! I cannot remember a time that I was not trying to play."

"That's wonderful. And you play from memory?"

"Only pieces I know very well. And I am always learning others. I have piles of music upstairs."

"I see. Well, you must use the instrument whenever you wish. I shall have it tuned tomorrow."

"Thank you, Lady Fanshawe. You are always so kind to me."

"Nonsense. My motives are thoroughly selfish. You must practice so that you can play to me in the evenings. Will you do another now?"

Smiling, Euphie nodded and turned back to the pianoforte. The countess leaned back in her chair again and prepared to listen.

After this, it became their habit to have music in the evenings. Sometimes Lady Fanshawe would bring fancy-work and sew as she listened, but most often she simply sat still, her head back. She seemed to enjoy these sessions at least as much as Euphie, and she always thanked her warmly. Euphie found that she knew quite a bit about music, and they had many lively dialogues on this subject.

Thus, the days passed pleasantly in Berkeley Square, Euphie feeling more at home with each one. When she had been there two weeks, she and Lady Fanshawe were sitting at lunch one day discussing the possibility of going for a drive. "I should like to show you Kew," the countess was saying, "or perhaps Richmond. The flowers should be just coming up."

Euphie was about to express her willingness to see either when a terrific uproar began. Both of them swung around to stare at the door. "What is it?" said Euphie.

"Let us go and see," replied Lady Fanshawe, rising and starting out of the room.

The sounds led them down the corridor toward the back of the house. As they went, the din grew louder, and when they reached the half-open door of the back parlor, they encountered a wide-eyed maid staring at it apprehensively. "I don't know what it can be, ma'am," she said. "I dusted this morning, like always, and there weren't nothing in there."

Lady Fanshawe moved forward and pushed the door wide. "I think," she said as she strode into the room, "that it must be Pug."

It was. In the middle of the carpet sat the dog, crouched down in a miserable hump and howling piteously. At intervals, he rubbed his nose gingerly on the carpet, as if to soothe some ache.

"Pug," repeated the countess, going to him. "Whatever is the matter?"

But the dog was beyond reasonable communication. He merely continued to howl, his bulging brown eyes fixed on her ladyship's face.

"Has he hurt himself?" asked Euphie, coming to join her.

"I don't know. He looks all right." Lady Fanshawe moved as if to pick him up, and Pug fell over on his back, his paws waving feebly in the air.

"Oh, do stop, you ridiculous animal," responded the countess. "How can I see what is the matter if you lie on your back?"

Pug howled again, but just as he was hitting his stride, a noise from the corner of the room made him leap up again and stand on stiff legs, his hackles rising.

The two women looked around, but they could see nothing. Then, without warning, a small white bundle shot from beneath the edge of a tablecloth and swooped under Pug's low belly. The dog leaped convulsively into the air and came down moaning and shivering.

"Nero!" exclaimed Euphie. "Stop it at once, you naughty cat."

The kitten had stopped and turned to see the effect of his joke. He sat now some distance away on the carpet, surveying the scene with sparkling blue eyes.

"Oh, Lady Fanshawe, I am so sorry," began Euphie, "I try to keep him shut away."

"No, indeed. It is quite Pug's fault." She turned to the dog. "Do you think I have not seen you stalking poor Nero about the house? I suppose you found him alone here and tried to fight him. And got your nose scratched. Serves you right."

Euphie, who was trying very hard not to giggle, put in, "But, Lady Fanshawe, Nero was teasing him. You could see that. And he mustn't."

"That is true," replied the countess judicially. She turned back toward the cat. "You must behave yourself, Nero, and try to humor Pug."

Unable to hold herself in any longer, Euphie burst out laughing.

Lady Fanshawe whirled and put her hands on her hips, though her lips were also trembling. "This is no laughing matter, young lady. All the members of my household must agree."

Encouraged by her severe tone, which he evidently took as a vindication of himself, Pug chose this moment to challenge Nero once again. He advanced toward the cat's position, growling and baring his teeth. But he prudently halted just beyond Lady Fanshawe's skirts, keeping the line of retreat open.

Nero, delighted at this renewal of their game, danced forward and batted at him playfully with one paw. The dog fled around the countess, and Euphie collapsed into an armchair, putting a hand to her mouth.

"Enough," exclaimed the older woman, and the tone of her voice made Nero stop and look up at her, blinking. Euphie tried to stifle her merriment. "It is all very well for you to laugh," the countess said, "but we must do something. Pug and Nero must both learn better manners. I will not have this fighting."

"N-Nero is only playing," the girl choked out.

"Possibly. But he must learn when a joke ceases to be amusing to its victim. Now, what shall we do?" She considered the problem.

Pug peered around Lady Fanshawe's skirts at Nero, who batted at him once again. The dog pulled back quickly. Then, assuming a look of great cunning, Nero sank down on his stomach and began to inch his way along the carpet in the opposite direction around the countess's dress. Euphie choked again.

"I have it," said Lady Fanshawe. "They must be taught to get on with one another, and I know just how it can be done."

"How?" replied Euphie. But just then Nero jumped out from behind her ladyship and attacked Pug from the rear, startling the dog into a convulsive somersault. Euphie doubled up with laughter as Lady Fanshawe sought to snatch up first one, then the other combatant.

When things were at last quiet again, the countess said sternly, "You will henceforth, Euphie, take both of these creatures on your walks. I will order Jenkins to contrive a double lead, so that they must go together side by side. In this way, they will learn to get along or they get no exercise at all." She looked satisfied. "I daresay this problem will disappear in no time."

Appalled, Euphie stood up. "But... but, Lady Fanshawe, I can't... they will..."

The countess fixed her with an implacable gaze. "Who brought Nero to this house?" she asked.

"Well, I did, of course, but—"

"And who has shown a lamentable levity over this latest outrage? Without, I may add, making the least push to stop it?"

Euphie smiled ruefully. "I have, I suppose."

"You have indeed. And so, I think it only right that you take charge of the problem. You do not expect *me* to walk the animals, I suppose?"

"Oh, no. But there must be some better way to teach them…"

"I am open to suggestion," answered the countess equably.

Euphie frowned. "Well, we might… uh…"

"Precisely. You will take them out together tomorrow without fail. I will speak to Jenkins." Lady Fanshawe turned to leave the room, but at the door she paused. "It will do you good, my dear," she added, grinning wickedly. "I daresay you will get twice the exercise you normally take. And you know you have complained that there is no room to really walk in London." With this, she was gone.

Euphie stood shaking her head and laughing a little. She bent to scoop Nero up off the floor, determined to shut him in her bedroom for the rest of this evening at least. "What a nuisance you are," she told him severely. "I begin to wish I had chosen some other kitten. Can you not be a little more sensible and sedate?"

The white kitten looked up at her, his blue eyes gleaming. "Rrrowww," he replied.

Euphie laughed again. "Yes, that is exactly what Aggie used to say to me, isn't it? Well, we must do our best. I hope you will *try* not to tease Pug on our walk." And she started up the stairs to her room.

Fifteen

THE FOLLOWING DAY, AFTER LUNCHEON, LADY Fanshawe sent Euphie to find Jenkins and the device he had been asked to procure. When they returned, she inspected the new lead curiously. "This will do nicely," she said. "Admirable, Jenkins. Did you make it yourself?"

"Thank you, ma'am, but no. Actually, one of the stable-boys contrived it. He is very clever with his hands."

"Splendid." The countess handed the little sewn leather straps to Euphie. "Out you go, my dear. A nice long walk, now, mind."

Grimacing, the girl took the double lead. "If I don't return, you may search the prisons," she answered. "I am certain Pug and Nero will do something monstrous, and I shall be clapped in gaol for it."

Lady Fanshawe laughed. "Nonsense, my dear. I'm sure you'll have a wonderful, invigorating time." With this, she turned and started up the stairs for her afternoon rest. Euphie remained where she was, staring distastefully at the lead.

After a moment, Jenkins gave a discreet cough. "I should be happy to help you, Miss Hartington, if you would like."

"Help me? You don't mean you will take them out, Jenkins?"

The large butler looked appalled. "Oh, no, miss. I meant I will help you get the animals in, ah, harness, as it were."

"Oh." Euphie's momentary hope faded. "Yes, all right. I suppose we should do Pug first. He is used to a lead, at least. Nero will hate it!"

The dog was duly fetched and fastened in without protest. Indeed, he seemed happy to see the lead; he enjoyed his sedate outdoor walks very much. The new straps hanging at his side annoyed him a bit, but he seemed prepared to be magnanimous and ignore them.

"All right," sighed Euphie, "you keep Pug here, Jenkins, and I will go get Nero."

"Yes, miss."

The kitten was in her room, and he frisked up happily when she appeared, and even licked her hand when she picked him up and started back downstairs. In the front hall, Jenkins opened the straps next to Pug and held him as Euphie attempted to buckle them around the cat. Pug was not at all pleased to see Nero, but Jenkins kept a hand over his eyes during the operation, so that he did little but wriggle and growl softly.

When an extremely reluctant Nero was fastened up, Euphie stood and took the other end of the lead from Jenkins. "There," she said, "let Pug go."

The butler did so, standing and stepping back.

Pug shook his head, his long dragging ears flopping, and stood up straighter in preparation for going out. Then, gradually, he became aware of Nero, practically pressed against his side.

Pug's already bulging brown eyes threatened to leave their sockets. His hair stood on end, and he himself seemed to rise on his toes in his complete outrage. A menacing growl began in his throat, only slightly tempered by memories of his last encounter with Nero, and he bared his teeth and slowly turned his head in the kitten's direction.

Nero, fully occupied with trying to chew through, or wriggle out of, the hated straps, ignored him. Euphie moaned. "What a fool I shall look, dragging these two through the streets. Jenkins, what am I to do?"

"Perhaps, miss, they will become accustomed to one another as you walk," replied the butler doubt-fully. "That is her ladyship's idea, isn't it?"

"So she says. But I think she is just punishing me for laughing at her." Suddenly she had an idea. "Jenkins, couldn't one of the footmen take them out? He needn't go far."

Thinking uneasily of the difficulty of keeping good footmen, Jenkins said, "I don't think so, miss. Her ladyship was quite firm. And the animals will be more comfortable with you, knowing you as they do."

"Will they indeed?" snapped Euphie. Then she sighed. "Oh, very well, I may as well get it over." She pulled a little on the lead. Nero hissed and dug his claws into the hall carpet. Pug, in response, jerked his shoulders convulsively, nearly pulling the kitten off his feet.

Reluctantly Euphie smiled. "It is so ridiculous," she said, and urged the animals toward the door.

Once outside, things were a little better. Pug, though still angry, was happy to be out. And Nero was fascinated by his first sight of the city streets. Thus they forgot for a while to fight with one another, and Euphie tried to set such a pace as would discourage them from beginning again.

They walked briskly across the square toward a small park where Euphie often went. One or two people glanced at them and smiled, but Euphie was so relieved to have peace that she didn't care. They reached the park without further mishap and entered a fenced enclosure, where Pug was always allowed to run for a while. Today, cunningly, Euphie released him alone, letting him dash about as much as he pleased before she replaced his lead and let Nero go. The kitten also enjoyed his unaccustomed freedom. He explored the fence, the grass, and the flowerbeds with gusto. Finally, when Euphie judged that he had had enough, she caught him again and put back the straps. Nero liked them less than before, if anything.

At this point, Euphie's habit was to continue her walk in a circuit around the house, giving herself some exercise as well. But the idea of another twenty minutes in the streets did not appeal today, and she turned back toward home as soon as they left the park.

Pug and Nero seemed docile. Euphie even began to hope that they *were* becoming accustomed to one another by the time they entered Berkeley Square once more. True, Pug still tended to twitch his left shoulder at intervals, in an effort to knock Nero off his feet. And Nero continued to make feints at Pug's long trailing ear. But all in all, Euphie began to think they would get home safely.

They were only fifty yards from the house when the disaster occurred. Nero made a final, more serious lunge at the ear, catching it between his teeth and biting down. Pug, enraged and in pain, yelped and struggled to turn his head and get his own teeth around the offender. He failed, but his abrupt jerk on the lead pulled it from Euphie's less vigilant grasp, and the two animals went tumbling forward onto the pavement in a growling, hissing ball.

At the same moment, a high-perch phaeton turned the corner into the square and bore down on Lady Fanshawe's house, heading straight for the spot where Pug and Nero grappled.

"Oh, no," gasped Euphie. She waved to try to stop the vehicle and moved into the street, but it swept up before she could do anything. The highbred team took instant exception to the battling pair on the cobbles, threw up their heads, and began to back and rear. In an instant, all was chaos.

"Oh, dear," moaned Euphie. She had a momentary craven wish to run and hide, but she pushed it away resolutely and turned to watch certain disaster.

She didn't see it. With consummate skill, the driver of the phaeton hauled back on the reins, bringing the horses to a dancing, snorting stop just inches from Pug and Nero, who had by now ceased fighting in the face of this greater peril. "Go to their heads!" the driver shouted to his groom, and the servant hastened to do so. In the space of a minute, all was quiet again.

The driver then looked down at Euphie, standing at the edge of the pavement with one hand to her mouth, and said, "Are those *your* animals?" in a tone that made her shiver.

Wishing she were anywhere else, she gazed up at him. And what she saw was not calculated to put her more at ease. The driver of the very fashionable phaeton was a large man, with the body of an athlete and the bored mouth and eyes of a Corinthian. His hair was black, his eyes blue, and everything about him fairly shouted elegance and disdain. Euphie had never seen anyone like him, but she knew instinctively that he must be of the haut ton. She swallowed, started to speak, then changed her mind. Finally she managed a cowardly, "No, they belong to my employer."

"Your *employer*?" he asked, sounding bored.

"Yes, Lady Fanshawe. We were just going in. And I… I am sorry they frightened your horses. They were fighting, you see, and they pulled away from me."

"Lady Fanshawe?" echoed the man in puzzled accents. He started to say something else, but Pug and Nero chose this moment to renew their combat, and he turned instead to look at them. His eyebrows went up. "Do you have a cat and a dog harnessed together?" he added, astonished.

"Well, uh, yes. That is, Lady Fanshawe thought…" Suddenly the task of explaining how this came to be to the magnificent stranger was too much. Euphie hurried forward, scooped up Pug and Nero with no concern for their comfort, and almost ran into the house. Inside, she did not pause but fled directly to the kitchen, there to lecture the dog and cat for several minutes on their manifold sins.

Her feelings somewhat relieved by this outburst, she went up to her room to leave her bonnet and shawl, then started back downstairs to the drawing room. Lady Fanshawe should have finished her rest by this time, and Euphie intended to tell her that she would never take Pug and Nero out walking together again.

In the drawing room doorway she paused at the sound of voices within. Who could be here? The countess had had no callers since she arrived. As Euphie hesitated, Lady Fanshawe noticed her and called, "Come in, my dear. I understand you have already met Giles."

Euphie stepped farther into the room and saw with amazement that the contemptuous gentleman from the phaeton was now sitting opposite the countess, sipping a glass of Madeira.

"This, as you have already heard, is my new companion, Giles," continued Lady Fanshawe. "Miss Hartington. Euphie, this is my son, Giles Fanshawe. I've mentioned him to you."

"Y-yes," stammered Euphie. "G-good day."

"Come in and sit down, dear. Giles took it into his head to visit us today, and we must be suitably grateful for the condescension."

"Spare me, Mother," murmured the man.

"Why should I?" She turned to Euphie. "I understand you had a small contretemps outside the door."

The girl flushed. "Yes, Pug and Nero—"

"Giles told me. What dreadful animals they are, to be sure."

"Your cat is called Nero?" asked Fanshawe, amused.

"Yes, er, Mr., ah…"

"Actually, he's an earl," laughed the countess. "I suppose you must call him Lord Fanshawe. Or perhaps simply Westdeane. How ridiculous."

Her son smiled sardonically.

"My aunt named him Nero," finished Euphie uncomfortably.

"How very odd."

"Well, she was odd," put in Lady Fanshawe.

"Yes, and I don't think she had the least idea what the real Nero was like. She can't have, because my sister Thalia told me that he was not at all the thing, and Aunt wouldn't have cared for that."

The gentleman smiled with real amusement for the first time.

"Sit down, Euphie," repeated Lady Fanshawe. "Giles isn't going to bite you."

Flushing, the girl slid into an armchair.

"Your name is original also," said the earl. "Did your aunt name you as well?"

Euphie's flush deepened. He spoke to her as if she were some curious alien creature, mildly interesting but no more. "No," she replied shortly, "my father did."

"Her full name is Euphrosyne," added the earl's mother.

"Ah, a classical gentleman, I see." Lord Fanshawe's sardonic smile reappeared. "But you are very young to be a companion, are you not? You look scarce out of the schoolroom."

Not unnaturally, this remark made Euphie's chin come up. "I think that is for your mother to say," she answered, rather spoiling the effect by adding, "I am seventeen."

"So old?"

"Now, Giles, don't be odious," said the countess. "I know it is your usual manner, but do try. And tell me what you want."

Real amusement lit Lord Fanshawe's eyes again, and they twinkled charmingly. "You are hard, Mother. May I not come for a visit without wanting something?"

"May? Oh, of course you *may*. But you never do. Out with it."

He laughed at her. Euphie thought that he looked quite a different person when he really smiled. "It is a rather ticklish family matter, Mother," he answered.

Euphie rose at once, turning toward the door.

"Nonsense," said her ladyship. "Sit down, Euphie. Giles doesn't know about any family matters I would not have you hear."

"Do I not?"

"Well, perhaps you do. But I am sure you have not come to talk to me about *those*."

The earl laughed again. "Actually, I wanted to speak to you about Dora. She has gone beyond the line this time."

"Dora?" Lady Fanshawe looked amazed. "But whatever has she done? She has always been the most conventional creature." In an aside to Euphie, she added, "Dora is my elder daughter, dear."

"She is driving me to distraction with her continual schemes to provide me with a bride," replied her son.

Her ladyship's perplexity vanished. "Oh, a bride. Well, that's all right, then. I *could* not imagine Dora committing the least indiscretion." She turned to Euphie again. "She was the most docile child, quite unlike Jane and Giles."

"It may be more likely, Mother. But it is excessively annoying," said the earl, torn between laughter and exasperation.

"Is it, dear? But of course there is a simple solution."

"And what is that?"

"Why, you need only marry, Giles, and then Dora, and all the mamas would leave you at peace. You know we have all begged you to for years."

Euphie, embarrassed at this frank family discussion, made another move to leave, but the countess waved her back.

"I shall marry in my own time, Mother, and I wish you will tell Dora so, and to stop throwing silly chits fresh from the schoolroom at my head."

"Does she, dear? Dora always was a bit foolish. Your taste has never run in that direction."

Lord Fanshawe heaved a sigh, and then laughed ruefully. "I might have known that you wouldn't help me."

His mother turned to look at him, eyebrows raised. "But of course I will help you, Giles. I shall write to Dora at once." She smiled. "Shall I summon her for a scold? I haven't seen her in weeks."

"Whatever you please, Mother."

"What do you think, Euphie? Would a note be best, or a talk?"

"I... I don't know, Lady Fanshawe."

Lord Fanshawe looked amused. "Miss Hartington is not in the habit of deciding such questions, I imagine."

"No. And she knows nothing about the marriage mart and our schoolroom misses. She is an original." The countess smiled at Euphie, who was flushing again. As she did, an idea seemed to strike her. She glanced at her son, then back at Euphie, and fell into a brown study.

There was a short pause. Euphie stared at the floor.

"And so, Mother, have you been well?" asked Lord Fanshawe finally.

"What?" The countess started and turned toward him. "Well? Oh, yes, indeed. Quite well. It is charming of you to ask, at last. But of course, we had important matters to dispose of first."

The earl shook his head helplessly.

"You know, I believe I shall call on Dora," continued his mother. "I suddenly feel I should get out more."

"So we have always told you. You insisted you are happier at home."

"Well, I have changed my mind. In fact, I think I should like to see a play. Will you escort me, perhaps on Wednesday next?"

The earl eyed his mother speculatively. "I?"

"Well, who should do so, if not you?"

"I can imagine many others. You have friends still in London, Mother." She started to reply, but he held up a hand. "Nonetheless, I should of course be honored to accompany you whenever you like."

Lady Fanshawe bowed her head regally. "Thank you. Wednesday next, then."

"I shall be here."

"Come to dinner first, of course."

He nodded his agreement. "And what play do you wish to see, Mother?"

"Oh, it doesn't matter. Any of them. Pick the most fashionable; I have a fancy to see the ton in full plumage."

He nodded again. After a moment he said, "I must be going. I have an appointment at Jackson's. You won't forget about Dora?"

"Oh, no."

"Thank you. I shall see you Wednesday, then." And he took a polite leave of both ladies and went out.

Lady Fanshawe sat silent for a moment, with a meditative smile, then turned to Euphie. "What did you think of Giles, my dear?"

Nonplussed, the girl hesitated. She had thought her employer's son sardonic and rather aloof, but she could not say so. "He... he is very elegant," she ventured finally.

The other laughed. "Oh, he is that. Top of the trees, in fact. But that hardly answers my question."

Euphie made another stammering effort, but the countess cut her off. "We will leave it for another time. Let me ask instead how you would like to go to the play with me?"

"I?"

"Yes, I should like you to come."

"Oh, Lady Fanshawe, I should adore it. I have never seen a play in my life."

"Haven't you?" The countess smiled meditatively again. "How fortunate."

Sixteen

THE DAYS BEFORE WEDNESDAY PASSED IN THEIR
customary routine. Euphie and Lady Fanshawe chatted
together at meals, and the girl usually played the pianoforte for her employer in the evenings. There were no
more walks with Nero and Pug, her ladyship having
given in to Euphie's vehement protests. Dora was duly
visited. Euphie was not present at their meeting, but
she was later told about it. "Dora is as stodgy as ever,"
sighed Lady Fanshawe. "She thinks it amazing that
Giles does not marry any of her candidates, awesomely
proper girls all. And I could not convince her that he is
quite uninterested in that type. As, indeed, what man
really is? I was astonished when Ellingford took Dora
off my hands."

Euphie could not restrain a giggle at this; her ladyship's expression was so comical.

"Indeed, my dear, I was. And now she is wringing
her hands over Giles, who is barely thirty. Why, his
father was a year older when we married." She smiled
reminiscently. "I have often wondered how two such
fascinating people as my husband and I could have

produced Dora. It is unaccountable. Of course, Jane and Giles are altogether different, and much more like us." Lady Fanshawe shrugged and changed the subject. "You know, Euphie, we must think about finding you a new dress for the play this week."

"A new… but I have scores of new dresses already, thanks to your generosity."

"Pooh! Scores. You have no such thing. A few simple gowns. Nothing fine enough for a real evening out."

"There are two evening dresses. I thought I should wear the white."

"No, no. The white is well enough in its way, but you must have something better." The countess looked at her measuringly. "Pale green, I think, with ribbons."

"But, Lady Fanshawe, I cannot allow you to buy me still more gowns. You have done far too much already. Indeed, I know I should have refused—"

"My dear companion," interrupted the older woman, "do you quite understand that I am a very wealthy woman?"

Euphie blinked. "Well, of course I know that you—"

"*Very* wealthy. My husband, the former earl, left me an extremely generous jointure. I never spend the half of it, even though I am not at all penurious."

"Yes, Lady Fanshawe, but—"

"*Furthermore*, I quite enjoy spending money. Particularly when the results are so wonderfully successful. Do you mean to deprive me of this plea-sure?" She looked at Euphie haughtily.

The girl smiled slightly and sighed. "You know very well that I cannot counter that argument. Still, I don't think it is right for me to accept so much from you. What have I done to deserve it?"

Lady Fanshawe dropped her mock anger. "For one thing, you have been, and are, by far the most charming and agreeable companion I have yet had. If you could know what a relief it is not to be managed or toadied to, you would not wonder that I wish to give you a few paltry gowns. And for another, it is perfectly absurd that a lovely young girl like you should not have some dresses and parties to go to. More than absurd, it is wrong!"

Euphie laughed. "I think you have contradicted yourself, Lady Fanshawe. How can I be a good companion and go out to parties?"

"There is no contradiction. What makes you charming is that you *are* the sort of person who should go out. Now, no more nonsense. We shall look for a dress at once."

And, of course, they did. Euphie didn't really have the heart to protest further. This time, they went to Bond Street, to the shop of one of the French modistes, and there chose an evening dress of the palest green crepe, trimmed with darker green ribbons at the sleeves and waist. When Euphie modeled it before the long mirror, further objections died on her lips. It was the loveliest dress she had ever seen.

"Yes indeed," agreed the countess. "That will do very well." The satisfied light in her eyes might have puzzled some of her friends, had any been there to see it.

◦✦◦

On the day of the play, Lord Fanshawe was invited for dinner at six, and the ladies went upstairs to dress right after tea. Euphie put on her new green gown and admired it once again in the mirror. With its tiny sleeves, scooped neckline, and sweep of skirt, it really was lovely. As she sat down in front of her dressing table and began to do her hair, there was a soft knock on the door. "Yes," called the girl, and Lady Fanshawe's dresser came in, carrying a small box.

"Her ladyship sent me to help you," she said. "She thought you might wish me to dress your hair."

"Oh, that's very kind," stammered Euphie. She was a little in awe of this very superior lady's maid. "I was just going to do it as you showed me."

"Yes, miss," responded the woman indulgently. She took the comb from Euphie's limp fingers and began expertly to arrange her curls. In a moment, they looked better than Euphie herself would ever have managed. "Her ladyship also sent these, miss," said the dresser then. She picked up the box she had brought and opened it, revealing a string of exquisite pearls clasped with an emerald.

"Oh," gasped Euphie, "oh, I couldn't!"

"Lady Fanshawe wishes you to wear them, miss. As a loan, you might say. She was very insistent. I was to tell you that you *must*, as a favor to her." The dresser surveyed Euphie. "You do need something for your neck, miss."

Euphie gazed from the box to the mirror, and put a hand to her bare neck. She looked back at the pearls. "But they are so beautiful, and so expensive, I am sure. I should be afraid of losing them."

"No fear of that. This clasp is tight. We just had

it checked." The woman picked up the string and fastened it around Euphie's neck. "There. Oh, that does look well, miss."

It was indeed the finishing detail. Euphie gazed at herself wide-eyed.

"You should be careful to see that the clasp stays at the side like it is," added the dresser. "The jewel does bring out the color of your gown. And your eyes," she went on diplomatically.

Speechless, Euphie continued to gaze.

"Well, if that's all, miss, I must go back to her ladyship."

"What? Oh. Oh, yes, of course. And thank you so much."

"My pleasure, I'm sure, miss." The lady's maid left the room.

Euphie stood up and turned slowly before the mirror. The toilette was perfect. She knew that she had never looked half so well in her life as she did tonight.

A sound near the doorway made her turn. Lady Fanshawe's dresser had not quite closed the door, and now Nero was pushing his way in, looking annoyed. Euphie went to help him, picking him up and setting him on the armchair. "Look at me, Nero," she said then. "Am I not *splendid*?"

The white kitten blinked up at her, then opened his mouth in a colossal yawn before curling up in the chair for a nap.

Euphie laughed. "Horrid." She gathered up her wrap and snuffed the candles, leaving the room illumined only by firelight. "I shan't tell you anything about the play," she told Nero as she left the room.

The drawing room was empty when she reached it. Her excitement had made her rather early. After walking about the room restlessly for a while, Euphie stood still. "How shall I wait a whole twenty minutes?" she asked aloud. "I wish it were time to go." With this, an idea seemed to strike her, and she went out and down the corridor to the back parlor, opening the recently tuned pianoforte and sitting down before it. Here, she knew, time would fly past.

She played a quiet piece by Haydn in a dreamily slow tempo. And as she had known she would, she soon lost all track of the time. Her wrap slipped off the stool as she bent over the keys, and her eyes grew faraway. When the last notes faded into the air, she sat back and sighed.

"Amazing," said a male voice in the dimness behind her.

Euphie started and whirled around. Lord Giles Fanshawe stood there, very elegant in evening dress, watching her.

"You have a real talent," he continued. "I compliment you. That Haydn was exquisite."

"Do you know it?" replied Euphie eagerly, her self-consciousness forgotten. "It is one of my favorites."

He nodded. "Like my mother, I have a love of music and little skill at making it." He came further into the room and leaned against the instrument. "You have been playing for years, I understand?"

"Always."

He started to say something else, then changed his mind. "Will you do another?"

Euphie looked at him. She could see no trace of

the mockery that had put her off when she had first met him. She nodded and bent over the pianoforte once again.

Lady Fanshawe found them here five minutes later. As she came into the parlor, there was a gleam in her eye, and it intensified when she took in the scene. She said nothing, however, until the music ended, merely watching the two young people closely. Then she came forward "Lovely, my dear, as always. Does she not play beautifully, Giles."

"Exquisitely," replied her son quietly.

"I ask her almost every evening. It is one of my chief pleasures now."

"I can see how it would be."

Flushing a little at this praise, Euphie rose. She started to bend to pick up her wrap, but Lord Fanshawe was before her, offering it with a little bow. Euphie's flush deepened.

"Shall we go in to dinner?" said the countess, reaching for her son's arm. "We must hurry if we are to go to the play."

Dinner was pleasant. Lord Fanshawe seemed less reserved than on his previous visit, and he and his mother joked throughout the meal. Once or twice Euphie ventured to join in, and her sallies were received with flattering smiles. Altogether, she enjoyed herself very much, and she looked forward to the evening's entertainment even more than before.

The earl had secured a box at one of the most talked-of plays, and they arrived and settled themselves in it just before the curtain went up. Euphie breathed a deep satisfied sigh as she looked around at the elegant crowd. The glitter of jewels and hum of talk was intoxicating.

Lord Fanshawe smiled at her. "You are looking forward to the play, Miss Hartington?"

"Hugely. I have never seen one before."

"Never?"

"No, my aunt thought them a waste of time."

"I wish I might have met your aunt. She seems to have been a very interesting person."

"Oh, no," said Euphie, "she would have hated you."

"I beg your pardon?"

The girl flushed and bit her tongue. Why had she blurted that out like a child? "I… I only meant… my aunt did not approve of the male sex. Except those in holy orders. Sometimes."

"Indeed?"

Euphie nodded miserably and turned back to the theater. All around her she saw groups of men and women chatting vivaciously, and she wished that she had half their skill. They never said such foolish things, she was sure. She watched a woman in the next box flip open a fan and flirt it dexterously in front of her face as she laughed at something her companion had said. For a moment, she envied her fiercely.

But then the curtain rose, and Euphie forgot everything in her enjoyment of the play. It was not a particularly polished piece, but to one who had never been in a theater, it was enthralling. Euphie saw and heard nothing else until the curtain dropped for the first interval.

When it did, she turned to her companions, blinking and trying to bring herself back to reality.

"I believe, Mother, that Miss Hartington liked the play," said the earl. His tone held only gentle teasing, with none of the sharp sarcasm she so disliked.

Lady Fanshawe smiled. "I believe so."

"I thought it was wonderful," exclaimed Euphie. "I know it seems like nothing to you, but I… well, I loved it!"

"And I enjoyed it more than any piece I've seen these twenty years," answered the countess, "simply watching you." She turned to look out over the crowd. "But now we must be on the lookout for acquaintances. That is what one does in the intervals, Euphie. And, Giles, you may go and fetch us some refreshment."

The earl smiled. "Yes, Mother," he responded meekly, standing. "And may I do anything else while I am out?"

"Impertinence. Yes. I see Lady Osbourne there. Pray take her my compliments."

"Osbourne? That—"

"Yes indeed. And let that teach you not to mock your mother." She laughed.

Lord Fanshawe smiled ruefully back and disappeared through the curtains at the rear of the box.

"This really is amusing," continued his mother as she scanned the opposite side of the theater. "But you mustn't be disappointed if we don't receive many visitors, Euphie. Most of my friends are getting on and don't leave their boxes."

"Oh, nothing could disappoint me tonight," answered Euphie.

The countess smiled again.

Despite her warning, they did have several visitors.

Two young men came to offer their mothers' compliments. And a middle-aged lady stopped for a moment
on her way out, scandalizing Euphie by informing
them that she was going on to an evening party instead
of seeing the rest of the play. Lord Fanshawe returned
with their drinks, bringing with him two friends, whom
he presented to the ladies. And finally, near the end of
the interval, a very large older gentleman appeared and
bowed ponderously. "Arabella," he wheezed. "'Pon
my word. Couldn't believe it when Waring said you
were here. Came right along to see for myself."

"Hello, Charles," said the countess without marked
enthusiasm.

"By Jove, it is you. Looking lovelier than ever, too.
I declare I haven't seen you this age."

Euphie stared a bit at this. Though she herself had
thought that Lady Fanshawe looked very fine this
evening, with her gray hair dressed in waves and a
gown of black lace, she was surprised to hear her
called lovely.

"You're looking stouter yourself," replied Lady
Fanshawe dryly.

The large gentleman chuckled. "Still a wit, I see.
Yes, my girth increases with the years, I fear. Nothing
like you." He looked around the box helplessly.

"A chair, Sir Charles," said the earl quickly. "Perhaps
Miss Hartington would give you hers and move back
here. So that you can talk to Mother more easily."

Lady Fanshawe glared at her son as Euphie stood
and said, "Of course."

"No, no," sputtered Sir Charles, "can't take a
lady's chair."

"It's quite all right," said Lord Fanshawe. "You will be more comfortable there. This is Sir Charles Grove, Miss Hartington. Grove, Miss Euphrosyne Hartington."

Euphie's name seemed to confuse the large gentleman further. He muttered a greeting as she went past him and sat in the fourth chair, then sank gratefully into the one she had vacated and leaned toward the countess. Lady Fanshawe continued to glare at her son for a moment, then turned courteously to reply to one of Sir Charles's sallies.

Lord Fanshawe suppressed a laugh. As he turned to Euphie, his blue eyes twinkled. "Sir Charles is one of Mother's old beaus," he murmured.

She gazed at them. The countess by this time looked resigned. "Really? She is not very happy to see him," she whispered.

"Oh, no. He was not a successful beau. But he claims he never married on her account. Nonsense, of course. He is quite happy as he is. Look at them!"

Sir Charles had possessed himself of one of Lady Fanshawe's hands and was bending over her solicitously.

"I think you are in for a scold later," replied Euphie.

"Oh, doubtless, but it is worth it to see her so. Society and admiration, even Sir Charles's, are good for her."

And seeing the countess throw back her head and laugh, Euphie had to agree. But she was more impressed by the real concern she heard in the earl's voice. In their constant bantering, she had not been quite sure what the mother and son felt for each other. Now she knew.

At this moment, the curtain began to rise again,

and Sir Charles had to hurry away. He promised to return at the second interval, earning Lord Fanshawe an outraged look from the countess, and indeed he did so. They had no other visitors during that time, and Euphie alternately chatted with her host and listened to the older couple's exchanges, some of which made her cheeks redden.

The end of the play came all too soon for Euphie. She was caught up in it to the last. And she said little on the drive home. Indeed, she had little opportunity to do so, as Lady Fanshawe filled the short time scolding her son for encouraging Sir Charles. The earl took this in good part, however, and when he escorted the ladies inside, he stood for a moment in the hall to say, "A pleasant evening, Mother, in spite of Sir Charles, was it not?"

Lady Fanshawe shrugged.

"Come, now, admit you enjoyed yourself."

Looking sharply at him, the countess said, "Did you?"

"I did. Perhaps we can do it again soon."

"Perhaps. We shall see."

"Can we not set a date?"

"You are very eager."

Lord Fanshawe paused, seeming puzzled, then replied, "I think it is good for you to get out."

"Oh, for me. Well, how is this? Come to dinner one day next week, and we shall talk further about the idea."

"Done," he answered promptly.

"Good. Let us say Thursday next. And now, I am tired. Good night, Giles."

He smiled and bid them both good night. When he

was gone, the two women walked upstairs together. "Yes, a pleasant evening," murmured Lady Fanshawe, "and most instructive, too."

Seventeen

THE WEEK PASSED CALMLY. EUPHIE ENJOYED HER QUIET life with Lady Fanshawe more and more as she began to feel closer to her employer. And she received happy letters from her sisters, which raised her spirits. Nothing marred the peace of the household save a few minor skirmishes between Pug and Nero. And even these were reduced in ferocity and duration. Pug was learning to avoid his frisky colleague, and though he sulked a good deal about this addition to his former kingdom, he no longer attempted to revenge himself on the cat.

On the day Lord Fanshawe was to come to dinner, Euphie was once again ready first. But tonight she sat contentedly in the drawing room waiting for the countess. She wore her white evening dress, a simple gown that set off her bright hair and eyes to perfection, and she had fastened a white rose in her curls.

She was still sitting alone when Lord Fanshawe was announced and came strolling in. She rose quickly, wondering what could be keeping his mother, and said hello.

"Good evening, Miss Hartington. You are looking very fresh and lovely tonight."

"Th-thank you."

"Mother is…?"

"She hasn't come down yet. I can't think why. I'll go and see."

"No need. I don't want to hurry her. Let us sit down."

They did so. Euphie searched for a topic of conversation.

"And so you enjoyed the play, Miss Hartington?" said the earl.

"Oh, yes, very much."

"I'm glad. Your amusements in London up till now have not been quite so conventional, I think?"

"What do you mean?"

"Your walks. When I first saw you, you were certainly having an unusual one."

Euphie laughed. "With Pug and Nero? I was indeed. But I have not done *that* again. I refused."

"Did Mother wish you to?" replied the man, amused.

"Oh, no, I don't think so. She only pretended to."

The earl looked at her more closely. "You begin to understand my mother very well, don't you, Miss Hartington?"

Taken aback, Euphie looked up at him.

"Oh, I am pleased by it, don't misunderstand. In fact, I meant to congratulate you on the very favorable change I see in her recently."

"Me?"

"Why, yes. Your coming here has had a marked effect. My mother has kept entirely to herself for years, even discouraging her children from visiting her. Now she seems to be making a change."

"But I have done nothing."

"I think you have. Seeing the play in your company recently showed me what it is, too."

Euphie stared at him. She did not think that she had had any effect at all on the countess. The older woman did just as she pleased.

The earl smiled. "You lend a fresh perspective to everything, Miss Hartington. You renew one's interest in life through your eagerness for it."

Euphie flushed. "You are roasting me, Lord Fanshawe."

"I assure you I am not. You are a very unusual girl."

"Unusual?" Euphie was uncertain whether this was a critical or approving comment.

"What is unusual?" asked Lady Fanshawe from the doorway. Euphie started and whirled around, wondering how much of their conversation she had overheard.

"Miss Hartington," replied her son, unruffled. "The more I see of her, the more I am convinced that she is quite out of the common way."

"Well, of course she is. Haven't I told you so?" The countess came into the room and sat down. "Dinner will be ready in a moment, so I shan't offer you anything now. Euphie has been shaped by a series of very uncommon occurrences. First, there was her odd name. It always makes a child think when his name is unlike those of his friends; I am an advocate of odd names myself."

Lord Fanshawe smiled. "That is, no doubt, why you named your children Dora, Jane, and Giles."

She waved this aside unconcernedly. "Then, Euphie

was reared by her aunt, a most eccentric woman, as far as I can tell. This also contributed to her originality."

Euphie, very embarrassed by this discussion of her character, kept her eyes on the floor and wondered how she could shift the conversation onto some other topic.

"Tell me more about this aunt," said the earl. "How, precisely, was she eccentric?"

"Oh, on the face of it, in the usual ways. She kept a houseful of cats, you know, and scarcely ever went out. But that is not what I meant."

"Wasn't it?" Her son appeared to be struggling with laughter. "I am almost afraid to ask what you did mean, then."

The countess eyed him severely. "I was referring to Euphie's education. Her aunt gave her, and her sisters, the freedom to study whatever they wished and as much as they wished. In this way, Euphie gained her quite extraordinary knowledge of music. Her talent, of course, would have developed in any case, but her training was very unusual for a young woman. She was not forced to anything, but she was allowed to study one thing in depth."

"Yes, I see. But I admit that this method of education seems dangerous to me. It was effective in Miss Hartington's case because she was inspired to study music. It would hardly do for all young people."

"We… we were made to learn all the usual things first," blurted Euphie, not wishing to be thought wholly strange. "And Aunt Elvira always encouraged us to read."

"Of course she did," agreed the countess. "One

of Euphie's sisters is a remarkable scholar," she told her son.

"Indeed? And the third?"

"Aggie is the sweetest, most amiable person in the world," replied the girl, meeting Lord Fanshawe's blue eyes almost defiantly. He smiled, and something in his gaze made her catch her breath.

At that moment, Jenkins came in to announce dinner, and they went in, to Euphie's relief. The talk of originality had made her very uneasy. She did not wish to be an original. On the contrary, she had always objected to their aunt's keeping them so close to home and not allowing them to do the things other girls did. She had hoped that her unconventional childhood was not perceptible in her behavior, but it appeared that it was, and this was dispiriting.

When the first course had been served, the countess turned to her son and said, "So, Giles, tell us what you have been up to since we saw you last."

"Up to, Mother?"

"Come, come, you heard what I said. Don't pretend to be dull. You are always up to some deviltry."

He laughed. "Indeed I am not. I promise you I had a prosy week."

"I don't believe you, but if you are going to be difficult, I will talk of something else. Let us hear the on-dits, then. I haven't gossiped in an age."

Though he looked gratified by his mother's wish to hear about society, the earl hesitated. "Miss Hartington…"

"Oh, la, Giles, not the scandals. Just the news."

Thus reassured, he complied, and amused them

throughout dinner with stories about various London personages and their doings. Euphie had heard of none of them, but Lord Fanshawe's lively descriptions nevertheless amused her. And Lady Fanshawe was soon laughing heartily.

"Old Geoffrey Danvers a great-grandfather," she crowed. "How he must hate it. Does he still dye his hair?"

"Jet black," replied her son, "and wears the tightest corsets in the Carlton House set, which is saying something."

Lady Fanshawe wiped tears of laughter from her eyes. "I must see him. You shall take me to Prinny's next reception, Giles."

"I should be delighted." He threw Euphie a triumphant glance, and she smiled in reply.

His mother rose, "Come, Euphie. Let us go to the drawing room. And you come along too, Giles. There is no reason for you to sit alone over your wine. A bad habit." With a wry smile, the earl also rose, and they walked back upstairs together and sat in the drawing room. "Ah," sighed the countess, leaning back in an armchair, "we shall sit a moment and digest our dinners, and then perhaps Euphie will play a little for us."

"Indeed, I hope so," agreed her son.

Euphie signified her willingness, and Lady Fanshawe nodded. "Giles," she added then, "didn't Julia Warrington's boy tell me at the play that she is giving a rout party next week?"

"I believe she is; it is one of the first events of the season."

"Hah. I think I shall go. The lad mentioned something about an invitation, and I brushed him off, but I shall write her and tell her I wish to come after all."

"That would be splendid, Mother. I am sure she will be happy to see you again."

The countess looked sidelong at Euphie. "Will you like to go, my dear? I daresay you would enjoy a London evening party."

"I? Oh, but…"

"Well, of course. You cannot expect me to go alone."

"But Lord Fanshawe will escort you, certainly."

"That's as may be. I shall want you."

"You mustn't force Miss Hartington, Mother," put in the earl.

His mother looked at him sharply, but he refused to meet her eyes. "Naturally not," drawled Lady Fanshawe, "but Euphie would love a party, wouldn't you, dear?"

"Well, I have never—"

"Good. That's settled, then. I shall write Julia tomorrow."

Jenkins came in with the coffee, and Pug at his heels. As the butler began to set out the cups, the small dog edged along the drawing-room wall toward the far corner, looking frequently over his shoulder and once starting at an unexpected sound. "What has happened to Pug?" the earl asked his mother. "He seems a changed animal."

Lady Fanshawe laughed. "Changed? I should say so."

Amused, the earl watched him slink into the corner and lie down. Pug did not relax, however; he kept both eyes wide and staring and scanned the room continually. "What is he searching for?" said the man.

The countess gave another crack of laughter. "Ask Euphie."

Lord Fanshawe turned inquiringly toward her, and Euphie shook her head. "Nero," she answered. "He *will* jump out at Pug and tease him; I can't make him stop, though I promise you I have tried my best."

The earl began to laugh. "Are they still at it, then?"

"They don't fight quite so much," she replied, "but they don't get on, either. I have tried everything I can think of, but Nero is, uh, lively, and Pug does not seem to understand that he is only funning."

The butler went out, and Lady Fanshawe poured the coffee. "Pug is only sulking," she said, "and the sooner he stops, the happier he will be."

"I have never seen such a transformation," said her son. "Look, there is the cat now." Indeed, Nero could be seen near the doorway. He was crouched down on the carpet surveying the room.

"Oh, dear, he must have gotten in when Jenkins went out. I'll get him," said Euphie, starting to rise.

"No, leave him. I want to see what happens," answered the earl.

Euphie looked to Lady Fanshawe; she knew only too well what would happen, but her ladyship said nothing. With a sigh, Euphie sat back.

Stealthily Nero made his way to a table in the center of the room. The cloth hung to the floor, and he disappeared under it. Pug was hardly five feet from the other side. They waited, and in a moment the inevitable occurred. Nero burst from beneath the cloth with a yowl, flying at Pug, claws outstretched. Pug, considerably startled, leaped up just in time to butt his head into these claws, and he began immediately to howl in outrage. The earl collapsed laughing, and Euphie jumped up to separate the combatants.

She snatched Nero from the floor and held him up. Seeing his opponent removed, Pug, who had been retreating, began to yap and leap up on her skirts. Euphie bent again and scooped him up, holding him in one hand while the other imprisoned the squirming Nero. "I shall shut them in separate rooms," she said and strode out.

The earl continued to laugh for several moments, and his mother watched him appreciatively. When he was calmer, she said, "You are very merry these days, Giles. I don't know when I've seen you laugh so much."

"You should have provided yourself with a kitten before, Mother, and you might have seen me laugh all you like. What a sight!"

"And a charming young companion?" suggested the countess.

"What?"

"I said, Miss Hartington is very charming."

"Oh. Yes, she is."

"Do you like her?"

"I? Well, yes."

His mother nodded. "I think I shall try to marry her off, Giles."

The earl sat up straighter. "What?"

"Yes. She is a lovely little thing. It shouldn't be

difficult to find a suitable match." She watched her son's face closely as she said this.

"But... but, she is your companion. If she marries..."

"You cannot think I am so selfish as to consider that. I *am* selfish, but when I look at that lovely girl..." Lady Fanshawe smiled. "And how amusing it would be."

"But, Mother..."

Euphie came back into the room. "I put Nero in my room and Pug in the library; they cannot get at one another now."

"Splendid, my dear," replied the countess. "And now perhaps you will play for us a bit? Only a little. I am getting tired."

"Of course, Lady Fanshawe."

The countess held out her hand for her son's arm, smiling sweetly up at him. Frowning, he gave it to her, and the three walked down the hall to the back parlor and the pianoforte.

Eighteen

JULIA WARRINGTON'S GATHERING WAS TO TAKE PLACE only three days later, and there was something of a flurry in Lady Fanshawe's household as a result. The countess bemoaned the fact that there was no time to get Euphie a new dress; the girl insisted that she would wear her pale green once again, scandalizing her employer thoroughly. The maids ran here and there with laundry and mending, and somehow, on the night in question, Lady Fanshawe and Euphie met in the drawing room after dinner completely outfitted for the party.

Euphie was wearing her pale green gown, and it looked as lovely as before. The countess, very grand in lavender silk and silver lace, had to admit that the girl looked well. "We shall simply hope that no one of consequence noticed your dress at the play," she said. "You can be sure that some odious cat did so, however. And I shall be astonished if it is not mentioned."

Euphie shrugged, further trying Lady Fanshawe's sensibilities.

The carriage had been ordered for nine, and they

went down to it a few minutes after. After considering the matter, the countess had rejected her son's escort, saying that he would more than likely be late and they could perfectly well go alone. Euphie had the impression that Lord Fanshawe was not at all displeased by this decision.

At the Warrington house, they left their wraps with a footman and walked up the staircase. At its head stood two women, one obviously the daughter of the other. Both were tall, with dark hair and eyes and exquisite ivory skin. "Arabella!" exclaimed the older one. "How wonderful to see you. You cannot know how flattered I am that you have come out of seclusion to attend my party."

"Hardly seclusion, Julia," responded the countess dryly. "Allow me to present a young friend, Miss Euphrosyne Hartington."

The three greeted each other politely.

"And this is my daughter, you know, Arabella. Charlotte, this is one of my oldest friends. I am bringing Charlotte out this season."

To these rather confused remarks, Lady Fanshawe replied only, "How I hate that phrase, 'one of my oldest friends.' Surely you have some friends who are older, Julia?"

"But, my dear, I did not mean—"

"No, no, I know it. Come along, Euphie. We are blocking the entry."

They walked on, into the drawing room, where the countess was welcomed by several people at once. She went to sit on a sofa by the far wall, and Euphie followed. She was duly introduced to a number of guests, most of the countess's generation, and she took up her station behind the sofa and settled to watch the proceedings with a lively curiosity.

It was a spectacle worth observing. Several groups stood about the room talking and laughing, and Euphie studied them interestedly. There were the young girls just out, and their admirers; Charlotte Warrington came in to join this circle after a while. They were a mass of pale colors and nervous shiftings. A little farther along were the young matrons and a sprinkling of gentlemen of obvious sophistication and address. A knot of older men held the far corner. Euphie smiled at their patent boredom. Unless she was much mistaken, they were about to decamp in search of a card table and a bottle. Their wives were in the group surrounding Lady Fanshawe; this stretched along the side of the room, and from the glances that were often cast across the floor, it was clear that it included the mothers of all the debutantes present. Euphie stifled a giggle; she had never seen anything half so amusing.

Lord Fanshawe came up to greet his mother. He nodded to Euphie and started to turn away, but she was so taken up with her observations that she didn't notice. "It is better than a novel," she told him, "watching the way they speak to one another and move about the room. That woman there"—she discreetly indicated one of the most dashing of the young married women—"is excessively bored. I have watched her try this group, then that, in hopes of finding someone amusing to talk to, but she has not succeeded."

The earl looked startled. "Have you indeed?"

"Yes, and that poor young girl there is terribly

shy and frightened. I almost went to speak to her a moment ago, but then that young man rescued her. Do you know who she is?"

Lord Fanshawe looked around without marked interest. "The one talking to young Warrington?"

"If he is the tall dark young man, yes."

He nodded. "One of the Deming girls, I think. I haven't met her, but she has the look of the family. They are all hopelessly shy."

"She looks very nice."

Fanshawe shrugged. "If you will excuse me, I must say hello to our host."

"Of course." Euphie watched him walk away, a bit puzzled. He seemed very different this evening from the man who had sat with them at the play and had so enjoyed her music. As he reached the center of the drawing room, the young matron who had been so bored accosted him.

The woman did not look weary now; rather, her eyes sparkled as she put a hand on Lord Fanshawe's arm. He stopped, smiled, and said something that made her laugh, and she slipped her hand through his arm and went with him toward the card room. Euphie frowned unconsciously and turned back to listen to the countess's conversation.

Some time passed in this manner. Refreshments were offered, and a small band of musicians began to play quietly in an alcove. Lady Fanshawe was obviously having a splendid time, and Euphie was content to stand behind her and observe the party. The earl did not approach them again, but moved among the other guests, chatting now with one, now another.

About midway through the evening, Lady
Fanshawe abruptly remembered Euphie. "Here," she
said, turning round to peer at her. "What are you
doing there? You must mingle with the young people,
get to know them."

"I am happy where I am, Lady Fanshawe."

"Happy? Nonsense!" The countess looked around,
caught Charlotte Warrington's eye, and beckoned
imperiously. The daughter of the house obediently
came over. "Charlotte, take Euphie and introduce her
to the young people," ordered the countess. "I don't
know any of 'em."

Charlotte bowed her head and motioned Euphie to
follow her.

"I really don't..." faltered Euphie, but Lady
Fanshawe pointed sternly, and she was forced to
go along.

Taking her to the younger group, Charlotte reeled
off a list of names that Euphie immediately forgot.
Appearing to think that her duty was done, she
returned to her conversation with a tall thin freckled
boy in amazing yellow pantaloons.

Euphie swallowed and looked around her nervously.
No one seemed to be paying her the least attention;
all of them were engaged with one another, talking
of things she knew nothing about. She looked at the
floor and tried to pretend that she was part of a three-
some on her left.

A striking blond girl came through an archway
and joined Charlotte and her friend. Her rather hard
blue eyes swept over the group, stopping briefly at
Euphie, and she turned to ask Miss Warrington a

question. Charlotte answered, and the blond girl looked surprised. Pulling peremptorily at Charlotte's sleeve, she strode over.

"This is Miss Euphrosyne Hartington," said Charlotte then, with poor grace. "Miss Hartington, Lady Agnes Crewe."

"How do you do?" said Euphie. Charlotte lost no time in slipping away again.

Lady Agnes did not answer. She merely stared at Euphie in a very disconcerting way.

"Is… is something wrong?" asked Euphie finally.

"Have you a sister who is a schoolteacher?" replied the other.

Surprised, Euphie smiled. "Yes. Do you know her?" She was delighted at the notion that she might have found a friend of Thalia's.

Lady Agnes gave a hard little laugh. "Know her!" And without another word she turned away to whisper to Charlotte.

"Come with me," murmured someone. Euphie turned to find the shy girl she had been watching earlier standing beside her. This slight dark person pulled at her arm, and she followed her willingly to a settee by the wall. "Oh, how horrid she is," the stranger went on. "I wish I could slap her!"

Euphie was bewildered. "I don't understand."

Her companion lifted large brown eyes to her face. "Didn't Miss Hartington tell you?"

"Miss Hartington? You mean my sister? Tell me what? Do you know her too?"

The girl flushed bright red. "Yes. I am sorry. My name is Mary Deming. I should have told you sooner.

I was at school with Lady Agnes, and your sister. She was a teacher there, I mean. A wonderful teacher! We just came down to London two days ago. Lady Agnes and I, that is. We took the same coach; it was hateful! We are both coming out this season. This is my first party."

In response to this rather disjointed statement, Euphie frowned. "I see. But what was it that my sister did not tell me? And why was Lady Agnes so rude?"

Mary Deming shook her head. "If Miss Hartington hasn't told of it, I shan't."

"What?"

But the other shook her head again.

"I assure you my sister *will* tell me whatever it is. We have always shared everything."

"I am sure she will. But I shan't." Miss Deming turned to watch the group they had left. "Lady Agnes is spreading some horrid lie. I must go and stop her."

Euphie looked from the arrogant blond across the floor to the obviously terrified Mary. "How will you do that?"

The girl shivered. "I don't know. She is so horrid. But I must try. Miss Hartington was so kind to me." And with this, she rose and went back.

Euphie watched the group curiously for some time. A new excitement was evident in it; some news was clearly being passed. But Euphie was preoccupied with the idea of her sister. What had happened to Thalia to make Lady Agnes act as she had? Euphie wanted to hurry home immediately to write to her sister, or better yet, to go to her, but she knew this was impossible. Frowning, she walked back to the sofa where

Lady Fanshawe sat and took up her station behind her.
She could do nothing but wait, with as good a grace as
she could muster, for the evening to end.

It seemed interminable. The countess did not
notice at first that she had returned, so Euphie was left
to herself. She watched the group of young people
continue their lively discussion. Lady Agnes Crewe
and Mary Deming seemed to have gotten involved
in a fairly public dispute, and the rest were reacting
with varying degrees of amusement, embarrassment,
or discomfort, depending on their characters. The rest
of the party went on, oblivious.

Finally, at eleven, Euphie could stand it no longer.
She bent over Lady Fanshawe and murmured, "Are
you not getting tired, ma'am? Perhaps we should go."

The countess started and turned to stare at her.
"Euphie! What are you doing here? I sent you off to
enjoy yourself with the other young people."

The girl grimaced.

"What is the matter?"

Euphie did not want to explain what had happened,
at least not until she could communicate with Thalia,
so she said, "I have the headache. I couldn't endure
the chatter."

Lady Fanshawe surveyed her with narrowed eyes.
"Headache? You never feel ill."

Euphie shrugged and looked at the floor. It was all
she could do to stand quietly when she wished only
to rush from the party and find out about her sister.

"Do you really want to leave?" asked the countess.

Euphie nodded emphatically.

The older woman continued to look perplexed,

but she shrugged slightly and rose. "It is true I am a bit tired. I am not used to this dizzy gaiety. Very well, then. We shall go."

They said their good-byes to their hostess and then went in search of Lord Fanshawe. The countess insisted she must bid him farewell also. He was not in the cardroom, as they expected, but when they came back to the drawing room, they saw him in the far corner, talking once more to the dashing young matron Euphie had noticed earlier. They walked toward them, reaching the earl just as another older woman and young girl did so. Euphie saw that it was Mary Deming, and a woman so like her that it must be her mother.

"Lord Fanshawe," said Mrs. Deming. "May I present my daughter Mary to you. She is my youngest, you know."

The earl's back was to his mother and Euphie, so they could not see his face, but the tone in which he replied was so blatantly discouraging that Euphie flushed in sympathetic embarrassment. Lord Fanshawe sounded unutterably bored at the idea of meeting Miss Deming, and he also managed to convey the impression that they had interrupted a much more agreeable conversation to push themselves upon him.

Mary herself blushed fiery red, and even her mother showed spots of color. The young matron beside the earl suppressed a smile.

For a moment, no one spoke. Euphie, though she very much wished to ease the situation somehow, could think of nothing to say. She was transfixed by Lord Fanshawe's rudeness. How different he was tonight!

Finally the earl himself drawled, "You are coming out this season, I suppose?"

"Y-yes," stammered Mary. She opened her mouth to continue, but only a strangled sound emerged.

Lord Fanshawe sighed. "It is amazing; there seem to be more debs each year. I cannot account for it."

Mrs. Deming's eyes flashed, but before she could speak, the countess moved forward. "How abominable you are, to be sure, Giles," she said. "You make me blush for you. Hello, Mrs. Deming. This is your daughter Mary? Charming. Have you met my young friend, Miss Euphrosyne Hartington?"

Mrs. Deming greeted Euphie, and the two girls managed to convey the idea that they had met.

"We are going, Giles," continued Lady Fanshawe. "We came to say good-bye, though I almost wish I hadn't. So nice to have seen you, Mrs. Deming." And with this, she and Euphie moved off, followed almost immediately by the Demings. Euphie noticed that the countess had ignored the other woman in the group completely, and wondered why.

Once they were in the carriage and headed home, Lady Fanshawe leaned back with a long sigh. "Well, it was an interesting evening. I enjoyed myself, but it also reminded me of all the things I hate about society. People are so artificial."

"Lord Fanshawe seemed very different," ventured Euphie. She could not reconcile the two pictures of him now in her mind.

Lady Fanshawe sighed again. "Yes, he is always so, among the ton. He is on the defensive, you see, and he does it so badly."

"The defensive?"

"Yes. He is very much sought after, not just by matchmaking mamas, but by everyone. For some reason, Giles is all the crack, in spite of his sometimes appalling rudeness. And so he is forced to hold people at arm's length, so as not to be overwhelmed, you see. And he is not at all good at it. I have seen it done with such address that the poor object does not even know he has been snubbed, but Giles can't seem to get in the way of it. I have seen exchanges like that one with the poor Deming child time after time." She shook her head.

Euphie digested this in silence for a space. Then she said, "You did not introduce me to the other woman there."

The countess's chin came up. "I did not. And I shan't, either."

Her tone was truculent, and Euphie had to be content with this rather uninformative dismissal.

When they reached home, the footman let down the carriage steps and helped Lady Fanshawe down, and Jenkins threw open the front doors. As Euphie walked inside, the butler stopped her. "A letter came for you while you were out, Miss Hartington. Brought by special messenger." He held out an envelope.

Thinking at once of Thalia, Euphie took it and tore it open. The note covered one full page, and she began to scan it rapidly. As she read, her eyes gradually widened, and finally she looked up with an expression of astonishment.

"What is it, dear?" said the countess. "Nothing is wrong, I hope?"

"No. It is all right. It is all all right somehow." Euphie sounded dazed.

"What is all right?"

"Everything!"

Frowning, Lady Fanshawe took her arm and began to lead her up the stairs. "Come to the drawing room this minute and explain what you mean."

In the drawing room, the countess pushed Euphie into an armchair and sat down opposite her. "Now, then."

A bit more composed, Euphie heaved a happy sigh and said, "The letter is from my sisters, both of them. They are back home, and they say there was a mistake over my aunt's will. I don't understand all the details, but she left us something after all, quite a lot of money, Aggie says."

For just a moment Lady Fanshawe's face showed chagrin; then she smiled and said, "My dear child, how wonderful."

Euphie nodded. "And Aggie and Thalia are coming to London. That is why they did not call me home too. They ask me to find hotel rooms for them. We are to have our own house and spend the season here." She sighed again. "Oh, I can hardly believe it. It seems too perfect." Then she sat up straight. "Do you know a good hotel, Lady Fanshawe? One suitable for Aggie and Thalia? I must see about it first thing tomorrow."

"But, my dear, they must come to stay here. I insist. I won't have your sisters going to a hotel."

"Oh, but you have done so much."

The countess waved this aside. "I have a strong desire to see your sisters, in any case. You will write tomorrow and ask them here." The very slight disappointment in her ladyship's eyes had disappeared. "I positively insist."

Euphie hesitated, then smiled. "Thank you," she replied. "I will."

IV.
THE THREE GRACES

Nineteen

AFTER A FLURRY OF LETTERS BETWEEN EUPHIE AND HER sisters, it was settled that they would stay with Lady Fanshawe for the present. And the two older girls arrived by private chaise on a warm late-spring afternoon when the countess was taking her post-luncheon rest. Their reunion was tender, and they were grateful to be left to themselves for a while, to pour out the stories of their weeks apart. Euphie and Thalia heard about the Wellfleets and their kindness and were pleased to know that they would have an opportunity to meet this amiable couple in London. Aggie and Euphie expressed outrage at Thalia's tale, the latter wishing to write a stiff letter to Mrs. Elguard. The older girls discouraged her, but when Euphie told them that Lady Agnes Crewe and Mary Deming were now in London and described her encounter with them, Thalia's green eyes glinted ominously. Finally, Euphie told them about her time in town, and Lady Fanshawe's kindness to her. "She hopes we will stay here for the season," finished the youngest sister. "I told her I must wait and see."

Aggie nodded "She may change her mind now that we are all three on her hands."

Euphie bounced in her chair. "But tell me about Aunt's will. What happened? Why did you not call me home?"

"I started to," replied Aggie. "But by then I had decided to come to London, and Mr. Gaines had everything so well in hand that I really needed no help. So I just summoned Thalia, and we came on to you here."

"What a relief it was to get that summons," put in Thalia.

"But the will?"

Thalia grinned. "There *was* a later one, after all. You will never guess how it came to light."

"I don't want to guess! Tell me."

"Hannibal found it!" Thalia's eyes twinkled. "Aunt Elvira must have been reading it just before she died, because it had slipped far down behind the cushion of her armchair. Hannibal was clawing at the chair one day, and he uncovered the document." She choked. "He chewed it up a bit, but it was still readable when the maid came upon him. She sent for Mr. Gaines, and he summoned Aggie."

Euphie had dissolved into laughter. "Aunt would be so pleased," she gasped out.

Thalia began to laugh too. She nodded.

Aggie smiled and shook her head at them. "At any rate, Euphie, Aunt Elvira left us half her fortune, and the cats the other half. Since she apparently had an immense amount of money, that leaves all of us very well off indeed."

Euphie sighed happily. "How comfortable."

"Isn't it?" agreed Thalia.

"And… and so, I thought you would wish to spend a season in London, you and Thalia, I mean. You must have a proper 'come-out.'"

"You too," replied Euphie. "Or you first, I should say. Perhaps… perhaps I should wait a year." She made this heroic suggestion with only the slightest tremor in her voice.

"No," snapped Aggie, surprising them all.

"What is it?" asked the middle sister. She turned to Euphie. "Something is wrong with Aggie. I've sensed it since I went home again. But she won't tell me."

"There is nothing wrong! And no one will wait a year for anything. We must all come out at once, I suppose."

The other two looked at her with concern. It was quite unlike their even-tempered older sister to snap like this. Euphie started to speak, but a subtle signal from Thalia stopped her. She frowned, then said, "Well, that will be a nine days' wonder. I daresay we will make a hit."

"I don't know that I want to," answered Thalia.

"Of course you do. It will be great fun."

Before Thalia could reply, there was a sound from the doorway of the drawing room, and all three sisters turned at once.

Lady Fanshawe was just coming in, and they smiled and rose. The countess, seeing them, stood stock-still, her hand on the doorknob, her eyes wide.

Lady Fanshawe had naturally thought Euphie a very pretty girl indeed, and when she had considered the matter, she supposed that her sisters would be pretty as well. But none of her speculations had prepared her for the dazzling sight that now met her eyes. Separately, each of the Hartington girls was striking, but when they stood together, the effect seemed to be multiplied much more than three times, and they were astonishing.

"Oh, my dears," said Lady Fanshawe when she found her voice, "I shall give a ball. I positively *must* give a ball at once!" She came into the room dazedly, as one who sees a heavenly vision, forgetting to close the door behind her. Pug trotted in at her heels.

Aggie and Thalia exchanged an amused glance as Euphie made the introductions.

When everyone had sat down again, the countess looked from one to the other, shaking her head. "Have you any idea how lovely you are?" she said finally. "You three are going to set London on its ear, and if you don't allow me to help you, I shall never recover from the disappointment."

Thalia laughed, then quickly suppressed it.

But Lady Fanshawe merely nodded at her and smiled. "Yes, I daresay I sound quite demented. I don't think you have any idea of the effect you create together."

"Effect?" echoed Aggie, a little bewildered.

"Never mind. Just do say that I may give a ball in your honor, to present you to society. Grant me only that."

The sisters looked at one another. "That's very kind of you, Lady Fanshawe," began Aggie, "but—"

"You will need a sponsor, you know. It is difficult

to meet members of the ton without an introduction, even when your connections are good. And a ball is the only proper way to begin a come-out. Really."

She looked so eager that the girls did not know how to refuse. Aggie again glanced at the others, and seeing no objection in their eyes, she shrugged and said, "You *are* kind. Very well, we accept, but you must let us share the expense with you."

The countess brushed this irrelevant concern aside. "It must be as soon as possible, and I think you should not show yourselves in town until then. What a coup it will be!"

Thalia frowned. "Not show ourselves? But I want to get some clothes, and have my hair cut." She put a hand up to her braids, still wound about her head. "Aggie and Euphie are ahead of me there."

"Oh, as to that, of course you will all wish to shop. I only meant that you should not attend any ton parties before the ball."

Thalia laughed. "Well, that is easy enough, as we are not invited to any."

"Splendid! I shall send out invitations today. How surprised everyone will be. I have not entertained in years. They will all come, out of curiosity. And then, we will have them, my dears." She chuckled. "What fun it will be to see some of the faces. I can scarcely wait."

The girls exchanged another amused glance, and in the far corner of the drawing room, Pug began to howl piteously.

All of them started and turned to see the dog backed into the corner, facing three varicolored balls of fur. Brutus, Juvenal, and Nero had found a collective sport which apparently dissolved any lingering suspicion among them. When first reintroduced after their separation, the kittens had shown little enthusiasm, but this was apparently a thing of the past. They advanced in a united front. Pug, at this multiplication of the terror of his existence, had completely collapsed. He cowered in the corner, making no effort to defend himself from the kittens' playful onslaught.

"Brutus!" said Aggie.

"Juvenal!" snapped Thalia.

"Nero, you beast!" cried Euphie, all in the same moment.

They went to retrieve the cats, holding them up and reprimanding them severely, but Pug's nerves were too shaken to enjoy this spectacle. He continued to huddle miserably on the carpet and howl.

"Blast that dog," said Lady Fanshawe finally. "This is beyond anything. I am sending him back to my daughter tomorrow."

"No, no," replied Aggie, "it is we who must do something about the cats. It is your house." A sudden vision of Brutus on a small scrap of wood, floating down a swift stream, rose before her eyes. She watched a tall young man step out to retrieve him, and her voice trailed off.

"Yes," put in Thalia, "we should…" But remembering Juvenal bounding through a forest to find a hidden glade, she too fell silent.

"No, I have made up my mind," said the countess, to several people's profound relief. "Pug must go. He has been clinging to me like a drowning man for days, and it is driving me distracted."

There was a pause. They all looked at the miserable Pug. He had stopped howling finally, but he still groveled and slobbered on the rug. None of them could feel truly sorry that he was to go.

"Tomorrow," repeated Lady Fanshawe. "And now Jenkins must shut him up somewhere where the cats cannot get at him." She went over and rang the bell.

When this had been done, and Brutus, Juvenal, and Nero set free once more, the countess became absorbed in plans for her ball. These were lavish, and the sisters were soon pulled in to help her. The afternoon passed quickly in this way, and all of them were surprised when they found it was time to change for dinner.

The next two weeks were a whirl of activity. The girls were first put in the hands of an expert haircutter, who achieved similar but slightly different styles for them under Lady Fanshawe's jealous eye. The general effect, on each, was of a cloud of russet curls, and the countess clasped her hands in joy when she saw them side by side. There were also innumerable expeditions to Bond Street, most particularly to the exclusive shop of a Frenchwoman who was commissioned to create wardrobes for the sisters. Her ecstasy at this assignment exceeded even Lady Fanshawe's, and she entered into it with such enthusiasm that the girls' heads were soon reeling from talk of French braid and Russian sleeves, silk lace and flounced hems, and countless other embellishments of which they had never heard. Soon, boxes began to arrive at Lady Fanshawe's house, and before long, each of their bedrooms was a wilderness of silver paper and new gowns.

The countess received a flattering number of

acceptances to her ball, in spite of the lateness of the invitations. The ton was indeed curious to see why she had come out of her self-imposed seclusion. She had made no mention of the Hartingtons on the cards, against custom, for she insisted that she would startle London. She did let it be known that she was presenting some young friends, and this mystery only increased the ton's urge to attend.

Three days before the event, all was ready. The gowns had been sewn, the flowers and refreshments ordered, and the ballroom was being scoured from top to bottom. The countess and the girls sat in the drawing room after another morning of shopping, and all of them looked fatigued. "None of us," Lady Fanshawe ordered, "must do another thing before the ball. We must rest the whole time, so as to be ready."

Euphie laughed. "I don't think I *can*. After all the excitement of the last two weeks, I am too agitated."

"I know, dear, I feel the same myself, I could hardly keep from snapping at Giles yesterday when he came to see what I was up to." She smiled. "But I didn't tell him. He may have his own ideas about this ball, but he knows nothing for certain."

"I didn't know he had called," replied Euphie in a colorless voice that made her sisters turn to look at her.

"Oh, yes. You were all out at Madame Verdoux's. He heard the rumors flying about town, of course, but I told him nothing to the purpose." She smiled again.

Euphie was spared from answering by the appearance of Jenkins. "A gentleman and a lady have called, ma'am," he said, handing Lady Fanshawe a visiting card.

"Oh, dear." She took it and read the names. "That's

all right. It's the Wellfleets. Those are your friends, aren't they, Aggie?"

"Yes." The older girl rose. "Oh, how good it will be to see them."

The countess nodded. "Ask them to come up, Jenkins." And as Aggie started to follow the butler, she added, "My dear, will you do me a kindness?"

Aggie paused. "Of course."

"Would you just stand here, with Thalia and Euphie? There, like that, side by side?" She lined them up near the fireplace, ignoring their puzzled looks. "Yes, that's it." The countess stood back. The Hartington sisters wore similar gowns of pale primrose muslin this morning; Lady Fanshawe had been encouraging them to dress alike, though they resisted. The dresses were simple, but elegant, and they brought out the deep blue and greens of their eyes. Their auburn hair was curled and shining, and altogether they made a dazzling picture. "Yes," said the countess again. "Stay there. I want to try an experiment." She stepped back and sat down as the girls looked at one another. And in the next moment the Wellfleets walked into the drawing room.

They stopped on the threshold. Alex Wellfleet looked stunned, and Anne opened her large blue eyes even wider, then clapped her hands. "Oh, you are the most beautiful creatures I have ever seen," she cried. "Aggie, why didn't you tell me?"

Unsure what she was supposed to have told, Aggie came forward and greeted them warmly, introducing the countess and her sisters and begging them to sit down. Lady Fanshawe looked very pleased with herself.

Mr. Wellfleet noticed it. "I congratulate you," he told her. "You will overset polite society."

Lady Fanshawe smiled back at him. "I mean to."

"What a lovely journey we had," Anne Wellfleet was saying. "The weather was perfect, and we stopped at the most cunning little inn. I am so excited to be in town. It has been three seasons since we came up. Your ball is the first event we attend," she told the countess. "I was so looking forward to it, and now, I can't bear to wait." She looked at the Hartington sisters again. "You will have every young man in London at your feet. Oh, I am so happy." She clapped her hands again.

"I hope not," responded Thalia. "Think how hard it would be to walk."

Alex laughed, as did his wife after staring at Thalia for a moment. "You must be the clever one," she said, bringing a look of chagrin to the girl's face. "And you," she told Euphie, "the musical one."

Euphie laughed and bowed slightly.

"What a family. I do wish you had convinced John Dudley to come with us, Alex. He would have enjoyed himself, I know."

Her husband made some commonplace reply, and only Thalia and Mrs. Wellfleet noticed Aggie's sudden flush. For the latter, it confirmed something she had wanted to know. Thalia was merely bewildered.

The countess offered refreshment and began to tell their guests about the ball. They were suitably appreciative, and when that subject was exhausted, Aggie asked about the children and received a full report. She had found that she missed George and

Alice very much, and she was glad to hear something of their doings.

After half an hour, the Wellfleets took their leave, promising to come early on the night of the ball and dine. When they were gone, everyone declared that they were among the nicest couples they had ever met, to Aggie's gratification. As the sisters walked together up the stairs to change for dinner a little later, Euphie neatly summed up everyone's feelings. "If the ball were not the next day but one, I should positively burst!"

The sentiment was so general that Aggie did not even reprove her for using slang.

Twenty

On the night before the ball, Lady Fanshawe went out alone. As she pulled on her gloves in the drawing room before going down to the carriage, she told the Hartington sisters, "I am sorry, my dears, not to take you to the duchess's musical evening, but it can't be helped. You know I want you to wait until tomorrow for your debut; the effect will be so much greater."

Euphie looked at the older woman speculatively. She understood the countess's plan for the ball, but she did not see why she was going out tonight. Lady Fanshawe was not fond enough of ton parties to go alone. "Is the duchess a particular friend of yours?" asked the girl innocently.

"Oh, no." Lady Fanshawe worked the final finger into her kid gloves and picked up her fan and reticule.

"I suppose the entertainment must be something quite out of the ordinary, then," said Euphie.

The countess smiled, "Hardly." And, seeing Euphie open her mouth to speak again: "If you must know, Euphie, I am going to this dreary party expressly to prepare the way for our ball tomorrow."

"What do you mean?"

Lady Fanshawe looked away. "Well, you know I have kept our plans very dark up to now. I didn't want the gossips nosing around and spoiling the surprise. Now it is too late for that, and our guests must know *something* about the three of you beforehand. Your family and your… your situation, you see. So, I am going…" She trailed off.

"You are going to this party to gossip about us!" cried Euphie. "Lady Fanshawe!" A smile, sternly repressed, played about her mouth. It was echoed by Thalia.

Her sharp eyes catching these signs, the countess chuckled. "You may put it that way, if you must."

"It seems, ah, a little devious," murmured Aggie.

Thalia turned to look at her older sister, and her smile faded. "Does it?"

"Well, it isn't," retorted Euphie very positively. "And even if it were, other people won't hesitate to gossip about us. We must fight back."

Thalia blushed painfully, reminded of Lady Agnes and the talk she had started.

Aggie paled a little but said, "Because others behave badly does not make it right for *us*."

The countess, setting her lips, replied, "Perhaps not. And you needn't. But I am all the more determined to go out." She turned toward the door. "I shall let them know, with great discretion of course, that you are three of the wealthiest girls in London, and from one of the finest families. We shall see what the Lady Agneses have to say to *that*. Spiteful little cat!" And with this, she went out.

Aggie made a small noise and put a hand to her throat.

"I know," responded Euphie. "But I really do think it is best. Lady Fanshawe can make everything clear, and then we won't have any more worries. How comfortable it is to be rich; no one will dare talk against us."

Thalia laughed shortly, but Aggie continued to look upset. Had her sisters been a little less preoccupied with their own concerns, they would certainly have noticed it, and made her tell them what was wrong.

The night of the ball was warm and fine. The Hartingtons ate their dinners in a daze and went upstairs immediately afterward to put the last touches on their toilettes. At the countess's insistence, they all wore the same model gown, a pale pale primrose with tiny sleeves and a wide skirt trimmed with ribbons of deep gold. With it, they wore matching slippers and strands of pearls purchased for the occasion, and carried small bunches of deep yellow roses. With their russet hair and glowing eyes, this scheme was dazzling. The countess, in lavender, looked elegant and superior.

By nine, they stood in the arched entrance of the ballroom. Lady Fanshawe had arranged the girls in a close line behind her, Aggie first. She had placed them so that an approaching guest would not see them until the last moment, and then he would see them all at once.

"Well, my dears," she said when they were ready, "now we shall see." In the next moment, Jenkins announced the first arrivals, and it began.

The next hour was everything Lady Fanshawe could have wished. Carefully primed by remarks dropped the previous evening, the ton turned out to see the three wealthy and wellborn sisters taken under the countess's wing. One by one, they were astonished by the Hartington girls' beauty and poise. There were murmured references to the dazzling Gunning sisters, who had taken London by storm fifty years ago. And in a very short time the combination of the Hartingtons' names and appearance had led to the inevitable result— they were "The Three Graces" forever after.

The Wellfleets had stationed themselves near the doorway to watch. Anne Wellfleet appeared delighted by each new reaction. A guest would come to the outer door, cross the hall as Jenkins announced him stentoriously, and walk smiling toward Lady Fanshawe. Just before he reached the countess, he would catch sight of the Hartington girls and freeze. Not even the most blasé and controlled managed to hide a pause, a blink, and a look of dazzlement. And many showed much stronger reactions. Alex Wellfleet laughed aloud at one young man, who was so overcome he couldn't even speak.

The arrival of Lady Agnes Crewe and her parents was a tense moment. The older couple exhibited the usual surprise, but Lady Agnes was absolutely astounded. She stared at Thalia, then at her sisters, with open mouth, and continued to look at them even after her group had walked into the ballroom beyond.

Euphie couldn't help giggling. "She looked exactly like a stuffed parrot," she whispered. "We have silenced her."

"I daresay she'll find her tongue," murmured Thalia dryly, as they turned to be introduced to the next guest.

No one else of note came in for several minutes. Then Thalia was amazed to see a tall imposing woman approaching, accompanied by a gangly blond girl. "Oh…" she gulped. Her sisters looked at her, and Lady Fanshawe said, "My dears, allow me to introduce Mrs. Elguard and her daughter Amanda."

Aggie and Euphie opened their eyes very wide; Thalia struggled for words, but before any of them could speak, Mrs. Elguard surged forward. Taking both Thalia's hands, she cried, "But we need no introduction, do we, my dear Miss Hartington? We are old friends! How *are* you? I am so delighted to see you in London." She cocked her head. "And so will someone else be, when I write and tell him of it." She attempted a roguish smile.

Thalia's jaw dropped. And her sisters stared at Mrs. Elguard incredulously. They had heard the story of this lady's treatment of their sister. But before they could say anything, Mrs. Elguard was sweeping her daughter on into the ballroom. "I shall look forward to a cozy chat later on," she cried over her shoulder.

"Cozy chat!" exclaimed Euphie. "Why, that old—"

"Shhh!" hissed Thalia.

"Why should I be quiet? She deserves that everyone should know how monstrous she is. She has heard about the money, of course."

"Perhaps so," whispered Thalia, "but I do not wish everyone to know my part in the business. Please."

At this, Euphie closed her lips tight.

Lady Fanshawe was looking about the room. "I think we may leave the door now. Nearly everyone seems to have arrived, and we must start the dancing. Come along, I will—"

But just then Jenkins announced, "Lord Fanshawe," and they all turned back to greet their hostess's son.

He held out a hand. "Good evening, Mother," he said. "You are looking…" At this point, he saw the Hartingtons. He blinked, but his control was so good that he did no more. Rather, he smoothly finished his sentence, "…splendid tonight."

"Thank you, Giles. You have not met Euphie's sisters, I think? This is Miss Aglaia Hartington, and Miss Thalia Hartington."

The earl bowed. "Your parents were prophets."

"That's what everyone says," replied Euphie rather rudely.

Lord Fanshawe smiled. "I am amazed they can manage so much, after the sight of the three of you. A magnificent arrangement, Mother. I compliment you."

"Yes. But we are going to open the dancing, Giles, if you will excuse me."

"Certainly. But might I still claim the dance, Miss Hartington? Or are you all engaged?"

They were not, but Aggie looked uncertain. It was very proper that he should ask her first, of course, as the oldest. But he was much better acquainted with her sister.

"That would be splendid, Giles," answered the countess. "I thought to get young Barrington, since you don't usually dance. But if you mean to tonight, you will do very well. Take Aggie along, and I will find partners for the others."

The earl offered his arm, and after a moment, Aggie took it and walked away with him. Lady Fanshawe shepherded the others toward a group in the corner and beckoned imperiously to first one young man, then another. They came very willingly. The countess performed introductions, sent the two couples to join Aggie, and went to speak to the orchestra.

The music began, and the Hartington sisters opened their first ball. With their pale dresses and bright hair, they made a lovely picture as they swayed in the movements of the dance. After a while, other couples joined in, and soon the ballroom was full.

Lord Fanshawe looked down at his partner with interest. The sisters did not really resemble each other, despite the first impression that they were alike. The eldest was probably the most beautiful, and her face showed a placidity lacking in the others. "You and your sisters have created quite a sensation tonight, Miss Hartington," he said, looking around the ballroom. Everyone's attention was on the girls.

Aggie looked down. "It was your mother's scheme."

"Did you not enjoy it?"

She raised wide blue eyes to his face. "Oh, well, of course."

Lord Fanshawe began to feel a little bored. "This is your first stay in London, I understand."

"Yes, we lived in the country for most of our lives."

"Do you like the city?"

"I, ah, hardly know. But I think I prefer the country."

"Why is that?"

"Oh, well, it is so much more, ah, pleasant."

Lord Fanshawe sighed and began to wish the set would end.

When at last it did, his mother was besieged by young men begging for introductions to her charges. She looked very pleased with herself as she selected three and presented them. And this scene was repeated each time the dancing ended; clearly the Hartington sisters had made a hit.

For the set before supper, the countess chose carefully. Aggie was paired with a very eligible peer and Thalia with an extremely wealthy young man who had no title but a charming personality. She was just looking for a suitable partner for Euphie when she saw her son approach the youngest sister and claim her hand. "That's all right, then," she murmured to herself, and went to see about the buffet.

"What a splendid party," said Euphie as they started to dance. "I always knew I should be fond of balls."

"Did you?" replied the earl, smiling.

"Oh, yes. Even when we were still at home with my aunt, I was sure of it. And I was right. I am so happy I could shout."

"Do," he urged.

"Oh, no. I mean to behave with the strictest propriety, so that those forbidding ladies will give us vouchers for Almack's and everyone will think the Hartington girls 'unexceptionable, my dear.'"

She said these last words in such a convincing and comic imitation of one of the more starched-up society dames that Lord Fanshawe laughed outright. "You are in high spirits," he said. "I have not seen you so animated before."

"Of course I am. How often does a girl attend her first ball? But don't tell anyone."

"Tell?"

"That I am excited. One is supposed to be very bored and take everything for granted, isn't one?"

He laughed again. "Who told you so?"

"Oh, no one. It is just the impression I get from some of the modish ladies. When your aunt introduced us to Princess Lieven and Mrs. Drummond-Burrell, I thought they would nod off in boredom."

He looked around to where these haughtiest patronesses of Almack's sat and then turned back to answer Euphie's smile. "I see."

"So we must try to seem quite drowsy too, I daresay." She assumed a comical expression of utter boredom. "I told Aggie and Thalia so."

"And what did they say?"

"Oh, Aggie said I was ridiculous, of course. She is so wonderfully proper. And Thalia quoted Pope."

"Alexander Pope?"

"Yes. She is always quoting. I forget what it was. Something about the fickleness of fashion."

"She is your learned sister, I remember."

Euphie nodded happily. She was suddenly conscious of an even greater feeling of contentment than that engendered by the ball. She realized then that this was the first time she had chatted with Lord Fanshawe in weeks.

"Daunting."

The girl looked surprised. "She isn't at all. How can you say so when you have hardly spoken to her?"

"I beg pardon." Lord Fanshawe watched her face

for a moment. "You were glad to see your sisters, weren't you? You are much happier and livelier now that they have come."

"Of course I am glad. We have always been together. And no one laughs with me as they do."

He nodded to himself.

The music ended, and the dancers slowly moved toward the supper room. Euphie urged the earl toward her sisters and their partners. "Let us all eat together," she said. He agreed.

Just as the group was passing under the archway that led to the dining room, a slight dark girl came up to them hesitantly. "Miss Hartington…" she began.

"Mary Deming!" exclaimed Thalia. "How glad I am to see you. Euphie told me you were in town, and I looked for you earlier."

"W-we were late. And then you were so busy dancing that I… that is, I didn't want to interrupt."

"Nonsense. Come and have supper with us. We must have a cozy talk."

"Oh. I… I don't know." Mary looked toward where her mother sat.

"Is your partner waiting for you?"

"No." The younger girl flushed. "I haven't one."

Thalia frowned, then took her arm. "Come on, then. We'll find a vacant table."

Supper was a jolly meal. Thalia and Euphie sparkled in their different ways, while Aggie watched with a smile and an occasional supporting word. After a while, even Mary Deming relaxed and joined the conversation. The two older girls' partners were obviously entranced, and Lord Fanshawe looked extremely entertained. He looked from one lovely face to the other.

When the meal was over and the rest had gone back to dancing, Thalia took Mary aside. "Let us find a vacant sofa and have a good talk," she said. "It seems so long since I saw you, though it has been only a few weeks."

"I don't want to keep you from dancing," said Mary.

"Nonsense." They went back into the ballroom and sat down. "Now, tell me how you are and how you like London," Thalia went on. "Do you find the season exciting?"

Mary sighed. "I fear I find it more daunting. I can't seem to get the knack of chatting with strangers."

The older girl looked sympathetic. "But surely you know some people. Some of your friends must be coming out this year also. Euphie said she met you at, ah, the Warringtons', was it?"

Mary blushed bright red.

"Euphie told me what occurred," Thalia added quickly. "You needn't worry about sparing me."

"Agnes Crewe is horrid," responded Mary.

"Undoubtedly. But do you know the Warringtons?"

Surprisingly, Mary's flush deepened as she nodded. "Yes, our families have been acquainted forever."

"So you know the children. There are a daughter and a son, I think."

"Y-yes. And another boy still at school. Charlotte Warrington is my age. She is coming out this season. And… and Alan is two years older."

She struggled so as she said this that Thalia was puzzled. "Don't you like them?"

"Oh, yes! That is, Charlotte and I have always gotten along well, and… and…"

Thalia dimpled. "And you and Alan Warrington?"

Impossibly, Mary became redder still.

"Aha! I see."

"I… I don't know what you mean. I… of course, I have known Alan since we were children, but…"

"Indeed. I understand you."

"You don't. There is nothing… he doesn't…"

"What is this, an old school gathering?" said a cool voice beside them. The two girls looked up to find Lady Agnes Crewe standing there. "How charming."

"Hello, Lady Agnes," said Thalia without enthusiasm. Mary murmured something unintelligible.

The blond eyed her measuringly. "I suppose you are very pleased with yourself. You have managed very well indeed. No doubt you'll get what you want now." She smiled thinly. "If you still want it, of course."

"What I want?" Thalia had some idea what she meant, but she refused to understand.

"Well, Mrs. Elguard is telling everyone what friends you and her son are. The inference is obvious. But will a 'competence' look as tempting now, I wonder?"

Mary gasped audibly. "How… how dare…?"

Lady Agnes laughed. "Dare? You'd be surprised. We aren't all quiet little mice, you know, Mary. Ask Alan." And with this she turned and walked away.

"Alan," echoed Mary automatically. She swallowed and stared at the floor.

Thalia looked at her. She was reluctant to speak, yet she wanted to find out more about this situation. "Does Lady Agnes know Alan Warrington, then?"

Mary laughed shortly. "Know him?" She laughed again, but she did not sound amused.

Thalia opened her mouth to speak, then shut it. She understood enough, and she could get more information without upsetting Mary further. But at that moment, she made a vow. If she could do anything for Mary in this case, she would. There was a short pause; then Thalia said, "May I meet your mother, Mary? You promised me an introduction, you know."

The younger girl brightened at once. "Oh, yes. She would like it above all things. I have told her about you." She rose. "Come."

They walked across the floor toward a group of older ladies opposite. On the way, they passed Aggie and the Wellfleets taking a brief rest from the dancing. Thalia smiled and nodded.

"I can't take it in," said Anne Wellfleet. "How can you all be so beautiful and talented? It doesn't seem fair."

Aggie smiled. "I am not talented."

"Nonsense. Of course you are. You are the most soothing person imaginable. Your talent is making people feel happy and at ease."

Aggie looked a little surprised.

"Doesn't she, Alex?" said Mrs. Wellfleet.

Her husband merely smiled.

"Darling Alex." Anne turned back to the ballroom. "And there is your youngest sister dancing with Lord Cranleigh. She is quite charming, too. Very lively."

Looking at Euphie, Aggie smiled and nodded.

Anne Wellfleet, watching her face, looked

concerned. "How do you like London, Aggie? Is it all you hoped for?"

"Hoped for? Oh, yes, I suppose so."

At an imperceptible signal from his wife, Alex Wellfleet excused himself to speak to a friend. When he was gone, Anne continued, "Of course, you didn't hope for very much, did you? You didn't want to come at first."

Aggie looked at the floor and made an uneasy movement.

"But now that you are here"—Anne indicated the ballroom—"you are having a good time?"

The other followed her gesture, "Of course," she replied.

There was a short pause; then Mrs. Wellfleet said, "We saw John Dudley just before we came to town. He is very involved with a new drainage project and talked of nothing else."

"Really? He is, ah, very taken up with such things." The tone of Aggie's response was clearly unnatural, though she tried very hard to sound as usual.

"He always has been. But for some reason, I felt his heart was not in it this time." Anne Wellfleet continued to watch her companion closely. She already knew what she thought, but she wanted a bit more confirmation before she did anything about it.

Aggie had nothing to say to this. And she could not entirely hide a look of distress.

With a small nod, the other woman changed the subject, and a bit later Aggie went off to dance once again. Anne Wellfleet remained where she was, looking after her, then turned to find her husband.

The sisters danced and talked with a host of new acquaintances, both male and female. Toward the end of the evening, they stood with a group of young people near the doorway, and laughter rang across the ballroom. A tall rangy blond girl approached them and stopped uncertainly beside Thalia. She looked acutely uncomfortable and seemed unable to summon the resolution to speak. Finally Thalia said, "Did you want me?"

The other girl nodded. "Yes. I beg your pardon, but my mother wishes to speak to you." Seeing Thalia's surprise, she added, "I am Amanda Elguard, you know."

With this Thalia recognized her. This was the girl who had come in with James Elguard's mother. She sighed.

Hearing this, Miss Elguard stiffened. "You needn't, of course. I told her so."

Thalia turned to look at her more closely. She couldn't decide whether the other girl was embarrassed or angry. "No, I'll come." She followed Miss Elguard over to a sofa by the wall and sat down beside her mother. The daughter at once left them alone.

"How delightful this is," began Mrs. Elguard. "Now we can have a proper chat. I haven't been able to get near you all evening, too many eager young men." She smiled.

Thalia looked at her with a mixture of puzzlement and amazement. She could not help thinking of the last time they had faced one another and how different that had been.

"I think I can promise that James will be among

them next week," the lady was continuing. "He was *very* disappointed when you left Bath so suddenly, you know." She shook a finger at Thalia while the girl wondered at her effrontery.

"He may wish to attend to his studies," she replied discouragingly.

"His studies? Oh, no!"

Thalia surveyed Mrs. Elguard. Her complete change of manner was too marked to go without comment. "I take it you no longer object to my friendship with your son?" she said.

"My dear Miss Hartington, I was just about to apologize for that terrible misunderstanding. I admit to allowing myself to be swayed by malicious gossip. I regret it immensely. I beg you will forgive me."

Her simpering expression was almost more than Thalia could bear, but she was too polite to say what she really thought. "Of course," she choked out.

"You are kind, but I knew you would be. And now we are all in London and shall see each other constantly, I do so hope that you and Amanda may become friends."

Thalia swallowed. She turned to look about the room, then said, "Oh, I believe Lady Fanshawe is looking for me. You will excuse me, Mrs. Elguard?" And without waiting for an answer, she got up and escaped.

Soon after this, guests began to take their leave, as it was by now quite late. In half an hour, only the sisters and Lady Fanshawe remained in the ballroom.

"Well, my dears," said the latter, "I am half-dead with fatigue, but what a triumph we have had!"

"It was great fun," agreed Euphie, and her sisters nodded.

"And it was only the beginning, mark my words. But now, we must go to bed. Come along."

Together, the four women walked out and up the stairs. As they separated, Lady Fanshawe repeated, "A positive triumph," and the girls walked on, smiling at one another.

Twenty-one

THE FOLLOWING MORNING WAS PLEASANTLY SPENT exchanging memories of the ball. The Hartington sisters gathered in the drawing room after breakfast for one of their customary talks, each telling whom she had met and what they had said. "How cozy this is," exclaimed Euphie after a while. "Just like we used to do at home. I wondered, you know, if we should ever be together in this way again." She sighed happily.

Thalia nodded. "Yes. I am very grateful to be here."

"I should think so. That horrid school! And what are we to do about Lady Agnes Crewe?"

"Do about her?" Aggie turned puzzled eyes to her youngest sister. "What can you mean, Euphie?"

Euphie looked mischievous. "Well, you know, she has been so rude and awful, we must do something."

"Nonsense. We shall simply ignore her. Shan't we, Thalia?"

"I suppose we should, but let me tell you something else." She explained her suspicions about Mary Deming. "I think she likes this Alan Warrington very much. And perhaps, who knows, he likes her too. But Lady Agnes is clearly interfering in the affair. Out of spite, I imagine."

"She may like him also," offered Aggie.

"So she may." Thalia grimaced. "But I find I care very little whether she does or not."

Euphie grinned. "So we shall cut out Lady Agnes and make sure that Mary Deming gets a chance at this Warrington. Splendid, Thalia!"

The two younger girls exchanged a glance of guilty glee.

"I don't know," answered Aggie slowly. "It doesn't seem quite right to push in. I mean, Mr. Warrington may—"

"If he is so stupid as to prefer Lady Agnes to Mary Deming," snapped Euphie, "then he *needs* our help. We cannot allow him to make such a mistake."

Thalia smiled, but she added, "There is something in that, Aggie."

The oldest girl looked from one to the other, a reluctant smile dawning on her lips. Finally, her deep blue eyes twinkled. "But how will you manage this miracle? From what you have told me, Mary Deming is almost too shy to speak to the man."

Two pairs of sparkling green eyes met hers. "That is what we must see," said Thalia. "We require a plan."

"Ha," said Euphie. "You will think of something first-rate."

"I hope so. As yet, I have not done so."

"You always do, Thalia."

Her sister's amusement at this complacent certainty was punctuated by the entrance of Lady Fanshawe.

"Girls!" she exclaimed as she walked in. "Only look at this!" She held out a double handful of envelopes. "Already! Only the day after our ball."

"What is it?" asked Euphie.

"*They*, my dear. They are invitations, of course. You have been asked to every important event of the season. And vouchers for Almack's! By the very next mail. I told you it was a triumph."

The sisters all laughed. "We owe it to you, Lady Fanshawe," replied Thalia. "You arranged the whole."

"I began it, yes. But you three carried it off. My arrangements would have been nothing without your efforts. And now, we shan't be home one evening in ten, I suppose. Just look. A rout party, a Venetian breakfast, another ball, two musical evenings, a party for Vauxhall…"

"I don't even know what most of those are!" wailed Euphie.

"You will, my dear. You will."

Thalia cast a bright glance at her sister and said, "I hope you won't be completely exhausted by all this, Lady Fanshawe. I know you don't care to go out much."

Euphie, who had told her sisters all about her former employer, looked sharply at her sister, then grinned.

"Nonsense," answered the countess. She avoided their eyes, turning back toward the door and adding, "I must go and look through these to see which to accept. I merely wanted to show you." And with this, she was gone again.

Euphie burst out laughing. "Wicked, Thalia! You shouldn't tease her so. She has been so kind to us."

"Of course she has. And I am immensely grateful. I didn't mean anything by it. And she knew it, too."

Euphie nodded. "I think she did. But it is exciting, is it not? All these invitations."

"It is what you have always wished for."

"I? What about you, Thalia, and Aggie, too? You cannot convince me that you have never longed for a little gaiety."

Thalia smiled. "I shan't try. I am quite pleased, for my part."

"Aggie?"

The oldest Miss Hartington started visibly and looked up. "What?"

"You have been somewhere far away," laughed Euphie. "I only asked if you are not pleased to be going out at last, after Aunt's restrictions."

"Oh. Oh, yes, of course. It is very pleasant."

Her tone was so forced that Euphie stared, and Thalia watched her with real concern. There was a pause; then Thalia said, "What is it, Aggie? You have not been yourself since we came to London. Is there something wrong?"

"What could be wrong?"

"I don't know. But I would like to help you. You know that."

"I too, of course," said Euphie.

"There is nothing wrong," said Aggie firmly. "I don't know why you say so. I suppose all this unaccustomed activity has rather tired me, that's all."

The younger sisters exchanged a glance. Thalia shook her head briefly, and after a moment turned the subject to some indifferent matter. But a resolve formed in that moment, and she determined to act upon it at the first opportunity.

At luncheon, Lady Fanshawe was full of plans. She had gone through the pile of invitations and chosen those she liked best. She now described the whirl of gaiety they represented to the sisters, while they smiled and shook their heads. She also enumerated the new gowns, slippers, gloves, and other wardrobe items they would need and suggested an immediate expedition to Bond Street.

"What about your rest?" asked Euphie.

"I am not the least tired," retorted her ladyship. "I never sleep in any case, you know, I simply lie down and read a bit. But today there are more important things to do. We must order you all new ball gowns; it will take some time to make them."

"But we just had new dresses for last night," protested Thalia, who hated fittings.

"You cannot wear those again! What are you thinking of?"

Thalia begged pardon with a rueful smile, and it was agreed that they would go out after their meal. At that moment the dining room door swung open and Jenkins came in, followed by two of the footmen. All three bore as many bouquets as they could carry, and the sight was astonishing. "These began to arrive half an hour ago, my lady," said the butler. "I have not had a moment to bring them in until now." As he finished, there was a ring at the front door, and he sighed. "Excuse me." Still carrying the flowers, he turned and went out. The footmen remained, rigid and uneasy.

Euphie burst out laughing. "What are they all for?"

"Why, for you, goose," answered Lady Fanshawe. "And your sisters. The gentlemen you met last night are expressing their admiration."

This was signal enough for a descent on the footmen. The sisters found the cards among the flowers and began to open and read them. After a moment, Jenkins returned with yet another bunch added to his load, and they investigated these as well.

"Twelve!" exclaimed the countess when they had been counted. "Wonderful. Though not in the least odd. I expected as much."

"But I am the winner!" cried Euphie. "Six are mine, four are for Thalia, and Aggie has only two. You must try harder, Aggie."

The oldest girl shrugged good-naturedly. "You are welcome to my share."

"And mine," agreed Thalia. "These roses are from Mr. Charles Dunne, whom I recall as one of the stupidest young men I have ever had the misfortune to encounter. He talked of horses all through our dance. And not particularly knowledgeably, either."

"Well, I am pleased," said Euphie. "You are just jealous."

This teasing accusation brought her sisters down upon her with laughing denials, and before the uproar died away, Jenkins had returned with yet another bouquet. This one was not as large as some of the others, but it was by far the most beautiful, composed of white roses and carnations among sprigs of fern and dark leaves.

"Oh," breathed Euphie, reaching for the card.

"Shall it be seven?" teased Thalia.

"No," answered her sister in a queer voice. "This one is to all of us. It is from Lord Fanshawe."

"Giles?" replied the countess. "How charming of him."

Euphie nodded, though some of her gaiety seemed to have evaporated. She handed the card round so that the others might see the general congratulation written on it.

"Jenkins can put these in water," said Lady Fanshawe then. "I don't know where we will find room for them all. But we must go if we are to do any shopping today. Come, get your hats." And the four ladies filed out of the room and up the stairs.

Their shopping was very gay, but it was also tiring, and Lady Fanshawe went straight to her room to rest when they returned. Euphie took her purchases to her bedchamber to look at them all again, and Aggie went to the breakfast room, to write letters, she said.

Thalia didn't believe her. But as the excuse left her alone, she didn't question it. Rather, as soon as everyone else had gone, she picked up her hat once more and went into the hall. Jenkins was still there, and she went up to him. "I understand one can hire carriages to take one through the city," she said.

He looked surprised. "Yes, miss. But if you wish to go out, I can send round to the stables. Her ladyship's barouche will hardly be—"

"No, no. I am going only a short distance, to visit the Wellfleets, who were here last night. So if you could find me…"

"A hackney, miss," finished Jenkins.

Thalia nodded.

"I'll send Tom out for one." He summoned one of the footmen and did so. "But the barouche would be more suitable."

"No. You see…" Thalia struggled to find a plausible explanation. "The Wellfleets and I are preparing a surprise for my sister; it is a secret between us. So I do not want everyone to know. In fact, Jenkins, I was going to ask you not to mention that I have gone out or where. Unless Lady Fanshawe should ask you, of course."

Jenkins eyed her sternly, then relented. "Yes, miss. Unless her ladyship should ask."

"Thank you."

Tom returned with a hackney and helped Thalia into it. As she sat back in the vehicle, she wondered if she were doing the right thing. But the memory of Aggie's uncharacteristic despondence made her shake her head. Something had to be done.

The Wellfleets' townhouse was not far away, and Thalia was fortunate in finding them at home. She was taken up to the drawing room at once and greeted effusively by Anne Wellfleet.

"Miss Hartington! How lovely to see you. But, are you all alone?"

Thalia nodded. "I wanted to speak to you about something."

At this, her husband rose. "I have some business to see to."

Thalia looked uncomfortable, but his wife said, "Yes, dear, do run along." Neither of them seemed the least put out, which made their visitor feel better. "Now," continued Anne Wellfleet when the door had closed behind him, "let us sit down and be comfortable."

They did so. There was a short awkward pause.

"I don't know quite how to begin," said Thalia then. "I've come to speak to you about a rather delicate matter, and I don't know…"

"Perhaps I can help. Is it about Aggie?"

Thalia stared at her.

"Well, it was not so hard to guess."

"You've seen, then, that she is not… oh, not herself. Since I first went home, I have noticed it. Something is wrong, but she won't tell me what."

Mrs. Wellfleet nodded. "I thought so too. I am glad to have your opinion on the matter. And I think I know the problem."

Thalia leaned forward eagerly. "What is it? I do so long to help."

The older woman nodded again and looked thoughtful. She seemed to be considering how best to frame her explanation. "Did Aggie mention a young man named John Dudley to you?" she asked finally.

"Certainly. We were all struck by the coincidence of their meeting. We knew him when we were very small, you know."

"Yes. She said nothing else about him?"

"No. Only that they sometimes met at your house and that he was a pleasant man." She smiled. "Greatly improved, in fact, since his grubby schoolboy days."

Anne smiled back. "Indeed. Well, in my opinion, he is the problem."

"John Dudley?"

"Yes. Aggie spent far more time with him than she

told you. I was certain he was about to make her an offer, and she to accept him. And then, something happened. I don't know what. And all was at an end. Aggie went away, and John will say nothing about it." Her pretty lips pouted. "I tried to make him, but Alex said I mustn't."

Thalia sat back, pensive. "You think Aggie is in love with John Dudley?" The notion was so odd that she needed a moment to take it in.

"I do. And that there is some obstacle. The thing I can't see is what. They seem perfect for one another."

"Tell me all about him," commanded Thalia.

Anne Wellfleet thought for a moment, then embarked on a description of John Dudley's character. Thalia was surprised at the detail and depth. She had more or less dismissed Mrs. Wellfleet as a pretty widgeon, but she saw now that her understanding of people was significant.

"I see," said Thalia when she finished. "And you think they were getting on very well? No quarrels or anything like that?"

"None."

"Hmm. Let me think." She went back over all she had been told, and tried to fit it with her observations of her sister. "You say you expected him to offer for Aggie on the night of your party?"

"Yes. His manner was unmistakable."

"And then she got the letter from Mr. Gaines?"

"Yes."

Thalia nodded. "I think I see. John Dudley sounds to me like the sort of man who would draw back from Aggie's sudden wealth."

"You mean if he had asked beforehand…"

"Then all would have been well. But he would not offer *after* she heard about the money, for fear of being thought a fortune hunter."

Mrs. Wellfleet considered this. "It could be, though John seems too sensible for such ridiculous scruples." She frowned. "I wonder if he also felt that Aggie should have a chance to try her riches. Perhaps he thought she would feel differently about things once she did."

Thalia shrugged. "Perhaps. Both reasons seem perfectly doltish to me."

"Yes"—Anne smiled—"but so like a man."

The younger girl smiled back. "The question is, what are we to do?"

"Oh, we must get John to town. If we can only throw them together again, all will be well, I think."

"How can we?"

"Of that, I'm not yet sure. I must think. Alex might be able to help."

"Would he?"

Anne smiled. "Oh, yes, if I ask him nicely. Leave that to me."

Thalia nodded. "Yes. *I* can't write him. So I shall count on you to produce Mr. Dudley. Meanwhile, I shall work on Aggie."

Their eyes met, and both smiled. "We shall bring it off," said Mrs. Wellfleet.

Thalia nodded once, decisively, and rose. "I must get back before someone notices I am gone. Thank you."

The other spread her hands. "Thank *you*. I am flattered by your confidence. I will set to work immediately."

Thalia smiled and took her leave, going home the way she had come. On the way, she thought of her sister and her trouble. Hard as it would be to lose Aggie to marriage, it was far harder to watch her unhappiness without trying to remedy it.

She got back to Lady Fanshawe's at four and hurried to the stairs. She wanted to take off her hat and tidy herself for tea before anyone commented on her absence. But Jenkins, who had opened the door for her, stopped her halfway up. "Oh, Miss Thalia, a letter arrived for you while you were out. Hand-delivered." He held out an envelope.

She took it and ripped it open as she continued up the stairs. It was only one sheet, a few lines of writing. When she had read them, she stopped stock-still on the landing. James Elguard had arrived in London.

Twenty-two

LADY FANSHAWE'S PARTY WAS TO GO TO ALMACK'S for the first time that evening, and the girls met in the drawing room at eight thirty to wait for her. They were not dressed alike tonight, despite the countess's earnest request, but they wore similar gowns of floating muslin, Aggie's blue, Thalia's peach, and Euphie's pale green. And they looked very fresh and lovely as they stood together near the fireplace.

They talked quietly with one another until the drawing-room door was pushed open and Brutus came in, followed closely by Juvenal and Nero. Euphie walked over and picked up the latter. "How they are growing," she said. "They are hardly kittens any longer."

Thalia, coming over to examine Juvenal, agreed. "What do they do with themselves all day? Since Pug has gone, I scarcely see any of the cats about."

"I think they stay belowstairs. Cook told me that Brutus caught a mouse last week. She is happy to have them there." Euphie held up her white cat and looked into his eyes. "Have you caught a mouse also, Nero, or are you too lazy?"

Nero stared at her for a moment, then began to squirm to be let down. Laughing, Euphie set him on the floor. "They have become so selfish that they care nothing for us anymore."

"Of course they do!" snapped Aggie from across the room. She had not moved since the cats came in. Both her sisters turned to look at her in surprise, and she flushed.

"Whatever is the matter?" asked Euphie.

"Nothing, nothing. I have the headache."

Euphie started to speak again, but Thalia squeezed her arm warningly, and she subsided. In the next moment, the countess came down, the carriage was called for, and they were on their way.

They walked up the steps of Almack's Assembly Rooms just before nine, well before the doors would close to careless latecomers. When they entered the ballroom, already thickly populated with members of the ton, their reception was flattering. A number of people greeted them, and before they had gone three steps into the room, they had all been solicited for the set then forming. As they moved out onto the floor, it was obvious that notice was being taken and that it was generally approving. Whatever disappointed mothers of less entrancing girls might say, society in general had taken the sisters to its heart.

For the second dance, their choice was even wider. At least two young men approached each sister, begging her to choose him as partner. And Euphie laughingly hesitated among four. But the third set was a waltz, and they had to stand back and await the approval of one of Almack's patronesses before they could join it, so they walked toward Lady Fanshawe's seat together.

"Isn't it splendid!" said Euphie as they went. "Oh, I could dance forever. I hope they will approve us right away."

As if she had been overheard, Euphie was stopped just then by Lady Jersey. "You are not dancing, Miss Hartington? May I present you with a desirable partner for the waltz?" She moved aside, revealing Lord Fanshawe standing behind her. "I think you are already acquainted, are you not?" Almack's most sprightly patroness smiled mischievously.

"Y-yes," replied Euphie. "Ah, thank you."

Lord Fanshawe offered his arm, and she took it to walk out onto the floor.

"Now I must see about you two," continued Lady Jersey. "Is there anyone you would particularly like for the waltz?"

"No, thank you,'" blurted Aggie. "I… I must speak to Lady Fanshawe."

She rushed off, Lady Jersey watching her curiously.

"My sister has the headache," said Thalia. "She isn't feeling at all the thing."

"No?" The lady turned her sharp eyes on Thalia.

"No. I should go to her."

"Just as you like, my dear." And she watched again as Thalia self-consciously followed Aggie to the side of the room.

"I'm sorry," said Aggie in a strangled voice when her sister reached her. "I did not want to dance."

"It doesn't matter. But, Aggie…"

"Yes, I know. I *will* tell you, but not now, please."

Thalia looked at her. "All right."

"I am going to sit with Lady Fanshawe. I am fine. Just let me be."

Thalia nodded, and Aggie walked across to the countess, looking despondent.

"I have written the letter," said a voice behind her.

Thalia turned quickly to find Anne Wellfleet. "Have you? Good."

"Yes, I think it is. Poor Aggie."

"She cares for none of this."

"I know. It is strange."

Thalia shrugged.

"Perhaps you don't care for it yourself?" responded the other.

"It is interesting, often amusing, but I think only Euphie really loves it. I should much prefer…"

"Yes?" asked Mrs. Wellfleet when she broke off. "What should you prefer?"

But Thalia found she couldn't speak. She had just seen the Elguard family enter the room, Mrs. Elguard and Amanda escorted by James.

On the dance floor, Euphie was savoring the novel experience of whirling about in a man's arms. She had practiced the waltz with her sisters, but this was the first time she had tried it in public. She found she liked it very much, once she was certain that she would not make a mistake. The earl was a skilled dancer, and she had no trouble following his steps.

For his part, he watched her passage from nervousness to exhilaration with amusement. When he saw that she was completely at ease, he said, "You waltz very well, Miss Hartington."

"I can't think why," she answered. "My aunt was scandalized by the dance and always forbade us to learn. We had to try it on the sly, and I never had proper lessons." Suddenly suspicious, she looked up at him. "But perhaps you were mocking me, sir?"

"Not at all."

"Well, I haven't trod on your toes or tripped on my gown, so I suppose I am getting on fairly well."

Lord Fanshawe laughed. "You remain an original, Miss Hartington."

"Do I?" She considered this. "I wonder if that's good? It sounds rather frightening. Shall I turn out to be as eccentric as my aunt, then?" As soon as she said this, Euphie was appalled. "Oh, no!"

He laughed again. "The two things are quite different. You are in no danger, I assure you."

"How are they different?"

"Well, ah… you do take one up, don't you? Let me think. An original shows freshness, an attractive unspoiled quality, which is unusual without being at all odd. An eccentric, on the other hand, is, well…"

"Eccentric," finished Euphie with a laugh.

"Precisely." He smiled down at her, thinking that she was clearly the most charming of the charming Hartington sisters.

"Well, that does not tell me a great deal, does it? But as I think it over, I believe I shouldn't mind if I *were* eccentric, so long as it was in some kindly way. In fact, I think I *shall* be, when I am older."

"And what will your particular eccentricity be? Not cats?"

"Like my aunt? Oh, no. I haven't decided." She

paused a moment, then added, "Perhaps I shall keep an orchestra always at the ready in my house, so that I can have music whenever I choose."

"A charming peculiarity."

"Isn't it? How wonderful it would be." Euphie fell into a reverie, and the earl watched her face. They continued to dance through a short silence; then Euphie looked up abruptly. "What nonsense I have been talking. You must turn the subject."

"Must I?"

"Yes, tell me something witty. What have you been doing since the ball?"

"Nothing very amusing."

"You always say that. How dreary your life must be." Euphie's eyes twinkled.

"Indeed yes. Unspeakably so. It is only when I can escape for a moment to Almack's, or balls like my mother's, that I find any amusement at all."

Euphie burst out laughing. "What a plumper! I know you must think Almack's abominably slow. All the men do."

"All?" he answered teasingly.

"They say so, and someone told me that you do not set foot here more than once or twice a season."

"Ah, that was in the past. The place somehow seems a great deal more interesting now."

Euphie raised her eyes to his, startled. This sounded very like the compliments she received from other partners, but she had not expected such from him. And her own reaction was unsettling. She found it difficult to breathe for a moment and had to look down again hastily.

Behind them, at the edge of the floor, Thalia stood in a window embrasure and tried to look inconspicuous. She felt both agitated and ridiculous, but when she had seen James Elguard actually walk into the room, she had suddenly found herself unable to face him. In the weeks since she had left the Chadbourne School, through all the changes in that time, she had convinced herself that the episode with Mr. Elguard had been just that—a transitory friendship. Even her meeting with his mother had not altered her position, but now that she saw the man himself, she realized that she had been mistaken. For her response to Elguard's presence in the ballroom was far beyond what she would have confidently predicted. And because of this, she was confused and upset.

James Elguard, for his part, had been scanning the room alertly since he came in. He did not seek a partner for the waltz, but stood beside his mother and watched the dancers. At last, seeming impatient, he said something to her and started to stroll along the wall. Thalia, seeing him, swallowed and wondered if she could reach the exit without being seen.

She could not. And while she stood irresolutely alone, Elguard saw her and hurried over.

"Miss Hartington!"

"H-hello," Thalia managed, though she could not seem to raise her eyes. Silence fell and lengthened. At last, able to bear no more, she looked up. James Elguard, as blond and handsome as ever, was surveying her with a mixture of embarrassment and annoyance.

As their eyes met, a flood of recollection hit both. Thalia flushed, and Elguard's mouth moved uncertainly. "I hardly know what to say to you," he ventured then. "I have heard about everything from my mother, of course." Now he flushed. "I should perhaps apologize, or—"

"Don't."

He looked at her, then agreed. "No. That is irrelevant." There was another silence. He seemed to gather himself. "Why did you run away from me without a word?" he said then, his voice full of emotion.

"From you?" Thalia was startled into retorting.

"Didn't it amount to that?"

"Of course not."

"Ah."

There was a somewhat longer pause. Thalia felt a desperate urge to say something, but she could not frame a sentence.

"I haven't congratulated you on your good fortune," said Elguard stiffly then. "I was very glad to hear that your aunt did not fail to provide for you after all."

"Yes," murmured Thalia, then cursed herself for stupidity.

"Your situation has changed radically." He indicated the ballroom. "And for the better, of course. I am very glad." As he repeated this commonplace, he did not sound very glad.

Thalia summoned all her faculties and replied, "It is a very superficial change, however. My sisters and I remain the same despite a few new gowns."

He seemed to find this encouraging for a moment. "Indeed, externals cannot really alter the character." But then his face fell. "In the eyes of the world, however, the change is complete. You will be treated differently, and this will eventually change you as well."

"It won't," she said, with more conviction than politeness.

Their eyes met again, more easily this time; some understanding seemed to pass between them. "Nonetheless," he went on, "my position…"

Thalia shrugged and turned a little away from him. "Money has nothing to do with friendship," she said.

He hesitated, watching her face. "Indeed, with friendship, very little."

"How are your studies progressing?" asked the girl determinedly. "Were you not sorry to leave them again so soon?"

Mr. Elguard sighed imperceptibly and replied, "Not entirely. They are going well, and I can work here in London too, of course."

She nodded. "Tell me—"

But a voice broke in just then to wish them good evening. They turned to find Lady Agnes Crewe on the arm of her partner, coming away at the end of the set. "Isn't it a lovely dance?" she added, her tone poisonously sweet as she looked from one to the other of them.

Thalia nodded briefly. Elguard looked bewildered.

"Not as pleasant, of course, as meeting old friends," added Lady Agnes. She had dropped her partner's arm by this time and showed signs of settling next to James Elguard. The other young man, unintroduced, hovered uncomfortably nearby. "I think that is one of the nicest things there is, don't you, Mr. Elguard?" Lady Agnes raised her blue eyes meltingly and touched Elguard's arm.

The gentleman, obviously mystified, muttered, "Ah, yes, to be sure."

Lady Agnes gave him a blinding smile and moved still closer. "Why, Mr. Elguard, I do believe you have forgotten me. And you said you never would when we met in Bath, at your mother's evening party. You *do* remember?" She gazed up at him again, her fingers still resting on his forearm.

Thalia, her jaw clamped tightly, said, "I think my sister is beckoning; if you will excuse—"

"By Jove," burst out Elguard, "so is my mother. Allow me to escort you, Miss Hartington." He hurriedly offered his arm, and Thalia, with one brief upward glance, took it. Lady Agnes's silvery laughter followed them across the floor.

"Who in blazes was that?" asked James when they were out of earshot. "I've never seen her before in my life."

"Haven't you?"

"No, I haven't!"

Thalia looked at him. "That is Lady Agnes Crewe, one of my former pupils."

"Crewe? Wasn't she the one...?"

"Yes."

"Well, of all the dashed impudent... I've half a mind to go back there and tell her so."

Thalia shrugged. The scene just past had suggested something to her. "Mr. Elguard, do you know a family called Warrington? Most particularly a Mr. Alan Warrington?"

He frowned down at her, puzzled. "What has that to do with—?"

"It does."

He shrugged. "I know Alan. He was up at Oxford

with me. He came to town, and I stayed on to work for a fellowship."

"Will you introduce him to me, please?"

"Why are you interested in Warrington?"

"Because of Lady Agnes, and another friend of mine, who, I think, is fond of him."

The man digested this. "I see. Or, rather, I don't see, but I have some idea." He looked around the room. "I don't think he's here... No, wait, there he is. Come along, if you're serious."

"I am," replied Thalia positively, and they started across the floor toward a group of young people which included the Warrington children.

Twenty-three

THE NEXT MORNING, THALIA CAME TO AGGIE'S bedchamber after breakfast and heard the whole story of John Dudley. It was told haltingly and with many pauses, but she listened in silence to the end. "And so, you see," finished Aggie, "he changed. And I don't know why. I think that is the worst part, receiving that cold reply to my letter and not understanding what I had done."

Thalia looked at her. Aggie's skin was paler than usual, and there were dark smudges under her eyes. She seemed more tired with each day in London. "My dear Aggie," she began, "don't you see that—"

But before she could complete the sentence, there was a knock at the door. Aggie opened it, revealing Euphie in the corridor outside. "Oh," said the youngest sister. "I was looking for someone to help me pin up this flounce. Am I interrupting? I'm sorry." She looked a little hurt.

Thalia looked at Aggie, who said, "Of course not. Come in. I was just telling Thalia about something that happened to me in Hampshire. She asked."

Euphie looked from one to the other of her sisters.

"I meant to tell you, too, of course," continued the oldest. "I suppose I must say it all again."

She looked so gloomy at the prospect that Euphie said, "You needn't if you don't want to."

"No, no."

"Well, perhaps I can make it easier by saying that I think I know why he acted so," put in Thalia.

Aggie turned abruptly toward her. "Why?"

"Tell Euphie the story, then we will see what both of you think of my idea."

Aggie obeyed, speaking more rapidly this time and adding detail in response to questions from Thalia. When she had finished, she turned back to her and said, "Well?"

"The more I hear, the more I am convinced that I am right," answered the other. "It was the money, you dear goose."

"Money?"

"Yes, I see," said Euphie.

Aggie frowned. "You mean, Aunt Elvira's money?"

"Yes. Think back. According to your story, Mr. Dudley changed radically just after you got the letter. And nothing else happened. It must be that. He didn't want to be thought a fortune hunter, you see."

"But that is ridiculous!" exclaimed Aggie.

"Of course it is," agreed Thalia. "But very possible, don't you think? Here is a man about to offer for a charming girl without a penny, and suddenly he finds she is a great heiress. If he had spoken before he knew, all would be well. But to speak after?"

"It didn't make the least difference," insisted Aggie.

"I know, dear. But men have such queer notions of honor, don't they?"

This gave Aggie pause; she frowned and considered it.

"You must be right," said Euphie then. "Nothing else explains it. But what are we going to *do*?"

Thalia smiled at her. "Your perennial question."

"Well, that's the important thing, isn't it? How are we to rid this poor man of his silly idea?"

Thalia laughed.

"It isn't silly," retorted Aggie. "I think it is very noble."

The other two sisters grimaced. "There's no doubt she's in love," added Euphie.

Aggie frowned at her.

"Yes," said Thalia. "And as for what we are to do, I have already done something."

Euphie looked interested, Aggie alarmed. "Thalia, you haven't…!" began the latter.

The middle sister moved self-consciously in her chair. She felt a bit embarrassed about her talk with Mrs. Wellfleet. "I haven't done anything terrible. Anne Wellfleet has written to Mr. Dudley. She is going to get him to come up to town."

"Anne?" Aggie looked surprised.

"Yes. She noticed you were looking, uh, unhappy, and we talked it over." To Thalia's relief, her sister did not seem offended.

"And when he gets here," said Euphie, "you must let him know that the money doesn't matter a jot. And then everything will be as it was."

Aggie was thoughtful. "Yes," she replied slowly, "but how?"

"That must be up to you."

Thalia agreed. "But now that you know the problem, you will be able to deal with it."

After a moment, Aggie nodded meditatively. "Perhaps I will." She drifted into reverie. The other two sisters exchanged a smile.

After a pause, Euphie said, "Now, will someone help me with this flounce?"

Thalia laughed, and Aggie started. "Here, I will," said Aggie. "Give it to me."

"And I shall leave you to it," added Thalia, rising, "How I hate sewing."

They all laughed, and Thalia went out and walked down the corridor to her own bedchamber. At the door, she met one of the housemaids. "Oh, miss," said the girl, "I just left a letter on your dressing table. Mr. Jenkins told me to bring it up, being as the messenger said it was private."

Puzzled, Thalia thanked her and went into the room. She took up the envelope and tore it open. It was from Mrs. Wellfleet, and as she read it, Thalia began to smile. It went:

> *Dear Thalia,*
> *Such news! John Dudley has arrived in London all on his own. He left before he got my letter. Poor dear, he looks ghastly. Isn't it wonderful? It is my belief that he couldn't bear to stay away any longer. I shall bring him to the Butlers' evening party tonight. I leave the rest to you.*
>
> *Affectionately,*
> *Anne Wellfleet*

Thalia put the sheet down, her smile broadening. This was splendid. All would be settled very quickly indeed. And she turned to go back to Aggie and tell her the news.

Thus, it was an excited group that left Lady Fanshawe's townhouse for the Butlers' later that day. Aggie, in particular, was distracted, but she looked far happier than she had in days. The other two girls watched her with pleasure, and the countess asked plaintively what they were up to, to be so gay.

They arrived early; only a few guests stood about the Butler drawing room. This was to be a musical evening, so there were extra chairs and a piano and music stand at one end of the room. The Hartingtons greeted their hostess and then went to join a group opposite the door, where they could see all who entered.

They saw many acquaintances. Lady Agnes came in soon after them, and Mary Deming and her mother. Thalia noticed the Warringtons and, with a slight tremor, the Elguards. But there was no sign of the Wellfleets until just before the entertainment was to begin. Then, they came in with a rush, as if afraid they were late. And behind them, diffidently, walked John Dudley.

Aggie's fingers tightened on Thalia's arm when she saw him. Mr. Dudley did not seem aware of the girls at first. He looked rather nervous. And before they could make any move to reveal themselves, their hostess began urging people to chairs for the music, and all opportunity for private conversation was at an end.

More than one guest looked impatient during the

quite admirable program Mrs. Butler had organized. Aggie clearly did not listen, but spent the time twisting her hands in her lap. And though Euphie was soon wrapped up in the music, Thalia divided her attention between her older sister and John Dudley, whom she could just see on the opposite side of the room. She noted that he did not seem particularly enthralled either. And Anne Wellfleet met Thalia's eyes more than once, each time with a roguish smile. Out of sight behind the Hartingtons, James Elguard also exhibited signs of impatience.

At last the entertainment was over. Guests stood and began to walk about, some going into the adjoining room, where a cold supper had been laid out. The Hartington girls were soon surrounded by a crowd of admirers. But John Dudley was not among them. He had by this time discovered Aggie and her sisters, but after one stunned glance at the three of them, he had retreated to one of the window embrasures, there to stare painfully at Aggie and shift from foot to foot. Thalia was soon quite out of patience with him. But when she turned again and saw her sister's face, she said, "You must go and speak to him, Aggie. He is afraid to approach you among all these strangers."

"In front of everyone?" murmured the other.

"I see no other way."

Aggie nodded, swallowed, and excused herself to the young man who had been addressing outrageous gallantries to her for some minutes without effect. She took a deep breath and started across the room to Dudley. He, seeing her coming, stepped forward, and they met just beside the window.

"He is not so dashing as I would have imagined," whispered Euphie to Thalia as they watched the couple.

"No, not dashing. But his face looks kind and sensible, and I think he will do very well."

Euphie considered this as she surveyed Mr. Dudley. "Perhaps. But I should prefer a bit more… oh, something myself."

Thalia laughed "I daresay. Fortunately, what you prefer is not the issue."

Euphie smiled at her. "Or you?"

"Or me."

Their whispered conversation was interrupted, and they turned back to the group around them.

On the other side of the room, Aggie had said, "Good evening," and John Dudley had replied. Both were now looking at the floor.

At the same moment, Aggie began, "I hope you…" and Dudley said, "You are looking…" They both laughed uncomfortably. "Go ahead," said both at once. They laughed again; Aggie wondered miserably if their former easy friendship was gone forever.

"I was only going to say that you are looking splendid, Miss Hartington," said Dudley then. "Quite magnificent, in fact."

"Oh, that is all Lady Fanshawe's doing. She is very concerned with clothes and, and that sort of thing. I should prefer my old familiar gowns." Aggie excused this half-truth by telling herself that she did often miss her former quiet life.

"Really?" Mr. Dudley's face brightened a bit.

"Yes. I, I get so tired of the city, and of going out every night. My sisters enjoy it, of course. I came to town mainly for them. But I shall be very glad when I can return to the country and be done with all this." She made a vague gesture at the room around them.

"Indeed? Will you indeed?" The gentleman seemed transformed by this confidence.

"Oh, yes."

There was a pause; then Dudley cleared his throat and said, "Miss Hartington, I should apologize for not calling before you left the Wellfleets' house. I was, ah, very, ah…"

Summoning all her courage, Aggie put in, "I know why you did not."

"You do?" He stared.

"Yes, and, and although I think it was very noble, you were mistaken!" This was so bold that she drew in her breath sharply and put a hand to her lips.

But Mr. Dudley did not seem at all shocked. He looked very steadily at her, then, unconscious of the eyes around them, reached for her hand. "I think perhaps I was," he replied. "And I am sorry for it, though I could not help feeling as I did. I still feel it a little."

"You mustn't," answered Aggie intensely. "It does not matter a whit." Her deep blue eyes met his.

"No?" Mr. Dudley smiled down at her; then some noise made him aware of the crowd around them and he let go of her hand. "This is no place to talk privately. May I call upon you tomorrow? I want particularly to ask you something."

Aggie's answering smile was radiant. "Yes, please."

Their eyes held for another moment, and a clear understanding passed between them. Then Dudley said, "Would you like some lemonade or, ah, something?"

Aggie laughed. "Yes." He offered his arm, and they strolled toward the dining room together.

Thalia, who had been keeping one eye on her sister from across the floor, sighed audibly. "And that, I hope, is that," she said to herself.

"What is what?" a deep voice replied.

Thalia started. She had thought she was alone. Indeed, she had been only a moment before, when her companion went to fetch a glass of ratafia. She turned and found James Elguard standing behind her.

"What is what?" he asked again. "You sounded uncommonly pleased about it, whatever it is."

"I am. But I can't tell it yet."

"Ah. I suppose it concerns your sister and that unknown young man with brown hair?"

Thalia looked surprised.

"It wasn't so difficult to tell that. I saw where you were looking. And I think I know what you can't tell, so you needn't worry over it." He paused briefly. "Did you enjoy the music?"

Still a little startled at his divining of her thoughts, Thalia stammered, "Uh, yes."

"Really? I didn't. I had far too much to think about to pay any heed."

"Did you?"

"Yes. And I mean to tell you what it was, even though you don't ask." He looked into her eyes, and Thalia's heart beat rather faster.

But before he could speak again, they were interrupted. "Mr. Elguard," said Lady Agnes Crewe caressingly, "how lovely to see you again." She came up behind them and took his arm. "I was so dull only a moment ago, and now here you are to amuse me." Her glance flicked over Thalia. "Hullo, Miss Hartington."

Thalia nodded, wishing she could slap Lady Agnes's impudent face.

But the younger girl was gazing meltingly up at James Elguard and saying, "I was just longing for some lemonade, too. Why don't we go and get some supper? I should so like to talk to you about, oh, everything. I met your charming sister last night, and she told me how wonderfully intelligent you are."

Thalia gritted her teeth.

Elguard slipped his arm out of hers. "You flatter me. And I fear Miss Hartington and I were in the middle of a discussion, so I must beg to be excused."

The total lack of interest in his tone made Thalia's eyes glow, but she still said nothing.

"Oh," answered Lady Agnes sweetly, "I am sure Miss Hartington would release you. She has so *many* beaus."

At this, a small sound escaped Thalia. She was immediately furious with herself, because Lady Agnes surely heard it and gloated.

"Nonetheless," replied Elguard stiffly, "I should prefer to continue our discussion."

Thwarted, the blond girl looked at him. Their gaze locked for a moment; then she shrugged slightly and said, "Oh, very well." She started to turn away, but threw a flirtatious glance over her shoulder. "Perhaps we can have a 'discussion' later on."

James Elguard made an almost inaudible sound of exasperation, and Lady Agnes walked away. "That girl is abominable," added the man.

Thalia was almost too angry to speak. "Look, she

is going over to Alan Warrington. Mary Deming is talking to him, but that will not last. Oh, I could just—"

"What difference can it make?" interrupted her companion. "No doubt Warrington will discover what she really is soon enough. But we have more important things—"

"Will he indeed?" retorted Thalia. "Only look at him."

Impatiently, Elguard did so. He saw a young man besotted, a triumphant interloper, and a slender miserable third, Mary Deming. "It is too bad, to be sure. But as there is nothing we can do, I do not see—"

"Oh, I am determined to do something. Mary is my friend, and I don't mean to see her made unhappy because she is too shy and young Warrington too silly to know Lady Agnes's true nature."

"Look here, Miss Hartington," replied Elguard, so insistently that Thalia had to turn back to him. "I want to talk to you, about something rather important."

A bit nervous, Thalia said, "It will have to wait. I can think of nothing but Lady Agnes's monstrous conduct now."

"The deuce!"

Thalia stiffened. "I must help my friend, and if you don't care for that, well, then…"

"No, no, I understand your feelings." He sighed, then considered a moment "Look here, if I help you, will you listen to me then?"

"Help me?"

"Yes, help show up Lady Agnes as she really is. Warrington would be a fool to care anything about her after that."

Thalia stared up at him. "Would you… would you do that?"

"Why not? It's a worthy undertaking. And I want to help you." He smiled. "That most of all."

"But how can we…?"

"Leave that to me. I shall think of some scheme."

"Will you?"

"Of course. You must allow me a little time to think, however. I cannot pull ideas out of thin air all in a moment."

"But that you *would*." Thalia gazed up at him with a new look, and James Elguard smiled again. This was more like it.

"I care about fairness too, you know. And I must say that Lady Agnes's style of conversation has given me a pronounced aversion to her."

Thalia laughed.

"So, I will think of a way, and tell you tomorrow."

"Oh, yes. Thank you."

"A pleasure." He looked at her closely and seemed to come to a decision. "Would you like some lemonade? Or perhaps a bit of supper?"

"Yes, thank you." Thalia took his arm, and they walked off together, the gentleman looking more pleased than he had all evening.

❦

There was another musical program planned for after supper, and as the hostess began to shepherd her guests toward the chairs once more, several gentlemen were seen to slip out of the room. Among them was Lord Fanshawe, who had come late and shown little enjoyment of the entertainment. "Fanshawe," said another man, following him out, "what about a hand of piquet? I understand there is a card room hidden somewhere in this house."

Lord Fanshawe shook his head. "I mean to go back when the soprano finishes."

"Indeed?" The other man, a tall sardonic buck, looked at him with a smile. "But I had forgotten. It's said that you are pursuing one of your mother's ingenues. It's a sign of senility, you know, Fanshawe, sinking to the schoolroom."

The earl, who had stiffened, now shrugged. "So I have heard. I don't believe I've reached that state yet, however."

"No? Yet I understand she's a taking little piece. Better men than we have fallen before wide blue eyes. Beware, Fanshawe, the ton is avid to see you stumble."

The earl merely gave him a brief haughty look from under lowered eyelids and excused himself to go back into the drawing room. His companion laughed shortly and pulled out an enameled snuffbox.

When the second musical interval ended, the guests began to take their leave. The Hartington sisters were following Lady Fanshawe into the hall when she stopped to speak to her son and commanded him to escort her to her carriage.

"Did you enjoy the music?" Euphie asked him as they walked.

"Yes," he replied coolly.

"I thought the soprano rather off."

He shrugged, and Euphie looked up at him in perplexity. What had happened to make him so cold?

There was some confusion when they reached the front door. Lady Fanshawe's carriage, supposedly summoned quite ten minutes ago, had not come round, and they had to wait while a footman went to find it. The countess was tired, and sank down in a chair. Aggie was lost in a dream, and Thalia seemed little better, so Euphie and Lord Fanshawe were left to each other. The girl ventured another comment on the program, but receiving a bored reply, she fell silent. All her enjoyment seemed suddenly to evaporate.

The silence lengthened until Euphie could endure it no longer. "You look terribly bored," she said to Lord Fanshawe.

Some other guests went out behind them as he looked down. His expression was unrevealing. "Do I? I beg pardon."

She frowned at him. "You hardly spoke to us tonight," she blurted. Then, appalled at herself, she shut her mouth with a snap and flushed bright red.

A muscle at the corner of the earl's mouth jerked, but another group of guests crossed the hall at that moment, and he answered merely, "Did I not? I must beg pardon again, then."

Cruelly embarrassed, Euphie turned away. "Not at all," she murmured. To her intense relief, the carriage finally appeared at this moment, and they all moved to get in. Lord Fanshawe bade them all good night uninterestedly and turned away.

Twenty-four

As HE HAD PROMISED, JAMES ELGUARD CALLED BETIMES the following morning and asked for Thalia. There was some confusion on his arrival, for Aggie came hurrying down to the hall at the first ring of the bell. But when she saw who it was, she retreated again, passing Thalia on the stairs without a word.

Both Thalia and Elguard watched her retreat. "I hope I haven't come at an inconvenient time," said the latter.

"Oh, no. I believe my sister is expecting someone else, that is all." Thalia smiled to herself.

"Ah."

"Come into the library. I can hardly wait to hear if you have an idea."

They walked across the hall and into this room. Thalia shut the door and faced him. "Well?"

"Well, I have a scheme. You must tell me what you think of it." And he proceeded to explain at some length. "You understand I won't draw her out," he finished. "That would be despicable. But I doubt it will be necessary."

Thalia nodded. "But do you think it will do? Will Alan Warrington see?"

"If he does not, then your friend is mistaken in his character, and she should try to forget him as soon as may be."

"Yes, I suppose you are right. Still…"

"If you have some better plan, or any modifications to suggest, I am only too willing to hear."

"No, I don't." Thalia looked up. "This must work. It is a good idea." She smiled. "And I do thank you for making this effort, and for a girl you don't even know. It's splendid."

"I am not doing it for a girl I don't know, charming as Miss Deming may be. I think you know that."

"Yes, well… let us go over it all again, so that I am certain of what I must do."

He looked at her with a slight frown, then nodded. "All right."

They went over the scheme several times, trying to find flaws and correct them. After half an hour, both were satisfied. "Splendid," said Thalia heartily again. She rose and held out her hand. "I shall see you tonight, then, and we will do the thing."

Elguard took her hand, started to speak, then changed his mind. He nodded.

"Good-bye," said Thalia quickly. "And thank you again."

Smiling a little, he took his leave. Thalia ran back upstairs wondering what was the matter with her, and why things that she did not at all mean to say kept coming from her mouth.

About an hour later, at midmorning, the bell rang

again, and Jenkins ushered John Dudley into the house. He asked for Aggie and, when invited to step up to the drawing room where the young ladies were sitting, refused incoherently. Jenkins eyed his nervous expression, then smiled benignly and took him to the library. "I shall see if Miss Hartington can come down," he said.

She could. Indeed, the butler found her lingering on the upper landing, afraid to come down again but longing to know who had called. When he told her, her answering smile was so radiant that Jenkins smiled back. "I've put him in the library, miss," he added. "You'll find him there."

"Thank you. Oh, thank you," said Aggie, and she nearly ran down the stairs.

In the hall she paused a moment, running a hand through her russet curls and glancing in the mirror. She wore a dress of white muslin trimmed with blue ribbons this morning, and excitement had made her cheeks glow. She walked to the library and went in. Dudley stood before the fireplace looking uneasy.

At first, he only stared at her. He seemed struck speechless by her eager beauty. Then she said hello, and he muttered something in reply.

"Shall we sit down?" said Aggie, doing so.

He took the opposite armchair and continued to look at her. "You are so lovely," he said after a pause. "I am never prepared for it somehow."

Aggie blushed with pleasure.

"You deserve a setting like this," he continued, gesturing around at Lady Fanshawe's opulent room. "And parties and lots of admirers. I almost didn't come today; my nerve nearly failed." He smiled wryly.

"But I told you…"

"Yes, yes, I know what you said. I even flatter myself that I know what you meant. But did you?" She started to answer, but he held up a hand for silence. "You've only been in London a few weeks, you know. And you came with perhaps a, er, fixed idea in your head. I've talked with Anne Wellfleet, and she says… well, never mind. The thing is, you have to give town life a chance. You might find you like it very well, you know, and then…" He made a helpless gesture, and stopped.

Aggie had recovered her self-possession as he spoke, and now she looked at him steadily. "So I might," she replied evenly.

He stared at her, looking half desperate.

"Do you hate being in London, Mr. Dudley?"

"I? Why, why, no. That is, I enjoy it occasionally. Coming up to see a friend or two, going to the theater."

Aggie nodded. "Yes. That is exactly what I think I should like myself. To live in the country and to come up to town sometimes."

He shook his head. "Perhaps you think so now. But you are so young; you may change your mind. And with your fortune, you should be free to do as you wish."

Aggie rose majestically. "If you came today only to criticize me, Mr. Dudley, then we needn't continue this conversation, I think."

"Criticize?" He gaped.

"Indeed. Clearly you think me both frivolous and silly, unable to make up my own mind about what I like and do not like. I wonder that you care to talk with such a ninnyhammer as you believe me to be."

"Never! I did not mean that."

Aggie raised her eyebrows. "Indeed? Well, I admit I am glad, for though I may be young, I have never had any difficulty deciding what I like. My sisters could tell you so. I haven't their talents, but I have a great deal of common sense, and I believe I know myself quite as well as anyone could wish to."

"I didn't mean…" repeated Dudley, "that is, I am sorry."

Aggie sat down again, shrugging slightly.

He watched her for a moment, then blurted, "Can't you understand how I feel about all this?"

Aggie raised her blue eyes to his. "In a way, I do," she answered, not attempting to pretend she didn't know what he meant. "But in another, I don't. My fortune should make no difference, it seems to me. I am the same."

"No difference! Why, you may have your choice of… of anything."

"And, given that, it seems to you that my choice must be different? I disagree."

He leaned forward and took both her hands. "But, Miss Hartington, Aggie, don't you see? You must take the time to see everything. You had seen so little before; now you must make certain. I meant to wait, until the end of the season perhaps, and then come to see… but I couldn't stay away. It was torture. Every night, I would wonder if perhaps you had met someone else. I pictured the balls, the parties…"

"I haven't," said Aggie, quietly.

"You can't know—"

"I *do* know," she interrupted. Looking down, she added, "It sounds horrid to say so, but my sisters and I have had quite a success, you know. I have met a great many people and received a great many compliments. I didn't care for any of them." She looked at him from beneath her lashes. "Of course, you are not very complimentary, Mr. Dudley. You force one to insist upon an attachment. I blush for myself."

"How can you say so! Gods, I can't keep still any longer. Will you marry me, Aggie?"

She smiled. "Why, Mr. Dudley, this is so sudden." She laughed at his expression and added, "Of course I will, you great dolt."

There was an instant of stillness in the room; then he was on his feet and pulling her into his arms. "I pray you may never regret this," he said thickly. "I swear I will do everything to see that you don't."

"I shan't," replied Aggie serenely. And then she found herself being quite thoroughly kissed.

After a while, they sat down again, both on the sofa this time, and Mr. Dudley's arm remained around Aggie's waist. "Who would have thought," mused the girl, "all those years ago when you used to call me Uglea, that we would end here?"

"Do you still throw that in my face?" He laughed.

"Of course. I am marrying you only so that I may make you pay for your past sins. I shall mention it once a day, at least, for the rest of our lives."

He laughed, but said, "I can't believe that we shall really spend that time together. I have felt such despair. I still feel I don't deserve you."

"Now, no more of that. I won't hear it." Aggie put a hand to his cheek. "You deserve a great deal more."

Clearly there was only one answer to this. And the newly engaged pair spent a very agreeable quarter hour on the sofa exploring the subject. Then Aggie put a hand to her tumbled curls and said, "We should tell my sisters, and Lady Fanshawe."

"I hope they will be pleased."

"Oh, there's no doubt of that. I know that Thalia and Euphie, at least, are waiting for us now. I daresay Euphie is wondering what can be taking so long."

"You told them...?"

"They could see for themselves."

"Ah. Well, let us get it over, then."

"Silly. You will like them immensely, and they you."

"I don't doubt it. But the first meeting is daunting. And Lady Fanshawe, well, she struck me as formidable."

Aggie rose and held out her hand. "Nonsense. Come along."

They walked through the hall, receiving a positively fatherly smile from Jenkins, and up the stairs. Aggie, entering the drawing room first, found there was no need to say anything. Her sisters took one look at her face and jumped up to hug her, Thalia crying, "I am so glad," and Euphie, "My dearest sister!"

Aggie pulled Dudley forward. "This is John," she said simply. "I hope you will come to love him as I do."

Thalia held out a hand, and Euphie giggled. "I shan't promise *that*," she said, "but I daresay I shall manage to be a trying younger sister to him as well."

"Never," responded Dudley gallantly.

"Wait and see."

"Now, Euphie," said Thalia, "we must welcome John into the family properly."

"Indeed, we are very glad," said the youngest sister. "I wish you and Aggie very happy."

"Where is Lady Fanshawe?" asked the latter.

"She just went out for a moment, and here she is." Euphie indicated the doorway.

The countess was duly told the news and added her congratulations to the others'. She looked once closely at Aggie's face and, impressed by the change she saw there, sat down to discuss the wedding with great relish.

They had by no means exhausted this subject when Jenkins came in to announce another visitor. "Lord Fanshawe," he said, and stepped back to reveal this gentleman behind him.

"Hello, Giles," called the countess. "Come in and hear the splendid news."

Eyebrows raised, the earl came forward, and as he did so, Euphie quietly slipped from the room and went upstairs. She was determined to avoid him, after his chilling behavior the last time they met.

Twenty-five

IT WAS A VERY LIVELY PARTY THAT SET OUT FROM LADY Fanshawe's that evening to attend an informal ball. John Dudley was with them, and he and Aggie looked so happy that the others could not help exchanging smiling glances now and then. They had thought of staying home and having a quiet family dinner to celebrate the engagement, but they had promised weeks ago to attend this dance, and the hostess was a particular friend of the countess's, so they went.

The first person they encountered when they walked in was Anne Wellfleet. She looked once at Aggie and came hurrying forward. "My dear, I am so glad!" she exclaimed.

Aggie laughed. "Is it so obvious?"

"To me, yes. But I have been longing for it forever. Come, tell me everything." And she led Aggie over to a sofa by the wall. John Dudley, smiling sheepishly, followed them.

Their hostess came up then, in the process of organizing the dancing, and carried Thalia and Euphie off. Soon, nearly twenty couples were on the floor, and the music began. "Hardly 'an impromptu hop,' as she said it would be," Thalia said to her sister when they passed close to one another.

"No, but it isn't a ball, either."

Thalia laughed as they moved away from one another again.

Two sets passed pleasantly. And as the third was forming, James Elguard approached Thalia. "May I have the honor?" he asked.

She had half promised this dance, a waltz, to someone else, but she did not see him, and she very much wanted to speak to Elguard. She held out her hand, and he took it, leading her onto the floor.

"Is everything ready?" she asked when the music had started.

"As much as it can be, yes."

"It will be a matter of timing, I suppose?"

He nodded. "We must be careful to set the thing properly."

"But when?'"

"Just at the interval, I think. When everyone is starting to go down to supper. I hope to try when there are few people about."

"Yes." Thalia shivered a little. "I can scarcely wait, though I am not at all certain I want the moment to come."

"I know." There was a short pause; then he added, "I should tell you that I have chosen the place, over there in the corner."

"By the curtained arch?"

"Yes."

"Very well."

There was another pause. Thalia looked uneasy, yet determined.

"I heard the news about your sister," said Elguard. "I must offer her my felicitations."

"Thank you. We are very happy."

"It must be gratifying to see two people who are well-suited and who care for one another come together."

Thalia nodded silently, not meeting his eyes.

The music ended, and they stepped apart. "So," said Elguard, "we are decided?"

"Y-yes."

"Yes. I will arrange my part by the archway just before supper."

The girl nodded. "I will be there."

"Good. Well, thank you for the dance." He bowed slightly and walked away, leaving Thalia gazing after him uneasily.

Later in the evening, however, she talked with Mary Deming, and her resolve was strengthened again. For though Mary said nothing, she looked pale and tired. And when Thalia asked her if she was feeling well, she valiantly insisted that she was fine. Yet Thalia caught her watching a group of young people wistfully, among them Alan Warrington and Lady Agnes.

Thus when the interval came, she was ready to do her part. She saw James Elguard approach Warrington and engage him in conversation, drawing him toward the corner of the room. When they were nearly there, she looked around for Lady Agnes and found her talking to another girl and several gentlemen nearby. They looked ready to go downstairs, so Thalia took a deep breath and hurried over.

"Lady Agnes," she said when she reached them, "could I speak to you?"

The statuesque blond girl turned, looking very surprised when she saw who it was. "I beg your pardon?"

Thalia flushed slightly, but she repeated her request.

"To me? I suppose so. What is it?" Her rudeness was so patent that one of her companions stared.

But Thalia felt hardened by it. "It is a private matter," she said.

"We'll go down to supper," said the third girl. "You can join us there, Agnes. We'll keep a chair."

Lady Agnes looked annoyed. "Oh, very well."

The others walked away. "Let us go over here," said Thalia, moving toward the corner.

"Whatever for?" But as Thalia paid no heed to this, Lady Agnes was forced to follow. "I cannot imagine what you should have to say to *me*," she added as they walked.

They reached the corner and stood just beside the curtained arch. Thalia turned a little nervously, wondering if all would go as planned, and at that moment James Elguard came through the arch and let the curtain drop behind him. "Oh!" said Thalia, feigning surprise.

"Miss Hartington," acknowledged the gentleman. "And Lady Agnes. Good evening."

The blond girl smirked. "Why, Mr. Elguard. How fortunate to come upon you here." She cast a sidelong glance at Thalia, who tried to look put out, and sidled closer to Elguard. "I haven't seen you this age. You never call—naughty!"

Thalia's jaw tightened, and she no longer needed to pretend annoyance.

"I have little time for social calls," replied Elguard. "I am continuing my studies while I am in town, and they keep me occupied."

"You are so clever." Lady Agnes took his arm and gazed up at him. "But surely you can spare a few moments for special friends." She smiled. "And I am a special friend, am I not?"

Elguard raised his eyebrows. "We are not, perhaps, well enough acquainted to say that, Lady Agnes."

"And who is to blame for that? I have certainly done everything possible to forward our acquaintance. Did your sister tell you I called last week?"

"I, I believe she did."

"And you were out. After your talk of studies." She cocked her head playfully.

He had flushed very slightly. "I was... ah..."

"Oh, no. Don't give me a lame excuse. But if you were to call upon *me*, I promise you I should be at home."

This was so bold that Thalia drew her breath in sharply. Lady Agnes noticed, and smiled. Then she looked up at Elguard again. "I must tell you," she said confidingly, "that you are the most interesting man I have met in London. So many of the others seem young and dull. They have nothing to say for themselves. But you—you are quite different. You are the only man I know who can truly be said to be fascinating." She breathed this last word very softly, leaning closer to Elguard and parting her lips.

"Is he, by God?" said another voice. And Alan

Warrington pushed back the curtain and stepped into the room. He looked very angry indeed. "I daresay I must have misheard you when you said the same to me, then. I suppose you tell every man that. Gods, what a fool I have been!" And he stalked off.

Lady Agnes had paled and stepped away from Elguard. Now she turned toward Thalia and hissed, "You! You did this!"

The older girl met her eyes squarely. "I did nothing. I had no need to; you did it all yourself."

Lady Agnes's light eyes blazed. She started to speak, then whirled and ran after Alan Warrington.

There was a pause as the other two watched her disappear down the stairs.

"She won't get round him," said Thalia finally.

"No. I would say that young Warrington is thoroughly disillusioned."

"Perhaps now he will see Mary's good qualities; she is Lady Agnes's utter opposite."

"Perhaps," agreed the man.

"I know that I cannot count on it. But I do hope."

"Hope is always permitted," answered Elguard in a queer voice.

Thalia looked up sharply. "Shall we go and get some supper? I feel somehow exhausted by that encounter."

"In a moment. First, I must talk to you." Thalia made an involuntary movement, and he added, "I think you owe me a moment's attention."

The girl looked at the floor, nodding almost imperceptibly.

"Thank you. I think you must know what I am going to say. I have said it before."

"Please don't."

"Why?"

Thalia's cheeks reddened. "It is all so awkward."

"What is? You must be clearer if I am to understand you."

She took a breath and tried to gather her wits. "When we first met, we had such fun, talking of books and so on."

"And we can—"

"Please. Then things became so miserable, with the school and... and everything."

"And my mother," he added grimly.

Thalia made a gesture. "And it seemed there might be a scandal, and you came and asked... It was so awkward. And now..."

"Yes. And now?"

Thalia shrugged.

"It is still awkward? But why?"

"There won't be any talk," blurted Thalia. "Lady Agnes told the story, but others, like Mary, contradicted her account, and no one pays it any heed. You don't *have* to!"

"I don't... my dear girl, of course I don't *have to*. No one says that I do. Did you think that was my reason?"

"But it must... We hardly know one another."

"Perhaps that was true at Bath, though even then I think I knew enough. But now we have seen each other again and again. I do not feel that you are a stranger. Do you see me as one?"

"No," replied Thalia very softly.

"No. And as you say, there is no scandal. There couldn't be, for there is no basis for one. That motive, which never had a very strong hold on my mind, disappeared long since." He smiled down at her. "Indeed, I fear I am not the sort of man who could marry a woman simply to save her from scandal. I am too selfish." He leaned down a little to try to see her face. "I want to marry you, Thalia, because I admire and love you. As you said, when we met we saw immediately that we were kindred spirits. I have never found a woman with your intellect and talents, interested in the very things that interest me. And as I saw more of you, I realized that you had every other fine quality as well. Will you be my wife?"

There was a short silence. Thalia tried to speak, but her throat was too dry.

"Of course, I understand," he continued then, "that your fortune makes a great difference between us. You can now command every luxury, and I remain relatively penniless. I thought long and hard when I heard of it, and I decided that it should make no difference to my declaration. I feel the same. You, however, may not. I understand that. You may wish to—"

"No!" exclaimed Thalia. "Please don't."

"Don't? I fear I shall have to ask again that you be more explicit."

"Don't talk of money!"

"Ah." He looked relieved. "But I may talk of other things? How much I love you, for example?"

A gurgle of laughter escaped the girl.

"Yes?" He reached for her hands. "What is it, Thalia? Why won't you marry me? Is it my family? I admit that they have been appalling. Or at least, my mother has. But—"

"Stop, stop," laughed Thalia. "All right."

"All right?"

"All right, I will."

His hands tightened on hers. "Truly?"

She nodded. "I felt the same as you, when we met and, and after. But then so many horrid things happened. I was… oh… determined to put it all from my mind. And I did *not* wish you to feel obliged—"

"Oh, I rarely feel obliged," he interrupted cheerfully. "I do just as I please about most things; ask my sisters."

"I shall. And more."

"Aha, a termagant, I see. I had better enjoy my selfish habits while I can." And he pulled her through the curtained opening behind them into a small antechamber and bent to kiss her.

Thalia, shocked, started to move away. "Someone will see!"

"Nonsense. They are all at supper. And no one comes in here." He grinned. "Except lovers and conspirators."

Seeing that he was beyond rational argument, Thalia took the only possible course and gave in. She found that her arms crept up around his neck very naturally.

A good deal of time passed unnoticed; then a sound from the room behind recalled them to their position, and they moved apart. "I expect to continue this interesting dialogue very soon," he said, smiling down at her.

Thalia laughed, flushing a bit. "Indeed, sir, it seems a fascinating study."

He held out a hand. "Shall we look for our families?"

She nodded. "We know, at least, that yours will approve."

He grimaced. "Lavishly. Do you mind very much?"

"I don't mind anything tonight!"

Mrs. Elguard was, indeed, effusive. She insisted upon telling two of her particular friends at once, in fact. And Thalia was glad when they could escape from that chattering group. James's sister was more subdued, and she seemed genuinely glad to hear of the engagement, though she said little. Thalia told herself that she must improve their acquaintance as soon as possible.

They found Aggie and John on the dance floor, and told their news as the set was beginning. Aggie looked very directly at Thalia, who blushed, then took both her hands and squeezed them. Her sparkling eyes spoke volumes.

"Welcome to the family, old man," said John to James Elguard. He held out a hand as the other three laughed.

Elguard shook it. "Thank you. It is always comforting to know that the old established members accept one."

They laughed again.

"What good times we shall have!" exclaimed Aggie.

Thalia nodded, but said, "There is Euphie with Lady Fanshawe. Let us complete our round."

They did so. Euphie heard them out with an uncertain smile and warmly wished them happy. The countess, after one brief blink of chagrin, joined her. Lady Fanshawe had cherished the hope that her charges would make brilliant matches, and this second falling short of that goal was a blow. But as in Aggie's case, the look on Thalia's face banished any objections.

And once reconciled, the countess became expansive. "A double wedding, Thalia, you must!" she said. "At St. George's. I beg you to allow me to help. Two engagements in your first weeks out; it is beyond anything! And what a ceremony we can have. You and Aggie in clouds of white. It almost makes me cry to think of it. You *will* let me, won't you? Oh, there is Giles. Giles! Come here; I have something to tell you." And she conveyed this new intelligence to her son while Thalia and James laughed beside them. Euphie, catching the eye of a young man she knew, gave him a subtle signal and was soon being led onto the dance floor. Lord Fanshawe, glancing up from his mother's eager discourse for a moment, followed her figure with an unreadable expression.

Twenty-six

THE FOLLOWING EVENING, THALIA WENT TO DINNER AT the Elguards' to meet the other members of her prospective family. Aggie and John set off for Kensington, to call on his old aunt.

Lady Fanshawe, professing herself burnt to the socket by the unaccustomed gaieties of the past several weeks, retired to bed soon after tea, ordering dinner on a tray. Thus Euphie was left to her own devices and ate her dinner all alone.

Afterward, she went up to the drawing room and leafed through some illustrated magazines that lay on a table. But she could not summon any real interest in them, and after a while she sat down and put her chin on her hand. "Why do I feel blue-deviled?" she asked the empty air.

Receiving no answer, she sighed and stared at the wall. Presently she sighed again, and rose, making her way to the back parlor and the pianoforte.

When she sat down at the instrument, some of her glumness lifted. She ran her fingers lightly over the keys and then began to play very softly, so as not to disturb the countess upstairs. At first she played short passages from this or that favorite piece, along with a few of her own compositions that would have raised an approving eyebrow in certain musical circles. Then she bent over the keyboard and launched into a favorite sonata, very quiet and melancholy. Before long, she was lost in it, her worries forgotten, her surroundings irrelevant.

Though she continued to play softly, the strains filled the parlor and echoed in the passage outside. Euphie, wholly engrossed, did not hear footsteps approach or the door open. She went on playing until she felt a tug at her skirts and looked down to find Nero batting at a ruffle with one playful paw. She smiled and nodded absently, continuing to the end of the piece. Nero, offended at this lack of notice, began to climb up her muslin skirt.

She finished with a flourish, laughed, and bent to pick him up. Holding the cat out in front of her, she said, "Nuisance. Have you no appreciation of music? Nero was clearly an improper name for *you*. Or perhaps you prefer the violin?"

There was a tiny noise from the direction of the doorway, but Euphie did not notice it as she continued to talk to the cat.

"We shall soon be all alone here, Nero, you and I. You have enjoyed playing with Brutus and Juvenal, haven't you? But they will be going away. It is a lowering reflection. I suppose that is what depressed my spirits tonight."

"Wrrow," replied Nero.

"Don't think I don't wish them happy," added Euphie hurriedly. "Of course I do. It is just so sudden, you see. I lost them once. And now, when we are just back together again, both of them are engaged and starting a new life. And I remain as before. I haven't become accustomed to it yet; that is all."

Nero struggled wildly in her grasp, and she bent to put him down again. As she did so, she caught a glimpse of movement by the door and spun round. "Lord Fanshawe!"

"I'm sorry. I didn't mean to intrude. I called to see Mother, and when Jenkins told me she was resting, I heard the music. I couldn't resist coming to listen. You do play so exquisitely."

"You've... you've been here the whole time?"

"I'm sorry. I didn't mean to eavesdrop. But once you had begun, I didn't know how to make my presence known. And I was sure you would hear if I tried to leave the room."

Euphie stood. "It doesn't matter," she replied as grandly as she could. She started to move away from the pianoforte, took a misstep, and trod on Nero's tail. He jumped and yowled; Euphie started back and knocked against the piano stool with such violence that it toppled to the floor.

Lord Fanshawe began to laugh.

She gazed at him with incredulous rage. To her horror, tears filled her eyes, and in a moment, despite all she could do, she was crying bitterly. "Here, no," said the earl, coming forward. "Forgive me." He righted the stool and put Nero on an armchair nearby.

"I th-think you're b-beastly," sobbed Euphie. "Everything is b-beastly, and, and I h-haven't any handkerchief."

Suppressing a smile, Fanshawe offered her his. "You know," he said, "it's perfectly natural for you to be feeling some sadness at your sisters' engagements. It will be a great change. But I think you'll find it won't be as radical as you fear."

"I d-don't care what you think," wailed the girl, wiping her eyes and trying her utmost to stop crying.

"Yes, well, I suppose it really isn't any of my affair. Although…"

"Oh, why don't you just go away."

"But I came here tonight particularly to speak to you."

"To me?" This was surprising enough to check the flow of tears.

"Yes."

"You said you came to see your mother."

"Well, yes, of course. I meant to see her, too. But I wanted to talk to you about something."

"What?" Euphie blew her nose pointedly.

He smiled again. "Recently I have somehow gotten the notion that you are avoiding me. You seem to leave a room whenever I come into it. Have I offended you?"

Euphie, who had nearly regained control of herself, was further stiffened by this question. "How should you offend me, Lord Fanshawe?"

"I'm not sure. That is why I ask you."

The girl turned her head away. "You are mistaken. I am not the least offended. And now, if you will excuse—"

"But I won't." The earl came closer. "Tell me why you're angry."

"I am not—"

"You are. And I cannot think why. We danced together so pleasantly at Almack's, and—"

"And you snubbed me so thoroughly at the Butlers' musical evening," snapped Euphie before she thought. Then, angry at herself, she grimaced.

"Ah."

"There is no need to say 'ah' in that odious way. It was nothing but a trifle; pray forget it." Euphie started to turn away.

"Nonsense. You are right; I was rude. But I had a reason."

She turned back to look at him.

"Will you hear it?"

After a moment's hesitation, she nodded. His tone was so serious that she could not refuse.

"Thank you." He paused and appeared to think. "It is difficult to know how to say this without seeming a complete coxcomb. I must simply trust to your understanding. I have been on the town some ten years now, Miss Hartington, and in that time I have been pursued in every imaginable way by matchmaking mamas and their daughters. I learned early that it was a great mistake to pay any girl the slightest attentions, lest I then be expected to make an offer. I began to ignore the debs altogether. Because of this, I have acquired a certain reputation. And now, if I am seen to like a young girl, gossip begins at once. I was reminded of this on the evening you mention, and I realized that in my enjoyment of your wit and charm, I had allowed myself—"

Euphie had flushed bright red as he spoke, and now

she blurted, "Are you accusing me of setting my cap at you?"

"Of course not. But you are staying in my mother's house; it is a delicate situation. Particularly because I have come to—"

"You were rude to me because you were afraid people would think you interested, is that it? Well, you may be as rude as you please, I shan't care."

"I didn't mean—"

"Oh, you never mean anything, that's perfectly clear. You stand imperturbably above us all and smile at our silly foibles. Well, I have had enough, and I, I w-want to be left alone now." To Euphie's disgust, her speech was marred by renewed tears.

"My dear Miss Hartington…"

With an inarticulate sound, Euphie ran across to a sofa and threw herself down on it, giving way totally to tears. Looking distinctly upset, Lord Fanshawe followed her, though for the moment he could do nothing but make soothing noises and stroke her hair.

Gradually Euphie's sobs subsided. After a while she sat up, sniffing, and began to use the handkerchief again. When she could control her voice, she said, "There is really not the least need for you to stay. I shall be perfectly all right in a moment. I'm sorry for making such a scene." She tossed her head. "I'll have your handkerchief laundered and sent back."

"Blast my handkerchief." He sat down beside her. "I had no idea I seemed so offensive to you, and I promise I never meant to be supercilious. I have an unfortunate manner sometimes, I know. Others have mentioned it. But I never meant to exhibit it with you."

"Yes, yes, very well," said Euphie tiredly. "It doesn't matter. It was very wrong of me to speak as I did. But now, could you—"

"Don't you see," he went on, leaning forward, "I was anxious about gossip because my feelings for you are very deep. I could not bear having them mauled over by the ton."

"Your feelings for me?" echoed Euphie, astonished.

He laughed ruefully. "Now I've torn it."

She stared at him.

"Exactly so." He ran a hand through his hair. "You are very young, Miss Hartington."

"I shall be eighteen next month."

"And I am more than ten years from eighteen. It is a large difference."

Euphie shrugged.

He smiled. "It is. I had not thought to broach this subject with you for some time. I wanted to go slowly, to give you a chance to see things and form your own tastes and ideas."

Euphie's tears had nearly disappeared. "My tastes in what?"

"Everything."

She considered this. "Well, it is an odd circumstance, but whether because of my unusual childhood or because I found music very young, my tastes have always been very settled."

"Throughout your lengthy career?"

She looked directly into his eyes for a long moment Something she saw there seemed to reassure her, and she nodded, lips quivering. "And you know, I am quite determined to make a grand marriage."

"Are you indeed?"

"Yes. Aggie and Thalia never cared for that sort of thing, but I am different." She looked at him from beneath her lashes. "I should like a title."

"Should you?"

"Oh, yes. And large houses and lots of servants."

"What you deserve, minx, is a husband who beats you soundly."

"Oh, no." She raised great shocked eyes to his face, but her cheeks showed irrepressible dimples.

He laughed. "But as no such courageous candidate has presented himself, will you have me, impudence?"

Euphie's smile broke through, and she nodded shyly. He drew her close and took the handkerchief to wipe the remaining traces of tears from her face. This done, he kissed her very expertly.

After a while they sat back together on the sofa. "You *do* have a great house, don't you?" inquired Euphie.

"Several, my infuriating darling. Bulging with servants of all descriptions."

"Good," sighed the girl.

There was another hiatus; then Euphie said, "Oh, Giles, your mother will have an apoplexy!"

"I sincerely hope not."

"Three engagements in two days!"

"Well, we must break the news gently." A thought occurred to him. "And we will *not* participate in a multiple wedding in Hanover Square," he added.

"Oh no. I want my *own* wedding. A lavish one!"

"I daresay Mother will be satisfied with that."

At this moment Nero leaped from a shelf behind them onto the earl's shoulder, startling him into an oath. "I suppose you will say that this abominable animal must live with us," he continued, when he had plucked the cat off and set him down on the floor.

"But of course. He introduced us."

"Intro… Why, so he did."

They looked down at Nero, who was casting covetous glances at Lord Fanshawe's boot. Sensing their regard, he looked up and said, "Mmrrow?"

"You will grow to love him," laughed Euphie.

"I doubt it. You will have to be content that I love you."

This notion was so satisfactory that Euphie could not protest. Instead, she slipped an arm about his neck and smiled, which effectively put an end to conversation for quite some time.

Read on for excerpts from Jane Ashford's
brand-new Regency romances!

From *Once Again a Bride*

Available now from Sourcebooks Casablanca

CHARLOTTE RUTHERFORD WYLDE CLOSED HER EYES
and enjoyed the sensation of the brush moving rhyth-
mically through her long hair. Lucy had been her maid
since she was eleven years old and was well aware that
her mistress's lacerated feelings needed soothing. The
whole household was aware, no doubt, but only Lucy
cared. The rest of the servants had a hundred subtle,
unprovable ways of intensifying the laceration. It had
become a kind of sport for them, Charlotte believed,
growing more daring as the months passed without
reprimand, denied with a practiced blankness that
made her doubly a fool.

Lucy stopped brushing and began to braid Charlotte's
hair for the night. Charlotte opened her eyes and faced
up to the dressing table mirror. Candlelight gleamed
on the creamy lace of her nightdress, just visible under
the heavy dressing gown that protected her from drafts.
Her bedchamber was cold despite the fire on this bitter
March night. Every room in this tall, narrow London
house was cold. Cold in so many different ways.

She ought to be changed utterly by these months,

Charlotte thought. But the mirror showed her hair of the same coppery gold, eyes the same hazel—though without any hint of the sparkle that had once been called alluring. Her familiar oval face, straight nose, and full lips had been judged pretty a scant year, and a lifetime, ago. She was perhaps too thin, now that each meal was an ordeal. There were dark smudges under her eyes, and they looked hopelessly back at her like those of a trapped animal. She remembered suddenly a squirrel she had found one long-ago winter—frozen during a terrible cold snap that had turned the countryside hard and bitter. It had lain on its side in the snow, its legs poised as if running from icy death.

"There you are, Miss Charlotte." Lucy put a comforting hand on her shoulder. When they were alone, she always used the old familiar form of address. It was a futile but comforting pretense. "Can I get you anything…?"

"No, thank you, Lucy." Charlotte tried to put a world of gratitude into her tone as she repeated, "Thank you."

"You should get into bed. I warmed the sheets."

"I will. In a moment. You go on to bed yourself."

"Are you sure I can't…?"

"I'm all right."

Neither of them believed it. Lucy pressed her lips together on some reply, then sketched a curtsy and turned to go. Slender, yet solid as a rock, her familiar figure was such a comfort that Charlotte almost called her back. But Lucy deserved her sleep. She shouldn't be deprived just because Charlotte expected none.

The door opened and closed. The candles guttered

and steadied. Charlotte sat on, rehearsing thoughts and plans she had already gone over a hundred times. There must be something she could do, some approach she could discover to make things—if not right, at least better. Not hopeless, not unendurable.

Her father—her dear, scattered, and now departed father—had done his best. She had to believe that. Tears came as she thought of him; when he died six months ago, he'd no longer remembered who she was. The brutal erosion of his mind, his most prized possession, had been complete.

It had happened so quickly. Yes, he'd always been distracted, so deep in his scholarly work that practicalities escaped him. But in his library, reading and writing, corresponding with other historians, he'd never lost or mistaken the smallest detail. Until two years ago, when the insidious slide began—unnoticed, dismissed, denied until undeniable. Then he had set all his fading faculties on getting her "safely" married. That one idea had obsessed and sustained him as all else slipped away. Perforce, he'd looked among his own few friends and acquaintances for a groom. Why, why had he chosen Henry Wylde?

In her grief and fear, Charlotte had put up no protest. She'd even been excited by the thought of moving from her isolated country home to the city, with all its diversions and amusements. And so, at age eighteen, she'd been married to a man almost thirty years older. Had she imagined it would be some sort of eccentric fairy tale? How silly and ignorant had she been? She couldn't remember now.

It wasn't all stupidity; unequal matches need not

be disastrous. She had observed a few older husbands who treated their young wives with every appearance of delight and appreciation. Not quite so much older, perhaps. But... from the day after the wedding, Henry had treated her like a troublesome pupil foisted upon his household for the express purpose of irritating him. He criticized everything she did. Just this morning, at breakfast, he had accused her of forgetting his precise instructions on how to brew his tea. She had *not* forgotten, not one single fussy step; she had carefully counted out the minutes in her head—easily done because Henry allowed no conversation at breakfast. He always brought a book. She was sure she had timed it exactly right, and still he railed at her for ten minutes, in front of the housemaid. She had ended up with the knot in her stomach and lump in her throat that were her constant companions now. The food lost all appeal.

If her husband did talk to her, it was most often about Tiberius or Hadrian or some other ancient. He spent his money—quite a lot of money, she suspected, and most of it hers—and all his affection on his collections. The lower floor of the house was like a museum, filled with cases of Roman coins and artifacts, shelves of books about Rome. For Henry, these things were important, and she, emphatically, was not.

After nearly a year of marriage, Charlotte still felt like a schoolgirl. It might have been different if there were a chance of children, but her husband seemed wholly uninterested in the process of getting them. And by this time, the thought of any physical contact with him repelled Charlotte so completely that she didn't know what she would do if he suddenly changed his mind.

She stared into the mirror, watching the golden candle flames dance, feeling the drafts caress the back of her neck, seeing her life stretch out for decades in this intolerable way. It had become quite clear that it would drive her mad. And so, she had made her plan. Henry avoided her during the day, and she could not speak to him at meals, with the prying eyes of servants all around them. After dinner, he went to his club and stayed until she had gone to bed. So she would not go to bed. She would stay up and confront him, no matter how late. She would insist on changes.

She had tried waiting warm under the bedclothes but had failed to stay awake for two nights. Last night, she'd fallen asleep in the armchair and missed her opportunity. Tonight, she would sit up straight on the dressing table stool with no possibility of slumber. She rose and set the door ajar, ignoring the increased draft this created. She could see the head of the stairs from here; he could not get by her. She would thrash it out tonight, no matter what insults he flung at her. The memory of that cold, dispassionate voice reciting her seemingly endless list of faults made her shiver, but she would not give up.

The candles fluttered and burned down faster. Charlotte waited, jerking upright whenever she started to nod off. Once, she nearly fell off the backless stool. But she endured, hour after hour, into the deeps of the night. She replaced the stubs of the candles. She added coals to the fire, piled on another heavy shawl against the chill. She rubbed her hands together to warm them, gritted her teeth, and held on until light showed in the crevices of the draperies and birds began to twitter outside. Another day had dawned, and Henry Wylde had not come home. Her husband had spent the night elsewhere.

Pulling her shawls closer, Charlotte contemplated this stupefying fact. The man she saw as made of ice had a secret life? He kept a mistress? He drank himself into insensibility and collapsed at his club? He haunted the gaming hells with feverish wagers? Impossible to picture any of these things. But she had never waited up so long before. She had no idea what he did with his nights.

Chilled to the bone, she rose, shut the bedroom door, and crawled into her cold bed. She needed to get warm; she needed to decide if she could use this new information to change the bitter circumstances of her life. Perhaps Henry was not completely without feelings, as she had thought. Her eyelids drooped. Perhaps there was hope.

From *The Bride Insists*

Available March 2014 from Sourcebooks Casablanca

THE SCHOOLROOM OF THE BENSON HOUSEHOLD WAS agreeably cozy on this bitter winter afternoon. A good fire kept the London cold at bay, so that one hardly noticed the sleet scratching at the windows. In one corner, there were comfortable armchairs for reading any one of the many books on the shelves. A costly globe rested in another corner, nearly as tall as the room's youngest occupant. Scattered across a large oak table, perfect for lessons, were a well-worn abacus, pens and pencils, and all the other tools necessary for learning.

"I am utterly bored," declared seventeen-year-old Bella Benson, sprawled on the sofa under the dormer window. "I hate winter. Will the season never start?"

"You could finish that piece of embroidery for…"

"You are not my governess any longer," the girl interrupted with a toss of her head. "I don't have to do what you say. I've left the schoolroom."

And yet here you are, thought Clare Greenough. But she kept the sentiment to herself, as she did almost all of her personal opinions. Clare's employer set the tone of this household, and it was peevish. All three children had picked up Mrs. Benson's whiny, complaining manner, and Clare was not encouraged to reprimand them when they used it. "It's true that you needn't be in the schoolroom," she replied mildly. She sorted through a pile of paper labels, marked with the names of world capitals. The child who could correctly attach the largest number of these to their proper places on the huge globe would get a cream cake for tea. Clare had an arrangement with Cook to provide the treats. It was always easier to make a game of lessons than to play the stern disciplinarian, particularly in this house.

"I won't do what you say either," chimed in twelve-year-old Susan Benson, as usual following her older sister's lead.

"Me neither," agreed ten-year-old Charles.

Clare suppressed a sigh, not bothering to correct his grammar. Charles would leave for school in the spring. Only a lingering cough had kept him home this term. He was hardly her responsibility any longer. Bella would be presented to society in a few weeks, effectively disappearing from the world of this room. And Clare would be left with Susan, a singularly unappealing child. Clare felt guilty at the adjective, but the evidence of a year's teaching was overwhelming. Susan had no curiosity or imagination and, of the three children, was most like her never satisfied, irritable mother. She treated Clare as a possession designed to entertain her, and then consistently refused to *be* entertained. The thought of being her main companion for another four years was exceedingly dreary. Surely Clare could find a better position?

But leaving a post without a clear good reason was always a risk. There would be questions which Clare couldn't answer with the simple truth—my charge is dull and intractable. I couldn't bear another moment of her company. Inconvenienced, Mrs. Benson might well refuse to give her a reference, which would make finding a new position nearly impossible. Clare wondered if she could... nudge Susan into asking for a new governess? Possibly—if she was very clever, and devious, never giving the slightest hint that it was something *she* wanted. Or, perhaps with the others gone, Susan would improve? Wasn't it her duty to see that she did? Clare examined the girl's pinched expression and habitual pout. Mrs. Benson had undermined every effort Clare had made in that direction so far. It appeared to be a hopeless task.

Clare turned to survey Bella's changed appearance instead—her brown hair newly cut and styled in the latest fashion, her pretty sprigged muslin gown. At Bella's age, Clare had been about to make her entry into society. She had put her hair up and ordered new gowns, full of bright anticipation. And then had come Waterloo, and her beloved brother's death in battle, and the disintegration of her former life. Instead of stepping into the swirl and glitter of society, Clare was relegated to the background, doomed to watch a succession of younger women bloom and go off to take their places in a larger world.

Stop this, Clare ordered silently. She despised self-pity. It only made things worse, and she couldn't afford to indulge in it. Her job now was to regain control of the schoolroom. She shuffled her pile of paper labels. "I suppose I shall have to eat all the cream cakes myself then."

Susan and Charles voiced loud objections. Clare was about to maneuver them back into the geography game when the door opened and Edwina Benson swept in. This was so rare an occurrence that all four of them stared.

Bella jumped up at once and shook out the folds of her new gown. "Were you looking for me, Mama?"

"Not at present. Though why you are here in the schoolroom, Bella, I cannot imagine. I thought you were practicing on the pianoforte. Have you learned the new piece so quickly?"

"Uh…" Eyes gone evasive, Bella sidled out of the room. She left the door open, however, and Clare was sure she was listening from the corridor.

Mrs. Benson pursed narrow lips. "You have a visitor, Miss Greenough."

This was an even rarer event than her employer's appearance in the schoolroom. In fact, it was unprecedented.

"I do not recall anything in our arrangement that would suggest you might have callers arriving at my front door," the older woman added huffily.

Only humility worked with Mrs. Benson. She was impervious to reason. "No, ma'am. I cannot imagine who…"

"So I am at a loss as to why you have invited one."

"I didn't. I assure you I have no idea who it is."

Her employer eyed her suspiciously. Mrs. Benson's

constant dissatisfaction and querulous complaints were beginning to etch themselves on her features, Clare thought. In a few years the lines would be permanent, and her face would proclaim her character for all to see. "He was most insistent," Mrs. Benson added. "I would almost say impertinent."

You did say it, Clare responded silently. "He…?"

Mrs. Benson gave her a sour smile, designed to crush hope. "Some sort of business person, I gather." Her gaze sharpened again. "You haven't gotten into debt, have you?"

It was just like the woman to ask this in front of the children, who were listening with all their might. She was prying as well as peevish, and… pompous and proprietary. "Of course not." When would she have had the time to overspend? Even if she had the money.

Mrs. Benson's lips tightened further. "I suppose you must see him. But this is not to happen again. Is that quite clear? If you have… appointments, I expect you to fulfill them on your free day."

Her once monthly free day? When she was invariably asked to do some errand for her employer or give the children an "outing"? But Clare had learned worlds about holding her tongue in six long years as a governess. "Thank you, Mrs. Benson." Empty expressions of gratitude no longer stuck in Clare's throat. Mrs. Benson liked and expected to be thanked. That there was no basis for gratitude was irrelevant. Thanks smoothed Clare's way in this household, as they had in others before this.

Clare followed her employer downstairs to the front parlor. The formal room was chilly. No fire had been lit there, as no one had been expected to call, and obviously no refreshment would be offered to the man who stood before the cold hearth. Below medium height and slender, he wore the sober dress of a man of business. From his graying hair and well-worn face, Clare judged he was past fifty. He took a step forward when they entered, waited a moment, then said, "I need to speak to Miss Greenough alone."

Edwina Benson bridled, her pale blue eyes bulging. "I beg your pardon? Do you presume to order me out of my own parlor?"

"It is a confidential legal matter," the man added, his tone the same quiet, informative baritone. He showed no reaction to Mrs. Benson's outrage. And something about the way he simply waited for her to go seemed to impel her. She sputtered and glared, but she moved toward the door. She did leave it ajar, no doubt to listen from the entry. But the man followed her and closed it with a definitive click. Clare was impressed; her visitor had a calm solidity that inspired confidence. Of course she would endure days of stinging reproaches and small humiliations because of this visit. But it was almost worth it to have watched him outmaneuver Edwina Benson. "My name is Everett Billingsley," he said then. "Do you think we dare sit down?"

Clare nearly smiled. He *had* noticed her employer's attitude. She took the armchair. He sat on the sofa. Clare waited to hear what this was about.

For his part, Billingsley took a moment to examine the young woman seated so silently across from him. Her hands were folded, her head slightly bowed so that he couldn't see the color of her eyes. She asked no questions about his unexpected visit. She didn't move. It was as if she were trying to disappear into the brocade of the chair.

Despite her youth, she actually wore a lace cap, which concealed all but a few strands of hair the color of a fine dry champagne. Her buff gown was loosely cut, designed, seemingly, to conceal rather than flatter a slender frame. A shade too slender, perhaps, just as her oval face and pleasantly regular features were a shade too pale. Here was a female doing everything she could to remain unnoticed, he concluded. She even seemed to breathe carefully. Everett Billingsley certainly understood the precarious position of genteel young women required to work for their bread. He could imagine why she might wish to appear unattractive and uninteresting, to remain unobtrusive. Her attempt to impersonate an ivory figurine made his mission even more gratifying. "I have some good news for you," he began. "I represent the estate of Sebastian Greenough, your great-uncle." This won him a tiny frown, but no other reaction.

Clare sorted through her memories. Sebastian Greenough was her grandfather's brother, the one who had gone out to India years before she was born. She had never met him.

"Mr. Greenough died in September. It has taken some time to receive all the documents, but they are now in place. He left everything he had to you."

Clare couldn't suppress a start of surprise. "To me?"